REINCARNAL & OTHER DARK TALES

MAX ALLAN COLLINS

WOLFPACK PUBLISHING
— EST 2013 —

WOLFPACK
PUBLISHING
— EST 2013 —

Reincarnal & Other Dark Tales

Paperback Edition
Copyright © 2021 Max Allan Collins

Wolfpack Publishing
6032 Wheat Penny Avenue
Las Vegas, NV 89122

wolfpackpublishing.com

Paperback ISBN 978-1-64734-238-8
eBook ISBN 978-1-64734-237-1

REINCARNAL &
OTHER DARK TALES

For Phil Dingeldein –
who first suggested
"Teenage Truckstop
Hookers from Hell"

Contents

INTRODUCTION

While most of my crime and mystery novels include horrific elements, only two – *Mommy* and *Mommy's Day*, which I wrote based on the films I scripted and directed – might be said to fall directly into that genre.

But I have been a horror film fan since a childhood blissfully twisted by *Creature Feature* hosted by Dr. Igor (WQAD, Channel 8, Moline Illinois), and of course *Famous Monsters* magazine and all its imitators. Add to this discovering a handful of used EC horror comics when I was around seven or eight – yikes! These cheerfully bad influences led me to everything from Universal's monsters to Hammer Horror, from *Psycho* to *Halloween* and beyond. *Well* beyond – *Texas Chainsaw Massacre* and *Dawn of the Dead* beyond. Additionally, Richard Matheson and Robert Bloch were favorites dating back to junior high, and I recall reading Matheson's *Hell House* in one spellbound sitting.

So, over the years, when given the opportunity to contribute a horror yarn to an anthology – God bless you, Marty Greenberg...you too, Ed Gorman and Jeff Gelb – I did so eagerly. I've long wanted to gather those tales in one volume, and now, Wolfpack has given me that opportunity.

You will find all the classic boogeymen herein – vampires, werewolves and the Frankenstein monster – among other supernatural subjects. A few are horror tales that do not deal directly with the paranormal, but are still more horror than suspense or crime, at least in my view. A few are sexually explicit, and if that horrifies you, you have made an unfortunate purchase.

A number were adapted by me for the radio show, Fangoria's *Dreadtime Stories*, where Malcolm McDowell played host/narrator in grand crypt-keeper fashion, and full casts did a terrific job bringing them to life (and death). Thank you, Carl Amari, producer par excellence.

Two stories I wrote directly for that radio series are included here by way of their radio scripts. They, as well as *Reincarnal* and *Interstate 666*, were conceived with film in mind, and the latter two reached full screenplay stage but got sidelined in a long, unsuccessful (so far anyway) attempt to bring my *Road to Perdition* sequel, *Road to Purgatory*, to the screen.

So those two scripts are included as sort of bonus features, in the hopes you may seek out the glorious audio versions (two volumes of *Dreadtime Stories* are available on CD at Amazon).

I should also mention that "Open House" and "Not a Creature Was Stirring" were written for *Night Stalker* and *Dick Tracy* anthologies respectively and have been revised for inclusion here, with their licensed aspects edited out.

What's the best way to read these, you ask? Well, it's your choice, of course. But I'd prescribe one before bedtime...and then see what nightmare you can dream up for yourself.

Max Allan Collins
January 2021

REINCARNAL

Why, tonight, of all nights, did she have to get her period? Patsy Ann, in the claustrophobic restroom stall, her petticoats a nightmarish barrier, was doing her best to rid herself of one bloody tampon and insert a fresh one without getting blood on her white prom dress.

She would simply *die* if that happened! She'd saved so long, and worked so hard at the drive-in, to afford the daringly low-cut gown. Was it God's idea of a joke to have her period come a whole week early - on the night of the senior prom? To give her awful cramps and a heavy flow and make her miserable on this night, of all nights?

The night she and Jimmy were to finally go "all the way"...

She'd been nervous all evening, from when Jimmy

picked her up in his candy-apple red '56 Chevy, to the dance in the gym itself with the ancient Glenn Miller-style big band the parents had foisted on them. Even on the ferry ride to Coronado, she trembled, and not because of the breeze. The couple had stood at the rail looking at the lights of San Diego, the moon full and white, like a big peppermint Necco wafer.

"Here, babydoll," Jimmy said, slipping his white coat with its red carnation around her shoulders. Tall, with a blond pompadour, long-lashed baby blues and an overbite that Patsy Ann just loved, Jimmy was cute in a gawky way. She didn't even mind his Clearasil-caked cheeks.

"Thanks, honeybun," she said.

How could she break it to him that the curse was upon her? He was being so thoughtful - taking her to see her favorite singer at his late show at the Hotel Coronado, that gothic mansion of a fancy resort hotel Patsy Ann had only seen from the outside, before.

Now, as she stepped from the hotel ladies' room to rejoin Jimmy at their table, she heard the M.C. introducing the star.

"...Mr. Bobby Darin!"

The applause ringing in the room, and her ears, she clapped too as she moved to the table and she was happy, forgetting, for a moment, the disaster between her legs. Jimmy squeezed her hand and smiled at her as Bobby was singing, "Hello Young Lovers". Funny - this was a Big Band sound, too, but somehow it seemed so right, so cool, not at all ancient.

What a thrill to see Bobby in person - to see the face on all those pictures she plastered on her bedroom walls come to life before her very eyes. The only disappointment was the singer's refusal to do his biggest hit, "Mack the Knife".

"You're too kind," he said, a thin figure in a black tux with a roundish face, tie loosened, hand casually caressing the microphone, "but considering the current state of local affairs, performing that number would be in bad taste. Here's a new one I hope you'll like even better..."

She thought he was doing "Mack the Knife" after all, but instead it turned out to be a hip version of the old standard "Clementine," with funny new lyrics.

Patsy Ann could understand why Bobby declined singing his trademark tune. Just a week before, the fourth couple in a brutal series of lover's lane murders had been discovered, parked on a San Diego side street, slashed repeatedly; notes sent to the local papers, signed by "Mack the Knife," taking credit for the slayings, had found their way into the headlines, and into popular usage around San Diego - "look out old Mackie is back" was the equivalent around school for "Boo!" if some smart aleck wanted to get you going.

Thinking about it, Patsy Ann began to smile...the perfect excuse...

Hand in hand, as they walked to the parking lot, she said, "I *know* I promised...but I'm scared."

"Scared? Your Jimmy's right here to protect you."

"Tell that to those four couples that got killed!"

They were to the car. Jimmy opened the door for her.

"Babydoll, all those couples were *old* folks - in their twenties or thirties!"

She got in. "Maybe. But even so..."

"And ol' Mack the Knife may be back in town, but he's never been on Coronado Island, has he?"

"Well..."

He shut the door.

Soon they were parked along the beach, looking out at the moon reflecting on the water.

"Jimmy...we're just going to have to wait a while before we...do it."

"Wait! I've been waiting all semester!"

"Well, you're just going to have to wait a little longer...my *friend* is here."

"Your...aw. Aw, shit!"

"Jimmy! It'll just be a week or so. Then..."

His look of disappointment melted into a smile. He stroked her cheek. "You're worth waitin' a lifetime for, babydoll."

"Jimmy..."

"It's just...prom night's so special. It's a night for memories."

She loved him so. Impulsively, she kissed him. Deeply - thrusting her tongue into his mouth. He kissed her back with urgency, and their tongues dueled, the kiss a heated mixture of pleasure and desperation.

Reaching over delicately, she undid his pants and, with a boldness that shocked both of them, she found his erect penis - so hot, so thick - and caressed it with her hand.

She had never done this before. One of her girl-friends had told her about it, and her reaction had been horror, till her girlfriend explained it was fun, as long as you didn't let the guy "spurt" too soon, and besides, guys liked it even more than the *real* way.

So she kissed him, it, tentatively, kissed the tip, then opened her mouth and slipped her lips over it, suckling, then taking more of it in...

She heard, but didn't see, the car door behind Jimmy open, and he was still in her mouth when her eyes were harshly filled with the glare of the dome light. Patsy Ann reared back, her hand still on Jimmy, and the long gleaming butcher knife swung past her and into Jimmy, just above where he was rising out from her tender hand, and then Jimmy was spurting, but not in the way her girl friend had warned her about...

The screaming in her ears was hers, and Jimmy's, and she looked up past Jimmy's pain-distorted fea-tures to see a face she would never forget - a thin face with one blue eye and one brown eye and a smile so wide it seemed wider than the thin face should be capable of, and sadder than any smile should be.

Then the butcher knife flashed, like a lightning bolt of cold steel, blood splashing, and she was floating like Supergirl, over the car, looking down at it, down through it, with Supergirl's X-ray vision, and seeing the blond-haired husk in a white, blood-spattered prom dress, a husk that used to be her as the thin-faced man flailed with the knife in the moonlight, then slipped his hand up under her prom dress as, high above, she floated away, looking skyward.

"What did I *say?*" Nora Chaney asked.

The lanky brunette, dressed in beatnik black that bespoke some other era, lay sprawled on the couch in her loft apartment. Scattered around the apartment, amidst her '5Os deco furnishings culled from second-hand shops, were half a dozen guests, all of whom looked ashen.

Bearded, bespectacled Will Wyman sat in a chair beside her, looming over her, his cow-like eyes filled with concern. The heavyset psychology professor wasn't easily shaken, but he looked that way, now.

"Are you all right?" Will asked.

Nora sat up; she touched her forehead. "Tell you the truth...I'm not sure."

"You *should* feel fine. I gave you a post-hypnotic command...you shouldn't remember a thing..."

"I don't, Will." She shook her head. "But the memory of it is tugging at me...I know I've gone through something disturbing. It's...clinging to me, like a...taste in my mouth, from a meal I can't quite remember eating."

Mary, the heavyset lesbian who ran the bookstore downstairs, brought Nora a beer, which Nora took eagerly.

Over the last several weeks, on their regular Friday

night get-together, the little group had been eagerly going along with their old psychology prof Will's hypnosis party games. Nora had proven to be the best subject among the group, and just last week had been stretched out like a board while two hundred-pound Ted sat on her stomach; had several pins stuck in her arm, painlessly; and responded to a post-hypnotic suggestion in which she placed two bananas in her purse while preparing to leave the party, which really brought the house down.

This week she had agreed to let Will regress her, to what might be a previous life.

"No one really knows," Will had said, "whether hypnotic regressions are merely the subconscious playing games, or evidence of reincarnation, or perhaps something else - maybe tapping into the psyche of some ghost who's just passing through...but it can be damn interesting, whatever the hell it is."

Now it was time to find out just how "damn interesting" she had been tonight.

"Play the tape," she said.

The party guests looked at each other, as if sharing some awful secret.

"I won't be left out of the fun, when I *was* the fun," Nora said, stubbornly, and went to the cassette recorder, hit "rewind" and then "play" and stood, listening to her own voice, as she identified herself as "Patsy Ann".

The place was quiet as a church as she - and her friends - listened to the bloody tale of Patsy Ann and

Jimmy's ill-fated prom night.

She clicked the machine off, glancing at her long-faced guests; even Wyman looked as if his cat had died.

"You guys aren't *buying* this?" she asked, laughing.

Wyman, still seated near the couch, shrugged. "Who's to say you aren't the reincarnation of this poor girl?"

"Oh, please!" Nora got herself another beer from the fridge. "If anything, this fairy tale is proof *against* reincarnation - it's obviously my subconscious having a field day!"

Mary was squinting in thought. "You've always had a thing about the '5Os," she said, gesturing to a boomerang-shaped coffee table.

Rodney, the rail-thin eternal hippie art dealer, said, "And I guess we all know Bobby Darin is your favorite singer. You've forced his records on us, long enough..."

"He's been my fave since I was a little kid," she said, nodding.

Wyman stood. "But when you were a child, it was *after* that particular pop idol's period of popularity... perhaps you were attracted to his music because..."

"Because in another life I cut his pictures out of fan magazines?" Nora flopped back on the couch. "Please. The Hotel Coronado - isn't that in some famous movie?"

"'*Some Like It Hot*,'" Mary admitted.

Nora nodded, vindicated. "And as for this 'Jason Goes to the Prom' yarn that I spun...we *all* know where *that* comes from."

The local media was understandably obsessed, currently, with a series of similar murders, dubbed by the *Sun-Times* the "Chicago Ripper," and both the papers and TV had likened this serial killer to the "Mack the Knife" slayer who hit San Diego back in the '50s.

"It's obvious that some part of my brain," Nora said, "assembled these and other elements, forming this 'American Graffiti' ghost story - and you ate it up like kids around the campfire. I'm surprised I didn't go on to say that every year since, on the night of the prom, Patsy Ann is seen riding the ferry back and forth between San Diego and Coronado, looking for Jimmy!"

There was general laughter - although Wyman himself never seemed to shake off the moment - and for the rest of the evening, the topic of Patsy Ann and Jimmy did not come up.

Throughout the night, Nora maintained a cheerful, even giddy persona, which she dropped when she was down to her final guest - Wyman.

"I gotta admit, Prof - I'm kinda shook up about your little experiment..."

"I don't blame you," he said gravely. "My dear, I've witnessed numerous regressions...and I've never seen one more convincing than..."

She walked him to the door. "Maybe we should come up with a new party game."

"Maybe we should."

She kissed his cheek and he left.

Now on her fifth beer, Nora sat glumly on the couch.

In explaining from where, in her subconscious, the elements of the "regression" had emerged, she had failed to elaborate to her guests on one possibility.

The sexual nature of the story could have been a reflection on her own sexual hang-ups. Nora Chaney - her background liberal, her lifestyle less-than-conservative - moved in circles that included students and teachers from the University of Chicago, other commercial artists like herself, as well as freelance writers and journalists. Living in this loft apartment in Old Town, smoking pot occasionally, hanging out in alternative rock clubs, attractive, with a raunchy sense of humor, Nora Chaney had one terrible secret.

She was a virgin.

A virgin with an interest in, but fear of, sex. She liked men - she was definitely attracted to some of them. She was certainly *not* gay, though she had tried that, to see if it would help; it was, if anything, worse.

She found that no matter how attractive a man, when the petting got below the waist, she would turn to ice. A literal cold would envelop her, a shivering cold that came from fear, as if she were some repressed frigid throwback to the goddamn '50s or something...

That night, Nora had the first dream.

She is a blonde woman of about thirty and she is fucking a graying man of about forty in the cramped front seat of a sportscar. He is a married man, and she is a married woman, but not to each other; they don't speak of this, but it is there, with them, in the car, like something between them, even as she sits astride him, pumping, pumping, and then waves of orgasm begin, building, and she's screaming...

And through the open car window the butcher knife flashes, slashes...the knife enters her, plunges into her chest, and she is screaming but it's a different scream as she falls back and sees that thin blue-and-brown-eyed face in the window, with its awful smile, as the knife plunges into her lover's body, just above his sex, and he and she are screaming, blood spurting, as a rough hand is reaching for her ankle, slipping off the panties caught there, as she floats away, above the car, looking down through it at her blonde self as the slashing continues, though she feels no more pain, and looks away, looks up...

She woke, sitting up now, like a jack-in-the-box. She got up, prowled her apartment; fixed some instant coffee. She sat at her kitchen table, sipping the coffee, remembering the dream vividly. Somehow, she knew that this dream, unlike most, would stay with her in its every detail.

The dream seemed remarkably realistic, or so she guessed: that must be what sex, what fucking, was like. And she'd had her share of orgasms, of course - her sexual hang-ups didn't extend to avoiding masturbation - but this was different than the self-induced variety...

A wet dream - literally. She was sopping between

her legs; and the rest of her body was wet, too, glistening with sweat, though the nearby air-conditioner was hurling cold air at her.

She looked at the clock: three thirty-three.

The next morning, Saturday, Nora slept in. She was sitting at the kitchen table again, glancing at the *Tribune,* sipping another cup of instant coffee, only half-listening to a mid-morning news report on the portable TV on the counter.

"The so-called Chicago Ripper has apparently struck again," the woman newscaster was saying emotionlessly.

Nora looked up from the newspaper.

"The bodies of Teresa Gibson and Robert Haller, both of Naperville, were found in Haller's sportscar, parked in..."

She spilled her coffee. Nervously, she got up, found a dishrag, and wiped up the spill, even as the details made her hands shake all the more.

"...time of death is estimated at three-thirty a.m." A few hours later, she found a late edition of the *Sun-Times* that included the murder story, and further details: the victims were a married woman of thirty-two and a married man of forty-one...married, but not to each other.

She tried to put it out of her mind. She caught the new Scorsese flick at the Biograph, in the company of her divorced friend, Carol Reed. But all she could think about, all night, was the dream.

Carol, blonde, thirty-something, her plain features unadorned by make-up, was just enough into New Age sort of things that Nora figured she might get a sympathetic ear.

But as they nibbled carrot cake at an expresso shop after the movie, Carol was dismissive.

"The trouble," she said, "is you don't make a party game out of something as serious as past lives."

"That dream didn't have anything to do with the party..."

"Sure it did. Your 'regression' triggered this other dream."

"I dreamed about a couple being murdered by this 'Ripper' at the same time it was happening!"

Carol shrugged. "You and how many other Chicagoans? The media's been bombarding us with 'Ripper' this, 'Ripper' that..." Carol touched Nora's hand, spoke softly. "Hey, I'm single...I have sex dreams. I wouldn't be surprised if the next one *I* have doesn't get interrupted by our Freddy Krueger-ish media star..."

"Maybe you're right."

"Eat your carrot cake. It's as close to sex as either of us is gonna get tonight."

Nora laughed, and so did Carol, but Monday morning, at her kitchen table, Nora found herself staring at two familiar faces: Teresa Gibson and Robert Haller. The photographs in the *Trib* matched the faces in her dream.

"I think you should go to the police," Wyman told her on the phone.

"They'll laugh at me. They'll throw me out a window!"

"You have to try. Besides, even the FBI has been known to work with psychics."

"Is *that* what I am?"

"I don't know. I don't honestly know anything except I wish I'd never put you under. I blame myself."

"Don't be silly, Will," she said, but secretly she agreed with him.

The first cop thought she was a crank; that much was obvious. He was young, probably mid-twenties, sandy-haired, overweight and a smoker; his bad health habits would catch up with him: the bullpen area, where this was just one of many desks, was air-conditioned cool, though he had sweated through his white shirt.

But when she had mentioned one certain detail, he had begun paying attention.

"How did you know the Ripper takes the underpants off the female victims?"

"I told you. I *dreamed* it."

At the desk next door, a female detective was clearly listening in. She was in her thirties, heavy-set with a short blonde pixie-hair and thick glasses, and seemed on the verge of putting her two cents in. But she didn't. "I...I, also, uh, have a drawing," Nora said.

"What?"

She opened the manila folder, took out the pencil sketch. "I'm a commercial artist. I thought this might be helpful..."

She put the drawing of the thin-faced man on the desk.

"I used watercolor because of his eyes," she said. "One's blue, one's brown..."

He looked at the sketch, briefly, then at Nora, for a long time. "Thanks for your time, Ms. Chaney - we have your address. We'll be in touch. I wouldn't go on any extended trips if I were you."

"Do you want this?" Nora said, picking up her drawing of the Ripper.

"You keep it...for now."

At the elevators, Nora waited, fuming, angry at being treated so condescendingly, but mostly angry at herself.

"You made Wayne suspicious."

Nora turned, and it was the chunky pixie-haired female cop. A name tag said DETECTIVE LISA WINTERS.

"And why is that?" Nora asked.

Winters shrugged. "You knew a key detail that's been suppressed from the media. That makes Wayne think you might be connected to the murders, somehow."

"What do *you* think?"

The detective smiled, barely. "I think you're sincere. Psychic, maybe. But Wayne and me, we agree on one thing."

"And what would that be?"

"We neither one know exactly what to do with, or about, you." Winters dug in her breast pocket for a card. "This has both my work and home number. But there's another number on the back."

Nora took the card, glanced at the back of it. "Dick Mathis? Who writes for the *Reader*?"

Winters nodded. "He's bylined several damn good articles about the slayings. He just might print your story - and that drawing you did."

"I'm not looking for publicity..."

"I know you aren't. My hunch is you're trying to do the same thing I am: help stop this bastard."

The chunky cop headed back to her desk.

Nora stepped on the elevator, studying the card.

Nora knew who Dick Mathis was - in fact, it was his article she had read, about the similarity of the Chicago Ripper to San Diego's Mack the Knife of thirty-some years earlier, that could have fueled her "regression".

"We have some mutual friends," she said.

"Yeah, I buy books from your downstairs neighbor," Mathis said. He was thirtyish, a wide-shouldered six-footer with a homely handsome face, thinning brown hair and Buddy Holly glasses. He could have been a cowboy in another life.

"You buy *lesbian* books?"

"There are a couple of lesbian mystery writers I follow, yeah," he said, with a grin. "I *like* women."

They sat sipping expresso in Old Town cafe, filling each other in about their backgrounds. She told him about her freelance commercial artwork. He told her about being a novelist and freelance journalist and working out of his apartment on the near North Side.

"Lisa Winters says you may have an interesting sidebar on the Ripper story," Mathis said.

"That's right. But when you hear it, you may take me for a flake."

"Maybe. But you seem like a nice enough flake, so go ahead."

She knew he wasn't taking her very seriously; she sensed he was attracted to her, but when she mentioned the Ripper tearing off the woman's panties, he perked up, just like the cops had.

"Detective Winters mentioned that detail to me, off the record," Mathis said.

"I guess holding back key info is common, in cases like this, huh?"

"Yes, it is." He picked up her drawing of the Ripper. "I want to print this. And I want to print your story."

"I'm...I'm afraid you haven't heard it all..."

And she told him about Patsy Ann and Jimmy.

For the next three days, Nora worked with Mathis on an article about her experience. The weekly *Chicago Reader* was a giveaway, *Village Voice*-style paper that was widely read in the city; in his article, Mathis kept her anonymous but planned to print her drawing under the heading *Is This Man the Ripper?*

Working from his apartment, where Nora sat exhausted on the couch, Chaney faxed his final copy over to the *Reader* office, just making deadline. He flopped on the couch next to her and heaved a satisfied sigh.

"What have we done?" she asked.

"Huh? What do you mean?"

"I have the sick feeling I've just made a colossal ass of myself."

"With my help."

She laughed and slugged his shoulder. "I hope you're not exploiting me."

"Can I tell you a secret?"

"Sure."

He leaned near her. His breath smelled of coffee, but it wasn't unpleasant; hers probably smelled the same way.

"Working with you these last few days... 'exploiting' you *has* crossed my mind a couple times..."

She smirked at him. "Maybe you should put a classified ad in the *Reader*..."

"'Divorced balding male writer seeks female companionship, psychic reincarnated beauty preferred'?"

"Something like that."

He kissed her. It was a sweet kiss. Gentle.

She kissed him back. Not so gently.

Then they were rolling around the couch, sliding

their hands under each other's garments, gasping for breath as they necked and petted like a couple of frantic teenagers...

She sat up, as if abruptly waking from a dream, straightening her clothes, embarrassed - not for what she'd done, but for what she couldn't do.

"Dick...I'm sorry...I'm sorry, I can't..."

"I understand."

She held her arms to herself, shivering. "For some goddamn reason, I just get this icy feeling..."

"I understand. I really do."

"You do?"

He tentatively placed his hand on her thigh; it was not a sexual gesture.

"Think about it," he said. "This...difficulty of yours..."

"Hang-up, you mean."

"Okay. Call a spade a spade: this hang-up may mean that you really *were* Patsy Ann in a former life, the life immediately previous to this one..."

"Oh, Dick - you can't be serious..."

"I'm a journalist - I'm a combination of cynicism and open-mindedness. And I'm merely suggesting that the trauma of Patsy Ann's death, at a moment of sexual discovery that turned into bloody fucking horror, is something she - you - may have carried along into *this* life."

"Suppose...suppose there's something to this," she said. "What the hell am I supposed to do about it?"

"Find Patsy Ann," he said.

"What? What do you mean...?"

"See if she existed. Maybe if you can come to terms with who you *were*, you can come to terms with who *are*..."

With a little arm-twisting, Nora shamed Will Wyman into another hypnosis regression session.

"A fishing expedition," he said, "and a reluctant one, at that."

But he put her under, though little substantial information resulted - no last name, no street address.

"San Diego," she said. "Patsy Ann. But we had that before."

Wyman, seated beside her on her couch, tapped a pencil on his notepad. "But we do have a specific year: 1959."

"I already extrapolated that."

"How?"

"By Bobby Darin singing 'Clementine' at the Hotel Coronado."

"Oh. Well, this combination of the specific and the vague is *not* unusual in hypnotic regression - and it's rather typical for regressed subjects to resist giving certain specific details, including last names. And it's *very* typical for a subject to immediately seize upon a traumatic incident in regression, like Patsy Ann's traumatic death."

"But why have I carried this with me? Particularly, this...connection with 'my' murderer?"

The professor looked very grave. "Sometimes, when a life is cut short...according to one theory...we can carry an agenda of sorts into our next life. A job left undone."

"You mean, we keep coming back until we get it right?"

"Or wrong. Who's to say someone evil, cut short in the midst of his or her evil pursuits, might not try to continue on in a future incarnation - finishing the job that got interrupted. I'm not saying I believe any of this, mind you..."

"I appreciate you sharing these thoughts, just the same, Professor." She nodded at the tape recorder. "Do you think we should try again?"

"I'm willing. But if you truly believe you have some sort of psychic link to the 'Ripper', I should think the sooner you do something to substantiate this, the better."

"I'd have to agree. So my next trip shouldn't be back in time, should it?"

"There are ways other than hypnosis," the professor said somberly, "to go back in time..."

In San Diego, Nora checked in at the Omni. Less than an hour later, barely noticing the beautiful weather, she walked up the steps of the public library, where she soon sat looking through the old papers on microfilm, following the trail of Mack the Knife.

She could have waited the week the inter-library

loan would have taken, to get the San Diego newspaper microfiches through the Chicago library system; but she felt she couldn't wait. She felt the increasing need to *stop* him...was it her own need, or Patsy Ann's?

She didn't know. She only knew she had to go to San Diego - had to make this journey into someone else's past, to see if the city itself touched off any memory switches; she would go to Coronado Island, to the hotel, to the beach where a teenage couple had been murdered, so long ago...but first, the library.

Where it didn't take long at all...

Their young faces were before her, in high-school graduation photos that accompanied the story of the latest tragic victims of Mack the Knife, teenagers, a week away from graduation.

Patsy Ann Meeker; James McRae. May, 1959.

She read the news account over and over, then moved on, scrolling ahead to the next day, when a gloating note sent to the newspaper, presumed to be from the killer, made more headlines.

Then Patsy Ann's mother made the front page, on the day of her daughter's funeral, by having a stroke.

A wave of sorrow washed over Nora - it was as if she were reading about her own mother. Which, if Dick and the professor were right, might be the case...

The Meekers weren't listed in the current phone book, but there was an address in the decades-old news accounts, and she tried that.

The little stucco home on San Rafael Boulevard was in a neighborhood that had turned Hispanic; it was a nice enough area, though, and she hoped the current tenants might remember the Meekers, or at least have a lead for her.

They did.

Mrs. Cavazos, a pleasant heavy-set woman in her fifties who Nora caught in the midst of preparing supper, said her family had bought the home from the Meekers.

"Very sad," Mrs. Cavazos said, standing in the doorway, as Nora wondered if the rooms beyond would stir any memories should she have been invited in."Mr. Meeker, he pass away about ten years ago - took his own life."

"Oh."

"Mrs. Meeker, she had one stroke after another... she's in a nursing home."

Hillview Care Center was stucco, too, a hacienda-style building up in the hills; Nora was glad she'd rented a car - the cab ride would have bankrupted her.

"I'd like to speak to Mrs. Meeker," she told the head nurse.

"You're welcome to try," said the nurse, a tired-looking woman in her forties, "but I'm afraid Mrs. Meeker hasn't spoken a coherent word in years."

Though still in her sixties, Mrs. Meeker (the nurse said) was an old, old woman, far older than her years - less than human, all but a vegetable. She could eat, feeding herself as if by automatic pilot. With the aid of a walker, she could make it to and from the bathroom. But that was the extent of her life.

"That," the nurse said, "and her TV playing soap operas that she may or may not hear."

The nurse led Nora to a little room, where a frail old woman - tiny, balding, a baby bird of a human - sat in an armchair next to the hospital bed, watching a blaring television.

"Mrs. Meeker," the nurse said, loudly, "you have a visitor -"

The old woman turned her head away from the TV, where a young soap opera couple was kissing. Her eyes were dim, cloudy...until they fixed on Nora.

Then the old woman's eyes came brightly alive.

Mrs. Meeker reached her quavering arms to Nora, and Nora went to her, kneeling before her, instinctively holding out her arms to the old woman.

Mrs. Meeker looked right in Nora's eyes and said, "Patsy Ann! Patsy Ann..."

Nora held the old woman in her arms for a long time. Then she sat, for an hour or more, holding Mrs. Meeker's hand. The old woman said nothing, just the name "Patsy Ann," occasionally, but her smile was beatific.

When the nurse came back around to collect Nora, and Nora rose to leave, the old woman's expression turned desperate.

"Don't go...Patsy Ann...don't go...."

Nora hugged the old woman.

"I'll be back," Nora said, calming her.

In the hallway, the nurse shook her head sadly. "That was her daughter's name. The poor old woman thought you were her daughter."

"Has she ever reacted that way with anyone else?"

"Well...no."

Their footsteps echoed down the hall, the sound of the blaring TV fading.

On the plane back to Chicago, Nora fell asleep; in her dream...

....*she is a redheaded woman, a flight attendant, in her early twenties, in a hotel room getting oral sex from, while giving oral sex to, a too-handsome man of about thirty who is (he says) a movie producer.*

"*Lick me!*" *she's saying.* "*Lick me!*"

"*Suck me!*" *he's saying.* "*Don't stop!*"

The man is still in her mouth when the butcher knife falls like a guillotine.

Nora woke suddenly, to see a flight attendant before her, shaking her gently awake.

Not the same flight attendant...not the redheaded one in the dream...

"I'm sorry, ma'am," the flight attendant - a pretty brunette - said. "You were making noise...I'm, uh...afraid you were alarming some of the other passengers..."

"Sorry."

"Can I get you something? Some soda perhaps?"

"Ginger ale."

The flight attendant smiled and nodded and went away.

Nora sat and breathed deeply. The businessman sitting next to her was looking at her warily out of the corner of his eye.

She wondered if she'd talked in her sleep.

Nora took a cab from the airport to police headquarters in the Loop. She asked for Lisa Winters and was soon sitting at the sympathetic cop's desk.

"I think the Ripper may have struck again..."

"Why's that, Ms. Chaney?"

"I...I had another dream."

Winters listened patiently, not even arching an eyebrow at the sexual nature of the dream, then said, "I don't think there's much to worry about...you were obviously influenced by being on an airplane, which is why you were a stewardess in the dream, and..."

"Winters!"

The young sandy-haired cop with the patronizing attitude was walking over, to interrupt them.

"We got another one," he said. "Ramada Inn near O'Hare - maid has discovered two bodies with the usual M.O. - missing panties and all. Really caught in the act - in your classic 69 position."

"Jesus," Winters said.

"It's a stewardess...sorry: *flight attendant.* And the guy's some Hollywood jerk." Now he noticed, and recognized, Nora. "What the hell are you doing back?

Have another dream?"

"No, thanks," Nora said hollowly. "I just had one."

In the police car on their way to the Ramada Inn, Nora drew a picture of the too-handsome Hollywood producer; she also drew a sketch of the woman, though having been within the woman's perceptions she was not sure how she knew what the dead woman looked like, except perhaps from some shared memory.

Nora was not allowed within the hotel room, though she knew full well what was in there.

Winters came out, looking pale, shaking her head, Nora's drawings in hand.

"Any doubts I may have had about you," Winters told Nora, "are gone."

"Then circulate the drawing I did of the Ripper to every cop in town!"

Winters laughed humorlessly. "That's exactly what I'd like to do. Far as I'm concerned, it's an eye-witness police sketch. But I can't."

"Why in hell not?"

"Picking up a suspect on that basis wouldn't begin to hold up in court - the guy would walk."

The sandy-haired cop came out and shook a Marlboro out of a pack and lighted it up. He walked over to Nora reeking macho and sneered.

"Hope you got a great fucking alibi, lady," he said.

Nora sneered back at him. "How does being thirty thousand feet in the air at the time of the murder strike you?"

Winters inserted herself between them and said to Nora, "I don't think you're needed here any longer. Thanks for your help."

"I'll stay in touch," Nora said.

"Do that," the sandy-haired prick said.

In Mathis' apartment, Nora sat beside him on the couch, unloading her frustrations on him; his arm was slipped gently around her shoulder. On the cluttered coffee table before them was a copy of the *Reader* with her portrait of the Ripper.

Nora slapped the paper face. "Why don't the police *do* something! I've handed the son of a bitch to them!"

"Maybe they will, pretty soon."

"What do you mean?"

He grinned at her. "I have some good news for you...we've had several phone calls at the *Reader* saying a man closely resembling your sketch has been seen in Evanston."

She sat up. "You think there's something to it?"

"One caller even spoke of noticing the man had one blue and one brown eye..."

"Damn! Do you think Detective Winters would pay attention to that?"

"Frankly, no. But I'll drive out to Evanston tomorrow, myself, and show the picture around."

"The police should be doing that."

"Hey. It's what *I* should be doing...I'm the reporter who's breaking this case, remember? There may be a book in this, and then I can afford to take in a roommate."

She smiled, stroked the hand that had settled on her shoulder. "Anybody special in mind?"

"I'll run a classified. How did San Diego go?"

She pulled her legs up on the couch and snuggled against him as she told him.

"Now that you've proved the Patsy Ann connection," he said, "maybe you can lay your demons to rest."

"I don't know about demons being laid," she said. "But *I'm* willing to give it a try..."

She kissed him, deeply, and he slipped his hands up under her sweater, filling his hands with her.

"I...I never made love to a virgin before," he said.

"Don't worry about it," she laughed, not afraid at all. "I lost it riding a bike as a girl..."

He nibbled her neck. "That's what they all say..."

She lay cozily in his arms, in his bed. The thrum of the air-conditioning was the only sound.

"The second time was even better," she sighed.

"Just wait'll the third."

"Dick...do you think...? Nothing."

"What?"

"The visions. The dreams. They've all been... sexual."

He sat up in bed; his chest, bare, was as hairless as a child's. "I wouldn't describe them as 'sexual', exactly..."

"Sex interrupted by violence. But now that...

now that you've helped me overcome my sexual hang-up, maybe..."

"Maybe the visions will stop?"

"Yes."

"Possibly. Or maybe they'll manifest themselves in some other way." He shrugged. "Maybe once the psychic floodgate's open..."

"God, I hope not."

"Well, try it out. Quit talking and go to sleep..."

She nestled against him and did. Her dreams were only of him.

The next day, Mathis drove to Evanston and asked around the neighborhood where the man who looked like Nora's picture had been sighted. Three people told him the same thing: a guy in his fifties resembling the drawing worked as a janitor at the Faith United Methodist Church.

The church was on the corner in a residential neighborhood of well-maintained turn-of-the-century mansions. The church was a massive brick affair that lacked the gothic character of the surrounding structures.

Inside, Mathis approached a pleasant, round-faced middle-aged man with black-rimmed glasses, dressed in sweater and jeans, who turned out to be the minister. Mathis asked if he could speak with the janitor.

"Delbert's out running some errands," the minister said. "But he'll be back shortly - he has a little apartment in the church basement."

"What sort of fella is he?"

"Quiet. Devout. Couldn't ask for a better servant of the Lord."

"Well...thank you for your help, Pastor."

"Should I say a friend dropped by, Mister...?"

"No. I'll catch him later."

But when the minister slipped back into his office, Mathis slipped down a side stairway into the basement.

Off a finished banquet room, the janitor's quarters were adjacent to the furnace - must've been hot as hell in the winter, down there, in the cement-walled space.

And "Delbert" certainly was devout: makeshift cement-block bookshelves were stacked with books on religion and philosophy; no pornography, in fact no fiction. Not even a television. No evil influences whatsoever. Nothing but a Bible school-style print of a Jesus painting.

A dead-end? Mathis wondered, and poked around, further.

Nora had a frustrating morning in her studio, trying to work on a plum assignment for *Chicago Magazine*, but unable to focus.

She had come back last night from Dick's, taking with her the small handgun he insisted she now carry in the wake of the *Reader* article - even though he'd kept her name out of it, Dick was worried the Ripper might somehow find out who Nora was.

She had humored him, though once she got home, she put the little revolver away in a drawer. She had no intention of carrying that thing around with her.

Working into the night, she'd come up with several roughs that didn't satisfy her. After several hours sleep, woken by sunlight streaming in the skylight, she started back in and finally got something, but was too tired to do any of the precision work - the inking, the airbrushing - that could turn the penciled drawing into a finished magazine cover.

After a lunch of microwaved soup, Nora took a nap on the couch, and began to dream...

She is a man.

She/he is alone in a small room; it's in a basement of some kind. The room is dreary, dank; the chest of drawers she/he's going through is old. In them are clothes, men's clothing, work clothes, a suit, all of it looking vaguely Good Will. In the bottom drawer, though, are some scrapbooks. She/he opens the top scrapbook and a headline leaps out: MACK THE KNIFE KILLS TEEN COUPLE. She/he leafs through the book.

More bloody headlines; another scrapbook has headlines, circa mid-'70s, of the Detroit Slasher; the bottom scrapbook, the newest one, the one in progress, details the continuing career of the Chicago Ripper...so do the stack of blood-spattered panties below the scrapbooks...

She/he glances up at the mirror over the bureau. She/he is Dick Mathis.

Somehow, through sheer will, Nora forced herself awake. Her heart was in her throat.

If she was Dick in the dream, Dick was in danger! But where the hell *was* he?

In that room.

What room?

She grabbed her purse and was half-way out the door when she thought of something: she took the revolver from the drawer, stuffed it in her purse, and hurried down the steps to the street, where she grabbed a cab.

"Evanston," she told the driver.

"Where in Evanston?"

"Just Evanston!"

"Oh-kay..."

They drove to Evanston; she heard herself giving the cabbie directions. She told him street names she didn't know she knew. Told him to take this right. That left.

Then, for reasons unknown to her, she found herself getting out of the cab in front of a church.

She threw money at the cabbie, and rushed up the steps and a round-faced man in a sweater and glasses approached her, pleasantly, but she pushed him aside, running to a stairway and running down, to a room near the furnace.

She stepped inside, and saw Dick, on the floor, half-conscious, holding his chest, blood bubbling through; the man with the thin face, in his late fifties now, a coveralled smiling Satan, was bending over Dick, the butcher knife poised to strike again. He looked back sharply at her with one blue eye and one brown.

"Remember me?" she asked.

He turned and looked at her, his eyes slitting, his face as long and narrow and sharp as the bloody blade.

He smiled his terrible smile and came at her with the knife high in his fist and she took the gun from her purse and shot him in the chest.

Astounded, he fell to his knees, in praying position, the knife tumbling from his fingers.

"I'm Patsy Ann," Nora said, standing over him.

He looked up at her with eyes that seemed to recognize her. It was as if he were awaiting communion.

"Patsy Ann Meeker," she confirmed. "I came back for you."

He glanced at the knife he dropped, not thinking of going after it, but (somehow she knew this) wondering why she didn't pick it up and make him suffer, before he died. Like he had made her suffer, her and all the others...

She answered the unasked question.

"I don't want you to suffer," she said, and fired the gun right at his forehead, and fired again, and again. An acrid fragrance wafted.

"I just want you to go away," she said. "Just get the hell out of here!"

But he already had. He was on his back, and both the blue eye and the brown one were empty.

She went to Dick, cradled him in her arms as the frowning minister appeared in the doorway.

"Get help," she said.

A week later, Nora brought Dick home from the hospital to Old Town, to her loft apartment, which they now planned to share.

"Make love to a cripple?" he asked.

"Any time," she said, and helped him disrobe, scattering clothes on their way to the bedroom, where they made love slowly, gently, and fell asleep in each other's arms. Nora, enveloped in a deep, sound pool of slumber, began to dream.

It is a dream unlike the others. She is no specific person. She is a presence in a white room. Doctors are standing around a table; a mother has her feet in stirrups. She is in a delivery room in a hospital. She watches as a baby is born, its first breaths turning into a wailing that builds into what seems almost a scream of rage.

Nora sat upright in bed, waking Dick, who looked with alarm into her wide eyes.

"He's back," she said.

THE NIGHT OF THEIR LIVES

I spent the first week in the shantytown near the 31st Street bridge, nestled in Slaughter's Run. The Run was a non-sequitur in the city, a sooty, barren gully just northeast of downtown. For local merchants it was a festering eyesore - particularly the ramshackle Hoovervilles clustered here and there, mostly near the several bridges that allowed civilization passage over this sunken stretch of wilderness.

For men - and women - down on their luck, as so many were in these hard times, the Run was a godsend. Smack dab in the middle of the city, here were wide open spaces where you could hunt wild game - pigeons, squirrels, wild dogs, and the delicacy of the day: Hoover hog, also known as jackrabbit.

In the 31st Street jungle, a world of corrugated metal and tar paper and tin cans, I met "former" everythings: college professor, stock broker, habidasher, and lots of steel mill workers, laid off in this "goddamn Depression". I don't know that I ever heard the latter word without the former attached.

Saddest to me were the families - particularly the women who were alone, their husbands having hopped the rails leaving them to raise a passel of dirty-faced, tattered kids. A ragamuffin-laden woman, even an attractive one, was unlikely to find a mate in this packing-crate purgatory.

Since Thursday of last week, I'd been wandering the streets near the Central Market, where hobos haunted the rubbish bins. The weather was pleasant enough: a cool late April with occasional showers and lots of sunshine. I hadn't shaved the whole time; I wore a denim work shirt, brown raggedy cotton trousers and shoes with holes in the soles covered by cardboard insteps. My "home" was a discarded packing crate in an alley off Freemont Avenue, behind a warehouse, in the heart of the city's skid row district.

When I talked the chief into letting me take this undercover assignment, he'd suggested I take my .38 Police Special along. I said no. All I'd need was a few personal items, in my canvas kit bag. I never went anywhere without my kit bag.

"It's a good idea," the chief had said. He was a heavy-set, bald, grizzled man who spoke around an ever-present stogie, frozen permanently in the left corner of his mouth. "As just another hobo, you can gain some trust...we can't get this riffraff to cooperate, when we haul 'em in on rousts. But they might talk to another bum."

"That's the theory," I said, nodding.

Of course, if I told the chief my *real* theory, he'd have fitted me for a suit that buttoned up the back - you know the kind: where you can't scratch yourself because your arms are strapped in?

It had been three weeks since the last body had been found. The total was at eleven - always men, dismembered "with surgical precision," whose limbs turned up here and there, washed up on a riverbank, floating in a sewage drainage pool, wrapped in newspaper in an alley, scattered in the weeds of the Run itself. Several heads were missing. So was damn near every drop of blood from each victim's jigsaw-puzzle corpse.

Because the butcher's prey was the faceless, home-less rabble washed up on the shores of this depression, it took a long time for the city to give a damn. But the Slaughter Run Butcher was approaching an even dozen now, and that was enough to interest not just the police, but the press and the public.

The mission at 4th and Freemont was always crowded - unlike a lot of soup kitchens, they didn't require you to pay for your supper by sitting through a hell-and-damnation sermon. In fact, I never saw anybody seated in the pews of the little chapel room off the dining hall, although occasionally you saw somebody sleeping it off in there; the minister was a mousy guy with white hair and a thin black mustache - he didn't seem to do much beside mill around, touching bums on the shoulder, saying, "Bless you my son."

The person who really seemed to be in charge was this dark-haired society dame - Rebecca Radclau. If the gossip columns were correct, Miss Radclau was funding the Fourth Street Mission. Though schooled in America, she was said to be of European blood - her late father was royalty, a count it was rumored - and the family fortune was made in munitions.

Or so the society sob sisters said. They also followed the movie-star lovely Miss Radclau to various social functions - balls, ballet, theater, opera, particularly fund-raisers for the local Relief Association. She was the queen of local night life, on the weekends.

But on week nights, this socially-conscious socialite spent her time dressed in a gray nurse's-type uniform with a white apron, her long black hair up in a bun, standing behind the table ladling bowls of soup for the unfortunate faceless men who paraded before her.

Even in the dowdy, matronly attire, she was a knockout. The soup was good - tomato and rice, delicately spiced - but her slender, top-heavy shape, and her delicate, cat-like features, were the draw. Men would hold out their soup bowls and stare at her pale face, hypnotized by its beauty, and grin like schoolboys when she bestowed her thin red smile like a blessing.

"I'd like a piece of *that*," the guy in front of me in

line said. He was rail thin with a white, stubbly beard and rheumy eyes.

"She seems friendly enough," I said. "Why not give it a try?"

"She don't fraternize," the guy behind me said. He was short, skinny, and bright-eyed, with a full beard.

"Bull," the first guy said, "shit." He lowered his voice to a whisper. "I seen her and Harry Toomis get in her fancy limo out back...it comes and picks her up, you know, midnight on the dot, every night, uniformed driver and the works."

"Yeah?" I said.

"Yeah," he said. "Anyway, I seen the night Harry Toomis got in the limo with her, and she was hanging on 'em like a cheap suit of clothes."

The other guy's expression turned puzzled in the maze of his beard. "Say - whatever *happened* to Harry? I ain't seen him in weeks!"

Somebody behind him said, "I heard he hopped the rails, over to Philly. Steel mills out there are hiring again, word is."

We were close to the food table, where I picked up a generous hunk of bread and took an empty wooden bowl; soon I was handing it toward the dark-haired vision in white apron and gray dress, and she smiled like a Madonna as she filled it.

"You're the most beautiful woman I've ever seen," I said.

"Thank you," she said. Her voice was low, warm, no accent.

"I feel I've known you forever."

She looked at me hard; her almond-shaped eyes were a deep brown that approached black - it was as if she had only pupils, no irises.

"You seem familiar to me as well," she said melodically.

"Hey, come on!" the guy behind me said. "Other people want to eat, too, ya know!"

Others joined in - "Yeah! This goddamn depression'll be over before we get fed!" - and I smiled at her and shrugged, and she smiled warmly and shrugged, too, and I moved on.

I sat at a bench at one of the long tables and sipped my soup. When I was finished, I waited until the food line had been shut down for the evening and found my way back to her.

"Need some help in the kitchen?" I asked, helping her with one handle of the big metal soup basin.

"We have some volunteers already," she said. "Maybe tomorrow night?"

"Any night you like," I said, and tried to layer it with as much meaning as possible.

Then I touched her hand as it gripped the basin; hers was cool, mine was hot.

"I wasn't always a tramp," I said. "I was somebody you might have danced with, at a cotillion. Maybe we did dance. Under the stars one night? Maybe that's where I know you from."

"Please..." she began. Her brow was knit. Confusion? Embarrassment?

Interest?

"I'm sorry to be so forward," I said. "It's just...I haven't seen a woman so beautiful, so cultured, in a very long time. Forgive me."

And I silently helped her into the kitchen with the basin, turned and went out of the mission.

The night sky was brilliant with stars, a full moon cast an ivory glow upon skid row, giving it an unreal beauty. An arty photograph, or perhaps a watercolor or an oil in a gallery, might have captured this land-scape of abstract beauty and abject poverty. Rebecca Radclau might have admired such a work of art, on her social travels.

From around a corner, I watched as her dark-win-dowed limousine arrived at midnight, pulling into the alleyway where an impossibly tall, improbably burly chauffeur stepped out and opened the door for her. She was still wearing the dowdy gray uniform of her missionary duties. A sister of mercy.

She was alone.

She slipped into the back of the limo, her uni-formed gorilla of a driver shut her inside, and they backed out into the street and glided away into the ivory-washed night.

Perhaps I'd misjudged her.

Or perhaps tonight she just wasn't thirsty...

For the next two nights I worked in the kitchen, washing the wooden soup bowls the first night, drying them the next - and there were a lot of goddamn bowls to wash and dry. She would move through the small, steamy kitchen as if floating, attending to the next night's menu with the portly, little man who was the cook for the mission, and in her employ.

Rumor had it he'd been the chef at a top local hotel that had gone under in '29. Certainly, the delicately seasoned soups we'd been eating indicated a finer hand than you might expect at a skid-row soup kitchen.

I would catch her eye, if possible. She would hesitate, our gazes would lock, and I would smile, just a little. She remained impassive. I didn't want to push it: I didn't repeat my soliloquy of the first night, nor did I add to it, or present a variation, either. I tried to talk to her with my eyes. That was a language I felt sure she was easily fluent in.

The next night, as I went through the soup line, she said, "We won't need you in the kitchen tonight," rather coldly I thought, and I went to one of the long tables, sat, sipped my soup, thinking, *Damn! I screwed up. Came on too strong. She needed to think she was selecting me.*

And just as this thought had passed, I felt a hand on my shoulder: hers.

I looked up and she was barely smiling; her cat-like eyes sparkled.

"How was your soup?"

I turned sideways and she loomed over me. "Dandy," I said. "I never see *you* trying any. Don't you like the company?"

"I never eat...soup."

"It's pretty good, you know. Rich enough even for your blood, I'd think. Want to sit down?"

"No. No. I never fraternize."

"I've heard that."

"I just wanted to thank you for your help." And she smiled in a tight, business-like way. Others were watching us, and when she extended her slender fingers toward me, and I took them, we seemed to be shaking hands in an equally business-like way.

Nobody but me noticed the tiny slip of paper she'd passed me.

And I didn't look at it until I was outside, ducked into my alley home.

Midnight, it said.

Written in a flowing, lush hand. No further instructions. No signature.

But I knew where to be.

She stepped out of the back door of the alley, looking glamorous despite the dowdy uniform being damp with sweat and steam, black tendrils drifting down into her face from the pile of pinned-up hair. The whites of her eyes were large as she took in the alley, looking for me, I supposed. She seemed perplexed.

When the limousine glided into the alley next to the

mission, and the tall burly chauffeur got out to let her in, I stepped from the recession of a doorway, kit bag in hand, and said, "You did mean midnight, tonight?"

She jumped as if I'd said "boo."

She touched her generous chest. "You startled me! When I didn't see you, I thought you'd misunderstood...or just stood me up."

I went to her; took her hand and bent from the waist and kissed her hand, saying archly, "Stand up a lovely lady like yourself? Pshaw."

I'd always wanted to say "Pshaw," but it never came up before.

She smiled slyly, a thin smile that settled in one pretty dimple of her high-cheekboned face. "Did you think this was a date?"

"I had hoped."

"Mister...what is your name?"

"Jones, or Smith, or something. Is it important?"

"Let's make it Smith-Jones, then."

"Sure! That's high-tone enough. And may I call you Rebecca?"

"I prefer Becky."

"All right."

The chauffeur was standing with the limo's rear door open. His face was shadowed by his visor, but I could make out a firm jaw and a bucket-like skull.

"Let's not stand out here talking," she said, suddenly glancing about, almost furtively.

"Why not? You're not mistaking a member of the Smith-Jones clan for the sort of riffraff you don't care to be seen with?"

"Please get in. What is that you have there?"

"Just my old kit bag. I don't go anywhere without my old kit bag - it contains what few possessions I still have."

"Fine. But do please get in."

The chauffeur moved forward, and I had the feeling that if I didn't get in, he'd toss me there.

"Ladies first," I said, bowing, gesturing, and she quickly ducked in.

I followed. The leather seats smelled new; they were deep and comfortable - like living-room furniture, not the back seat of a car.

"Mr. Smith-Jones, I wanted to express my gratitude to you, this evening."

She was unpinning the black hair; it fell in cascades to her shoulders. She shook her head and it shimmered and brushed her shoulders, flipping up at the bottom.

"Gratitude?" I asked. "For what?"

"For your help, these last several days."

"In the kitchen? Jeez, lady...Rebecca...Becky...it's only fair. You've been always good to guys like me, down on their luck, making sure we get a square meal once in a while."

"I've known adversity myself," she said solemnly. It sounded silly, but I managed not to laugh.

"So, uh...how exactly do you intend to express your gratitude?"

She touched my hand; she looked at me with those iris-less dark eyes. She seemed about to say something provocative, something sensual, something seductive. What she said was: "Food."

"Food?"

"Food. Real food. A real meal. Prepared by a five-star chef."

"No kidding. I had something else in mind..." I grinned at her lecherously and she just smiled, "...but I'll settle."

She didn't let it go. "What else did you have in mind, Mr. Smith-Jones?"

I sighed. Looked down at my tattered clothes. Shook my head. "I shouldn't even kid about it. How can you look at somebody like me...unshaven...dirty clothes...breath that would knock a buzzard off a dung wagon...and think of me in any other way but one of pity?"

She patted my hand. "That's not necessarily true, Mr. Smith-Jones. I can look at you and see...possibilities. I can see the man you were - the man you still are, underneath the bad luck and the hard times."

"That's kind of you to say."

Her cool hand grasped mine. "And I don't think your breath is bad at all...I think it smells sweet...like night-blooming jasmine..."

She leaned forward; her thin but beautiful lips parted - they were scarlet, but I wasn't sure she was wearing lip rouge - and she touched her lips to mine, delicately. Then she touched my unshaven cheek with the slender, long-nailed fingers of one hand and stared soulfully into me.

"You're a fine man, Mr. Smith-Jones. We're going

to clean you up...a bath...a shave...an incredible meal. You're going to have the night of your life..."

The Radclau mansion was a modern brick castle beyond a black wrought-iron gate; three massive stories, its turreted shape rose against the clear night sky in sharp silhouette, the moon poised above and to the right as if placed there for the sole purpose of lighting this imposing structure.

"This is really something," I said. "When was this built?"

"Just a few years ago," she said.

We were around the side of the building now, gliding into a garage which opened automatically for us - whether the chauffeur triggered it somehow, or someone inside saw us coming and lifted the drawbridge, I couldn't say.

"I recruited one of the top local architects to build something modern that would invoke my family home," she said.

"Where was the family home?"

"Europe."

"That doesn't narrow it down much."

"Just a little corner of eastern Europe. You probably wouldn't even have heard of it."

Maybe I would have.

We stepped from the cement cavern of the four-car garage into a wine cellar passageway that led to an elevator.

"I was never in a private home that had an elevator," I told her; the leather strap of my canvas kit bag was tight in my hand. The chauffeur - whose bucket-like skull turned out to have two dead eyes, a misshapen nose and grim line of a mouth stuck on it - was playing elevator operator for us.

"Why, Mr. Smith-Jones," she said, looping her arm in mine, smiling her wry one-sided dimpled smile again, "I find that difficult to believe."

The elevator, a silver-gray chamber, rose to the fourth floor and opened onto a red-painted door in the recession of a cream-colored plaster alcove.

"We're in one of the guest towers," she said. She stepped out into the alcove with me, still arm-in-arm. "These are your quarters...you'll find everything you need I think. I just guessed on your size. If I've got it wrong, just pick up the phone and ask for me. We can accommodate you. Then, let us know when you're ready to dine..."

She smiled - both dimples this time - and ducked back into the elevator, whose doors slid shut and she was gone.

"I'll be damned," I said, and in the little alcove, it echoed.

The red door was unlocked, and opened onto a vast modern living room - plush white carpet, round white leather sofa, deep white armchairs, sleek decorative figurines, black-and-white decorative framed prints, a fireplace, a complete bar, a radio console, you name it. Everything but the kitchen sink. Everything but mirrors.

Beyond the living room was a bedroom; it was another white room, with one exception: the round bed was covered with red silk sheets. On the wall, over the bed, was a huge, bamboo-framed, sleekly decorative watercolor of a black panther, about to strike.

In the closet hung a full-dress tux - white tie and tails, pip pip. And the size was right, down to the black size nine and a half shoes, so shiny I could see my face in 'em, but probably not hers...

I tossed my kit bag on the bed and checked out the bathroom; it was bigger than most apartments. On the white marble counter (and there was a mirror in here, at least) I found a straight razor, a brush and cup and shaving soap, and fancy French imported after-shave cologne. Also, deodorant powder, and toothbrush and Pepsodent.

She apparently wanted me clean and smelling good, for dinner.

I made sure the guest-room door was locked and stuck a chair under the knob to make double-sure, before stripping down to take a long, elaborate, very hot bubble-bath. After two weeks of the hobo life, I was ready to take advantage of Miss Radclau's hospitality and soak off the slime.

Dressed to the nines, looking like neither a hobo nor an undercover cop in my white tie and tails, I picked up the phone and said, "Mr. Smith-Jones is ready to dine."

Within minutes, a knock at the door announced

the chauffeur, who was serving as a room-service man this time; he wheeled in a cart with several covered dishes.

"Please wait for the lady, sir," the chauffeur said, in a voice as dead as his eyes. "Madam is still dressing."

"Sure," I said.

It was another ten minutes before another knock came, and I hadn't even peeked under the dull, non-reflective lids of the hot dishes. I didn't want to be an ungracious guest.

I answered the door, bowing, with an arch, "Enchante."

But it almost caught in my throat, because as I was bowing, I found myself staring into her round, ripe decolletage.

I backed up awkwardly. "You're sure a sight."

She floated inside. Madam still looked undressed: her astonishingly low-cut gown was a vivid dark red and clung to her as if wet. Her waist was tiny, her hips flaring, but she was too tall, too long-legged, to have an hour-glass shape; she was wearing open-toed heels that brought her to my eye level. Her toenails were the same bright red as the dress and her lips.

She gestured theatrically to herself, with both hands. "I trust this is better than the apron?"

"Than the apron and the gray uniform," I said. "Maybe not just the apron..."

Her laugh was long and sultry. She was draped in an exotic, incense-like perfume, which was making me feel woozy.

She gestured with a slender, red-nailed hand toward the tray with the covered food.

"Please dine," she said.

I pulled up a comfy chair that was a little short for the tray; it made me feel like a child. Before I sat, I asked, "Aren't you joining me?"

"I've eaten."

I doubted that.

"Please," she said, "I take great pleasure from watching you enjoy yourself. The carnal pleasures are so..."

"Pleasurable?" I offered, lifting a round lid; the fragrance of prime rib rose to my nostrils like a cobra from a Hindu's basket, only I was the one doing the biting, sinking my teeth into the tender, very rare, succulent meat.

"I know I promised you the work of a five-star chef," she said, perched nearby on the arm of the couch, legs crossed, giving me a generous view, hands clasped in her lap, "and that is the work of a master, but...I could tell that you had...basic appetites."

She rose and switched on the radio and drifted back to her perch on the couch arm. A dance band was playing "Where or When". She swayed gently to it, her black hair shimmying.

"This is swell," I said. The prime rib, Yorkshire pudding and browned potatoes were, in fact, delicious. No salad, no vegetable. But what the hell - it was free. So far.

She watched me with what seemed to be genuine pleasure, eyebrows raising as she savored me savoring every bite, her thin, pretty mouth tied up in a cupid's bow of shared bliss. Why she was getting such a vicarious glow out of watching me dig into the rare roast beef, I couldn't say. But I had a pretty good hunch...

I touched my napkin to my lips, sipped the red wine she had risen to pour for me, in a goblet-sized glass, and said, "This is a hell of a public service program you got here, lady."

"I don't single just anyone out, you know." She looked almost hurt by my remark. "Once in a while, working in that line, serving up soup...I see someone... special. Someone who shouldn't be there. Someone who...deserves better. Deserves more."

She leaned in and the incense-like smell of her was overwhelming; her mouth locked onto mine and her kiss was sweet, much sweeter than mere wine...

The lights were off, suddenly, as if she'd willed it, and she led me into the bedroom, where the red gown slipped off and confirmed my suspicion that there was nothing, not even the slightest, wispiest step-in, underneath. A window allowed some moonlight to filter in, and her slender, yet full-breasted, wide-hipped, long-limbed frame was like some artist's dream of female perfection. And a horny artist, at that.

She drew me onto her bed, and lay me down on the cool silk sheets, and climbed on top of me, to grant me yet another gift. The erect blood-red tips of her breasts were as hypnotic as the intoxicated and intoxicating almond eyes, as she rode me, and I kept waiting, lost in her as I was, with my left hand dropped down along the side of the bed, waiting for her head to dip toward my throat, but it didn't, and when her face lowered, it was merely to kiss me again, deeply, passionately, as we flew together to some high, fevered place...

Maybe she was just some rich-bitch society girl who felt sorry for (and had a yen for) poor down-and-out schmucks like me, or like the poor down-and-out schmuck I was supposed to be. Maybe the suspicions that had brought me here were unfounded. Maybe I was the only dishonest one in this bed.

It had seemed a reasonable theory - what better place for an ancient monster to hide than behind the mask of a modern monster? The mass murderer that the city took the Butcher of Slaughter Run for would be the perfect disguise for a demon of the night.

And how better for the beast to gather its victims than behind the mask of an angel of mercy?

She seemed to be sleeping; the perfect globes of her bosom rose and fell, heavily, gloriously, in what seemed to be slumber. But as I stared at her, leaning on one elbow, her eyes popped open, startling me.

"What's wrong?" she asked.

"Nothing," I said. "I was just...admiring you."

She smiled a little, a pursed-lipped, kiss of a smile. "In what way?"

"Physically. You're a handsome woman. The handsomest I've ever seen. But it's more than that."

"Oh?"

"I admire what you're trying to do. Helping guys like me out."

She laughed. "I told you - I don't make love to all of them."

I shook my head. "I didn't mean that. Not everyone who's...advantaged...takes the time to give a little back."

"I know. Please don't take this in a condescending manner, Mr. Smith-Jones, but the 'little people' of society, they're the life's blood of the 'advantaged'. It seems to me the least an advantaged person can do is, now and then, make life a little better for someone less fortunate."

"Well, you've certainly made my life better, tonight."

She smiled, and it seemed, suddenly, a sad, bittersweet kind of smile; the thin red lips looked black in the near dark. "Good. That was my desire."

She leaned forward and kissed me, gently, tenderly, then buried her face in my shoulder, and I had a sudden flash of what was about to happen and pulled away.

Her fangs were distended; her eyes were wide and there was no longer any difficulty in telling the pupils from the irises, because the latter were a ghastly yellow.

Naked, I jumped out of the bed; she was poised there, on all fours, as if mimicking the panther on the wall looming over her.

"You are from a privileged, moneyed family, aren't you, Miss Radclau?"

Her response was a deep, throaty snarling sound; I

wasn't sure she was capable of speech, at this point.

"You think just 'cause I'm a bum, I can't do a damn anagram?" I asked, and I swung viciously at her, and it landed.

A punch on the jaw, even with all my weight behind it, wouldn't be enough to knock her out - she had metamorphosed into something beyond human, stronger than a mere man – but it had surprised her, and threw her onto her back, which was where I wanted her.

The kit bag was out from under the bed in a flash and the pointed stake and the mallet were in my hands in another flash, and drove my knee into her stomach, and the stake into her heart. She yowled with pain; it was a wolf-like sound. Blood bubbled from around the stake, and I hammered it again, and it sunk deeper, and she yowled again, but her eyes weren't yellow anymore.

And they weren't savage, anymore, either.

Her expression was sad, and maybe even grateful.

She was still alive when I raised the machete - heaving under the pain, her hands clutching the stake but unable to remove it, slender fingers streaked with her own blood, a perfect match to her nail polish.

"I know you acted out of compassion," I said. "I know you gave me, and the other men, the best night of their lives, before taking those lives, when you wouldn't have had to. You could have just been a beast. Instead, you were a beauty."

She seemed to be smiling, a little, when the

machete swung down and severed her head from pale, pale shoulders. I had no trouble getting out of the place.

I took the elevator down to the wine cellar passage to the garage, with the bloody machete in hand in case I had to ward off the gorilla-like chauffeur or any other minions of the night who might appear.

But none did.

I found a button in the garage and pushed it and the door swung up and open and I ran out into a cool, clear night. At the first farmhouse, I called in to the station, and told them to wake the chief.

"He's not going to like it," the desk sergeant said.

"Just *do* it." I couldn't tell him I'd stopped the Slaughter Run Butcher, or I'd be up to my eyeballs in reporters out here. "Understand, Sergeant?"

I could hear the shrug in his voice: "If you say so, Lt. Van Helsing."

A GOOD HEAD ON HIS SHOULDERS

Louie Carboni was no monster.

Some people thought he was. He knew that. But they were stupid people. Ignorant people. Insensitive people. Uncultured. Unschooled.

As Carboni drew back the curtain to look out on the lake, the sky thundered and lightning threw a silvery glow on the baby-smooth surface of his round, thick-lipped face; his bright dark eyes glittered under heavy black brows and prominent forehead, thinning black hair slicked back over a massive skull. A thick, five-dollar cigar smoldered between the similarly thick fingertips of a hand heavy with ruby - and diamond-encrusted gold rings. Wearing a LC-monogrammed scarlet silk smoking jacket over creamy silk pajamas, his feet in soft lambskin slippers, the short, wide, solid mob boss looked like a beast somebody had dressed up for a joke. Of course, Carboni didn't see himself that way.

Carboni saw himself as a modern Napoleon, as a wall of books on the Little General and several busts around the otherwise rustic den of the cabin indicated. He was proud of what he had accomplished by the young age of thirty. He felt he'd smoothed his own rough edges, without losing his touch where keeping discipline was concerned.

Louis Alberto Carboni had come out of a rough Brooklyn neighborhood; his pop, who came over from Naples turn of the century, was a barber whose shop had been a hang-out for the local Black Hand boys. Good connections like this put Louie and his boyhood pal Carlo Gazia in solid with the Five Points Gang. By the time he was sixteen Louie was one of the most prosperous pimps in Brooklyn.

He'd come to Chicago to help Danny Torello run whorehouses. He and Carlo were Danny's righthand men, and when Prohibition came in, it was Louie and Carlo who convinced Danny to expand, even if it did mean war.

War was the natural process by which civilization found out who its real leaders were. That was Carboni's creed. He had waged every kind of warfare known to man - openly attacking some enemies in certain cases, and in others weeding out the competition from within. Deviously. Like that guy Machiavelli laid it out in *The Prince*, a book whose philosophies would have been beyond the intellectual grasp of his late friend Carlo Gazia.

Carlo had been no dummy - he had a good head on his shoulders; but what good did it do him? After all, Carlo couldn't even read. Made an "X" for his signature, and not a very good one. Tall, skinny, mustached, a real ladies' man, Carlo had street smarts, but that was it.

Carboni heard a rustling outside the window, and returned to draw back the curtain again, but figured it was just the fall wind, shaking the shrubs, bending the trees down by the lake. Lightning cut the sky like a jagged Z and turned the surface of the restless lake silver-gray.

"Exquisite," Carboni said, pronouncing the word slowly, correctly.

He'd set himself a goal: three new words a day. Ten years solid, he'd stuck with this program, and not even when the streets were running red with blood and the bodies were piling up like kindling did Louie Carboni not find a few minutes a day to improve his vocabulary.

He walked to one of his Napoleon busts and placed a hand on the shoulder of the Little General.

"It's hard being a leader of men," Carboni said. "You have to make sacrifices for the common good. Right, pal? Fuckin' A!"

He sat in the deeply-padded brown leather chair. Before him, in the cobblestone fireplace, a fire snapped, crackled, glowed orangely; he basked in its warmth. But in the flames, he saw faces. Faces of men he'd killed or had killed.

He shook them away.

"It's all right," he told himself. "Only a monster has no conscience."

He was sorry about them, or at least a few of them. Not the soldiers - a lot of them fell in any war. Pawns to be sacrificed. But some of the generals, who were getting too powerful and had to be gotten rid of, they were pals, and killing pals was never a picnic.

He'd killed Carlo in this room.

Carboni shivered a little, rose and threw a log on the dwindling fire. It perked up again.

Doing it here, just three months ago this weekend, killing this friend who'd been like a brother to him, dispatching him in this haven of trust, had been such a hard thing. Well...pulling the trigger hadn't been hard; he'd made up his mind, when he heard Carlo was cutting side deals, that his near-brother needed killing. And he'd staged that phony flare-up with the Gianni to have somebody to blame.

But when he'd fired the .38 and the round black hole appeared in Carlo's throat, and Carlo's eyes got round and wide, Louie had seen something terrible in those eyes: betrayal.

The shocked disappointment that had registered in Carlo's eyes before he dropped face down, revealing a bigger, more gaping, and bloody wound in the back of his neck, had haunted Louie Carboni. When he was alone in this room, here at the secluded cottage near

Lake Geneva, he should feel safe, secure, in a womb of warmth and trust.

But now, whenever he came here, he felt Carlo's accusatory gaze was always on him.

It had been business. It had been a necessary maneuver in maintaining the proper power structure. Nothing personal. Certainly not the monstrous act of some madman.

Yet those lousy stinking editorials (from the one "dry" paper in town, that conservative piece of shit, the *Sentinel*) dared to call him that. Just last week they'd compared him to that *real* madman, the Medical School Mangler. Imagine! The nerve! Comparing the Napoleon of the North Side to some mass-murdering slob!

He was offended by the...(he thought for a moment, his cat mind chasing the mouse of a right word) the *carnage*, the sheer brutality of this monster. And killing doctors - professors of medicine. Why do such a savage thing? Those guys were healers; they helped people, and more than that, they trained other people to help people.

This was the kind of beast the feds should be tracking down - not him. He was a business tycoon, not some homicidal mental case. This was the kind of fiend the papers should be stirring the public up about.

Well, actually, they were. The papers had been full of the Medical School Mangler. Seven deaths to date in as many weeks. Bodies torn apart savagely. Limbs flung around the quiet studies of cozy bungalows near

Hyde Park like a butcher shop that got up-ended.

One of the boys said a cop on one of the scenes told him that blood was splashed around like the work of some crazy modern artist.

How could that fucking piece of shit *Sentinel* editor put Louis Carboni in the same sentence with such a madman? And with this thought came the image of Carlo Gazia with betrayal in his eyes and a hole in his throat.

His cigar had gone out; he lighted it with a horse-head lighter and thought to himself, *I'll just sell the goddamn place.* Maybe it was childish, maybe it was weak, to be haunted by something; to feel...guilty. But that, Carboni decided, was what separated him from the monsters.

He was a man who could make hard decisions and suffer the consequences with dignity.

The sky growled, and cracked, and the room was momentarily bright with lightning, then rain began to batter the windows, like thousands of demanding, drumming fingers.

But the very incessantness of it became oddly soothing, after a while. He'd just drifted off to sleep in the comfortable leather chair when the sky exploded again, and as his eyes popped open, the room was washed with lightning's whiteness. At this very moment, a knock came at the door, and made him jump.

"*Yeah?*" he boomed irritably, making his own thunder.

Vinnie popped his bullet head in the door; the

narrow-eyed, needle-nosed, mustached hood was in rolled-up shirtsleeves and a loosened tie. He and the other boys were out there playing poker, Carboni knew.

"I know you said not to bother you, boss..."

"I require solitude, Vinnie. I told ya that."

"Yeah, boss, but..."

"Did I even ask you to have a girl sent out? No. Does that say anything to you when I don't want female companionship? It does. It says, I require solitude."

"It's just that Doc Stein's outside."

Carboni sat up, confused. "What the hell's the doc doing here? We ain't...haven't sent him any 'patients' in weeks."

Vinnie raised his eyebrows. "I dunno, boss. But he's acting kinda strange. All sweaty. Nervous. Looks like shit."

"I don't want to see him."

"Boss...he says it's urgent."

Carboni didn't like anybody pushing him, or contradicting him, and the heavy sigh he swallowed didn't taste good at all. But Doc Stein - minor minion though he was - knew where the bodies were buried. Hell - he'd buried most of the bodies! What was left of them after the doc's farmhouse crematorium got done with them, anyway.

And the doc was usually anything but pushy. Timid, even. If Doc Stein came around saying something was important, something was urgent, chances were, it was. Important. Urgent.

Carboni stood, waved a pudgy hand; the jewels on his rings winked with reflected firelight. "Send him in."

Vinnie went away, and a moment later, was back opening the door for the slender figure of Dr. Victor Stein, his wet fedora in hand, dripping, his raincoat dripping too, onto the wood floor.

"Get his damn coat, Vinnie! Have some fuckin' manners!"

"Sure, boss," Vinnie said, and did.

Stein was an average-looking man in every way - about five eight, slight of build rather weak-chinned with ordinary features but for piercing dark nervous eyes magnified by heavy lenses in dark frames; he was the kind of person who looks like a pair of glasses coming at you - you barely noticed the man behind them. Tonight, as usual, he wore his white doctor's smock, which was touched with splotches of red, as if the doc had been operating and called here, suddenly.

Carboni, still standing, gestured to a wooden chair against the wall. "Pull up a seat, Doc. You look damp. Sit by the fire. Warm your bones."

"Thank you, Mr. Carboni," he said. "You're very kind to see me at such short notice. I hate to impose."

"Doc, you're an important part of the team. Always time for you."

For the Carboni mob, a "staff" doctor was a vital team member indeed; when the bullets started to fly, you had to have somebody who could make the necessary repairs, and wouldn't be reporting gunshot wounds to the cops.

"I'm gonna have a little snifter of brandy, Doc. It's good stuff. That is...excellent vintage." Carboni rose and moved to the liquor cart. "Care to join me?"

"Certainly." Doc Stein was sitting now, closer to the fire than Carboni; he was holding his palms up and out, warming them. His face was orange from the flames; there were angles in Doc's face that Carboni had never noticed before.

"I have to ask you to be patient with me, Mr. Carboni."

He handed Stein a snifter of brandy. "Sure, Doc. As long as I'm not a 'patient' of yours." And he laughed.

Doc looked at him, either not getting it or simply unamused. "You're going to find what I have to tell you...incredible. Fantastic. I'm afraid - unbelievable."

With an expansive gesture and a benevolent smile, Carboni settled himself back in the deep leather chair. "Doc...I may just be a street kid made good. But I'm not a stupid man. I've educated myself." He gestured to the wall of books. "Give me a little fuckin' credit, okay?"

"I meant no disrespect. I ask only that you grant me fifteen minutes to present my case. Then, you may toss me out on my ass, as your boys might say."

"I'd never do that to you, Doc."

"Good. But again - I ask your patience. My story is a strange one..."

I believe you are under the misapprehension that I am a defrocked doctor (Stein began), but in fact I am a failed medical student. I had the highest marks in my class. I was attending on full scholarship. The dean of the medical college was my mentor. It was all too perfect, like something out of storybook.

I was a week away from graduation, ready to begin my internship, when I was...if I may use the phrase again...thrown out on my ass. Why? Because of my experimentation into areas where man is not meant to go...or so have said the unimaginative, petty medical minds of this so-called enlightened century.

One would think that the peasants who launched witch hunts against my forebears were endemic to the nineteenth century. Unfortunately, that is not the case. They exist, these feeble-minded modern-day peasants, amongst the highest level of supposed society, and the upper reaches of academia.

But I race ahead of myself.

I know, Mr. Carboni, that you have assumed I was either German or Jewish, or a German Jew. In fact, I am neither. My roots are in Geneva...and I do not refer to Geneva, Wisconsin, but Switzerland. My family name was once illustrious. It was distorted - courtesy of a cheap popular novel of another age, which unfortunately has endured - into some quite literally horrible.

My great-great grandfather, after whom I was named, was Victor Frankenstein.

And "Frankenstein" was not a monster...no matter

what school children who've seen that cheap, recent Hollywood monstrosity may believe. Frankenstein was a *man* - but more than just a man: a scientist, the most brilliant scientific mind of his age.

Oh, you've heard of the novel? You've read it? Yes, you're right...Mary Godwin Shelley's alternate title for that unfortunate work *was 'The Modern Prometheus'*. I had forgotten, for a moment, how well-read you are, Mr. Carboni. But I would encourage you to seek more enlightened, enlightening literature in the future than such travesties as Mrs. Shelley's gothic mockery.

Forgive my bitterness. I'll try to control myself. No...no more brandy. This is fine.

I will not bother you with any further critique of Mary Shelley's work. It would take hours to point out every lie, every distortion, each complete fabrication. Suffice to say that my great-grandfather did, indeed, manage to construct a living man out of bits and pieces of dead ones.

It is also quite true that he and his creation became... adversaries...and that they were lost to mankind, to science, on some polar ice cap, long ago...

No, no, you're right...that wasn't in the film. It's not important, Mr. Carboni. Please let me continue.

My father was not a scientist. He was ashamed of his heritage...it is he who dropped the prefix from our family name, condemning our family to a lifetime of Jew-baiting. A foolish man, my father. Perhaps vision skips a generation. At any rate, I stumbled upon my great-grandfather's papers in a trunk in our attic, when I was but sixteen. I already had a keen interest in science, and reading these brilliant, exciting documents inspired me further. I made medicine my goal - not to be some meager M.D., but to do medical, scientific research, in the tradition of my great-grandfather.

And even at that tender age I formed the ambition to confirm, and to continue, his data. To repeat, and perfect, his grand experiment.

It was toward this end that I was working (cadavers weren't difficult to come by) when the powers-that-be at the medical college discovered my research. The dean - my supposed "mentor" - instigated the proceedings that deprived me of my career before it had begun.

I was out in the cold, told that I was lucky the "good name" of the school had to be preserved, or I would have been turned over to the authorities, after which (so said the Dean) I would be languishing in a prison or, more likely, an insane asylum.

The only good turn my father ever did me was put me in touch with your late friend, Mr. Gazia. My father worked in the garment district and had business dealings with Mr. Gazia, and this was how I became a part of your family, Mr. Carboni, your "team".

Mr. Gazia said there was need for a medical man in your organization, and I was set up with my farmhouse surgery and since, when? 1928? I have been patching up bullet holes and stitching up knife wounds and, on a number of occasions, disposing of patients who didn't pull through.

Here, Mr. Carboni, is where you may truly lose patience with me. Here is where...frankly...I have possibly done you a disservice. I ask only that you withhold your judgment until my tale is told.

It is from the refuse of your organization, the soldiers who have died in battle, that I have found the...spare parts? The materials I needed to pursue my experiments. To be candid, these experiments have been dismal failures. These stitched-together patch-work men have remained useless piles of protoplasm on my laboratory table. One after another, they have been consigned to the crematorium.

Until three months ago.

My great-grandfather kept his notes in the language of his native land - *Schwyzertutsch*, Swiss-German, a dialect difficult for a speaker of true German to even understand; as a child, we'd spoken, even written, the language at home, to a certain degree. But my abilities were below that, I would say, of the average Swiss schoolchild. Later, I took a college German course, and felt I was capable.

But in truth I was not.

I took a crucial portion of my great grandfather's notes on his key experiment to a native speaker of the tongue. Out of context, these scientific ramblings were of no import to this woman; but to me, they were a revelation. They amounted to the key to the secret of creating life.

With the correct translation in hand, I set about to

assemble one more patchwork man. Last winter you had that outbreak with the Gianni brothers, remember? We lost five soldiers in that skirmish. They gave their lives to your cause, Mr. Carboni, but they gave me their limbs, their organs, their life's blood.

I created a giant. Your men were chosen for their physical prowess - remember Tony Lombardi? His torso became that of my giant. Remember Ange Berini's massive arms? Those formidable biceps, those powerful forearms? They are now my giant's.

You look as if you doubt me. Or my sanity. I can understand that. My story is almost over. Bear with me...

My giant was like a child. He had no memory of his former life. But he was not a baby: walking came easily, and just hearing my speech awakened something in his own speech center. We were conversing, normally, by the third week.

He wanted to know his purpose.

Can you imagine, Mr. Carboni? Look at that world out there - the rain lashing the windows, thunder cracking the sky, lightning making the night momentarily day. Can you imagine being face to face with the God who created all of that, and who created you?

Imagine how humble my giant felt in my presence. Unlike you and I, Mr. Carboni, my giant could face his creator. He could ask him the purpose of his life...a question we can ask the sky until it falls and never get an answer.

But I had an answer for him: revenge.

I had brought him into this world to serve me. And the goal I wished him to reach was complete, total vengeance upon those who would subvert science, those who called me mad, those who felt so threatened by my genius that they had to tear the future from my hands, and fling me into the trash heap of humanity.

But I fooled them. I fooled them all.

He killed the dean first. In front of the man's wife, who I instructed the giant not to touch, although I understand she is quite mad, now. She witnessed her husband's arms and legs being torn off as a naughty child might those of a grasshopper or beetle. The living room was sprayed with his blood, littered with his flesh, was filled with his screams, and he was only the first, the dean was.

There have been six more. Teachers. Board members. Those who wronged me. Those who denied the world...or tried to deny the world...my medical and scientific genius.

But a few days ago, something...unfortunate occurred.

You see, in my great grandfather's notes, he indicated that his creation's memory remained a blank slate. His creation knew only the *now* - had been "born again," but not in Christian sense, and was a sort of eight-foot child.

I assumed this would be the case with my giant, but after a time, he began having flashes of memory. At first, I deflected his questions, but finally he became... irritated with me.

Something else my giant knows that you and I never shall, Mr. Carboni, is what it feels like to pick your creator up by the throat and scare the living hell out of him.

I requested that he put me down, and pledged to answer his questions completely, and honestly. I told him who he had been, and it acted as a sort of triggering mechanism...a floodgate of memory opened, and the face of Nicky De Luca lighted up as the eyes of Willie Manzoni filled with the memories of Carlo Gazia.

Yes...Carlo Gazia.

You see, Mr. Carboni, as I mentioned before, your soldiers were men picked because of their physical nature. They were wonderful brutes, and perfect specimens for my research purposes in every way but one: their deficient mentality.

Fortunately for me, your good friend, your partner, Carlo Gazia was shot and killed just at the moment that I needed a man of superior intellect. Which compared to my other prospects at least, Mr. Gazia certainly possessed. In addition to which, he'd been shot in the throat. So many of your deceased, who passed through my hands and my farmhouse, were shot in the head. Which of course makes their brains quite unusable.

The problem we both have, now, Mr. Carboni, is the brain of Carlo Gazia. It is filled with what I schooled my giant in, in his first days, when he was taking his first steps: revenge.

And Mr. Carboni, it is my unpleasant but necessary duty to tell you that the object of my giant's quest for his own, personal vengeance is you, sir.

Carboni was standing, now. He looked down at Doc Stein, whose face in the firelight was as orange as a jack-o-lantern, and said, "This is all true?"

"Yes, sir."

"I thought you were mad for a while, but...Mother of Mercy, can it be true?"

"Oh, yes."

Carboni's tongue felt thick in his mouth; he went to his desk by the wall of books and got out his .45 Colt automatic. Worked the action - checked the clip.

"If it is, Doc - I owe you one, warning me like this."

"Think nothing of it."

He smiled tightly. "And unlike those medical-school bums, I take you seriously. I can see the benefits - a whole army of men like your mangler and there wouldn't be a mob on the face of the earth that could stop me."

"That's probably true."

A crack of what Carboni at first thought was thunder interrupted them. But it was from the room beyond, where Vinnie and the boys were playing poker.

Someone had kicked in the door.

Immediately, there was a barrage of ghastly sounds: screams, gunshots, thumps, overturning furniture, more screams, horrendous screams the likes of which

Carboni had never heard, and he had heard some.

He put one hand on the doorknob, the automatic tight in his other fat fist. A hand touched his arm.

Doc Stein, his eyes childishly wide behind the thick lenses, was waggling a lecturing finger.

"I wouldn't go in there, if I were you."

Whap! Something hit the door, impacting wetly. It was a sound that repeated, as something, or somebody, was being thrown here and there, against the door, against this wall, against that one, and through it all, the men were screaming. The gunshots had stopped.

And then, finally, the screaming stopped, too.

A noise that might have been the front door slamming made Carboni look searchingly at the doc.

Doc Stein nodded. "I think he's gone."

Carboni sighed. He cracked open the door, then he barreled in, ready to shoot.

He was not a squeamish man, but all his supper came up almost at once.

The large outer, lodge-style room, its poker table incongruously in place, was strewn with body parts, streaked with blood. One bloody arm was hanging over a stoic elk's head, sleeve caught in the antlers. An armless, legless torso that was Vinnie had its hysterical eyes open and was trying to talk but could only gurgle.

Carboni backed into the den. The .45 trembled in his fist. He shut the door. Hard.

Doc, who had not even ventured out there, said, "Not a pretty sight, I'd wager. He's strong, my giant is."

Carboni grabbed the little man by the front of his white smock. "How can I kill him?"

"I'm not sure. His organs are all technically dead, although I suppose well-placed shots of sufficient caliber might stop the heart from pumping. Trouble is, a side effect of my great-grandfather's creation process is a toughening up of the skin...a leathery effect, which most bullets can't even penetrate. Sorry."

Carboni slapped the doc, who went down hard.

"You didn't come here to warn me," the gangster said. "You came here to lead him to me!"

The little man shrugged. "I am sorry, Mr. Carboni. I had to. He did my bidding, seven times. I owed him this much."

"The only reason I'm not killing you," Carboni said through clenched teeth, waving the .45 at Stein, "is I might need you later. Stay put! I gotta get the hell outa here..."

Carboni went to the window, where the wind and rain was still rattling the panes. The storm was pelting the lake, as if God were firing down infinite machine guns; trees, barren of leaves, seemed about to snap. He put his hands up on the lock, to open the goddamn thing and climb out, when the awful face was suddenly before him.

Stitched-on ears. A skull-cap stitch-line where the brain, Gazia's goddamn brain, had been dropped in. Bits and pieces of various of his men were standing outside the window, staring at him, a grotesque face streaming with rain that might have been tears, and hands that used to belong to who-the-hell-knew, crashed through the glass and reached in and big fingers clutched Carboni's fat neck and squeezed, and lifted.

Carboni's head came off like the cap on a bottle of shook-up Coke, and his blood geysered the same way.

His body did a brief, shuffling dance before stumbling and falling, face-down, except there no longer was a face attached to the torso, the neck of which was spilling red like an over-turned paint can.

The giant, who was wearing a raincoat and dungarees, crawled through the window, workshoes crunching the glass underfoot, carrying Carboni's head by the left ear, the eyes in it moving wildly, as the howl of the storm provided accompaniment. The giant's footsteps shook the room as he strode to a pedestal where a bust of Napoleon rested. With a massive forearm, he swept the bust off and it shattered into countless pieces on the wood floor. He stuck Carboni's head on the pedestal, moving it around until blood and tissue provided some purchase. Carboni's eyes and his mouth were still moving. That would stop soon.

A thoughtful hand to his cheek, Dr. Stein considered this for future research. Reflex action only, or could Carboni's brain still be functioning, until the oxygen loss put a stop to it? A worthy topic to pursue...

"Ready, Doc?" the giant said. "We don't want to be here when the cops show."

"No, we wouldn't. What now?"

He patted his ex-partner's round skull with a huge hand.

"Now?" the giant said. "Now, there's gonna be a *new* head man in town."

WOLF

He had stalked them for decades, across every continent on the planet, across every racial and ethnic and theological line: he did not care who they were as long as they were women and spoke to the animal instincts within him.

They were his meat.

He preferred them young, of course - supple and sweet. But he had, on occasion, settled.

His name was Jack Wolff, and whether that last name was simple irony or a designation that defined him from childhood, he neither knew nor cared. He only knew, when the moon was high, he prowled for them, and had done so since that older woman had bitten him on the neck in the park that night when he was thirteen.

Since that night, he'd been biting back.

He was forty-nine years old but didn't nearly look it. He took care of himself; no drugs, no drinking, a full regimen of exercise, vitamins, natural foods. As for plastic surgery, he'd had his eyes done, twice; and one little lift. That was all.

He had only two vices: red meat; and women.

Fate had, in one respect, been kind to him. His parents were wealthy; his late father was a criminal attorney whose yearly retainer from a midwestern crime family had meant a comfortable life for the Wolffs. Jack was an only child, adopted, and had enjoyed an idyllic, almost Norman Rockwell-like childhood in the small Illinois city where he was raised.

Finding his victims had never been a problem. Jack was handsome. It was that simple. Tall, dark, with full widow's peaked black hair, Jack had the high cheekbones and finely carved features of a male fashion model only rugged, a Marlboro man made "pretty" by long-lashed green eyes that had an almost oriental cast.

It was summer and Jack was within a hundred miles of the small town he'd been raised in; but none of his family was still alive, and any of the friends he cared about had long since grown up and moved away. So, he didn't even consider "going home." The only reason he was in this neck of Illinois was that he knew the Wistful Wagon Lodge would provide good hunting.

The lodge dated back to the late '40s, and its heyday had been the '50s; Jack had been here often

parental mix of rage and concern, but the wife stopped him with a hand. *Let her be by herself,* the mother seemed to be saying.

Jack, who had finished his meal anyway, signed his room number to the check, and strolled into the lobby, just as she was coming out of the ladies' room. She'd been crying.

"Hey! Are you all right?" he asked. Putting concern into his voice was an old trick for Jack.

"No...no. Not really. Excuse me..."

She smelled so good, not like perfume - like soap. Yum.

"Has someone been bothering you?" he said. The young ones like a defender. He'd played that role so many times.

She swallowed, puffy lips trembling; she had delicate beauty, like something in a china shop. Defiling beauty like that was beyond pleasure.

"Just...just my dad."

"Your dad? Aren't you a little old to have to worry about that?"

"No. I'm...just fifteen."

"Really? I thought you were twenty, at least."

She beamed. She was at that rare age when girls liked to be mistaken for women.

"No. I'm just a kid. Without any rights."

"Kids have rights. Kids have very special rights." He offered his hand. "I'm Jack Wolff. I'm on vacation... getting away from my law practice."

He knew enough about law, from being around

his father, to fake that; he knew women didn't like to hear you were unemployed, even when you had money. "Lawyer" said money to a woman. Even to a girl, like this...

"My name's Anna Mullins, but everybody calls me Annie."

"Hi Annie," he said, warmly.

"Would you ever take somebody my age, for a client?"

"Sure. Why not?"

"Mr. Wolff..." She looked nervously over her shoulder, back toward the dining room entry. "Could we go somewhere for a moment?"

"Certainly," he said, and tried to keep the leer out of his smile. Good as he was at this, that was hard for him.

They sat under a tree on a bench made from a carved log, with a hedgerow on four sides, providing them a private chamber, out of doors though they were. A breeze shimmered through the leaves and the hedges; the sun dappled through the shade trees, making a lovely pattern on her creamy complexion. He kept his distance. For now.

"My father...he's a very bad man."

"In what way, Anna?"

"Annie - please. I want us to be friends."

"So do I."

"The trouble is...I think I may be bad, too."

"Why's that?"

"I...I like the things he does to me."

Well, that was good news and bad news. Jack had hoped she'd be a virgin; those were so rare - very precious blood to spill.

But an abused child, a victim of incest, was perfect for his game. Damaged goods - particularly goods that *knew* they were damaged - were easier prey.

"Did you ever tell your mother?"

"Once...a year ago...I did. She slapped me. Called me a liar."

He made his voice ooze compassion. "She doesn't want to believe it, Anna. That's so common."

"I've asked daddy to stop, but...but he knows once he starts, I let him. I *like* it. I'm so ashamed..."

"He's your daddy. You want to please him."

"I need help, Mr. Wolff."

"What sort of help, specifically?"

"Help me get away from them."

"Being a runaway is no answer, Anna..."

"I won't run away." She put her hand on his thigh and squeezed. "I'll go with you. Take me someplace safe, and then we'll *sue* that lousy...lousy...son of a..."

She couldn't say it.

"Even after all he's done," he said, "you still love him, don't you?"

Stupid little bitch.

"Yes," she said, and she clutched him, sobbing into his chest. "Please, Mr. Wolff...you've got to help me!"

Her sorrow was palpable, but mostly what Jack noticed was the feel of her large breasts pushed against him.

That, and the smell of soap.

That afternoon, he kept an eye on her. She and her family went to the swimming pool. So, did he. He sat in a deck chair opposite them, eyes behind shades, pretending to read the new Stephen King while he studied the pathetic father trying to cozy up to his daughter. *Have a Coke, honey? Is that chair at the right tilt? You need another towel?* But she wasn't speaking to him. It seemed to hurt the old man. The mother soothed him.

Sick, Jack thought. That sick son of a bitch. Screwing his own daughter...

On the other hand, Jack thought, God bless him: that perverted bastard was paving the way for Jack. He had his own hungers to satisfy, after all.

A finger tapped his shoulder, and he sat up, startled. "Mr. Wolff?"

The guy was beefy looking, with a round, red-blotchy face, and reddish-brown hair; he wore a rumpled suit and an egg-stained blue tie, his sunglasses the only concession to the warm summer day. Next to him was a uniformed state patrol officer.

"Yes?" Jack sat up.

The beefy guy pulled another deck chair around. He sat. "Beautiful day. Nice breeze. Some real pretty girls, 'round this place - will ya look at how high they cut those suits up above the hip-bone these days.

Wooo-weee."

"Do I know you?"

"I don't believe so." He smiled, showing no teeth, and dug a small wallet out of his suitcoat pocket, and displayed a badge.

"Sam Herrin," he said, putting the badge away. "But you can call me 'Lieutenant'."

"State crime bureau? What would you gentlemen want with me?"

The uniformed man, very young, sun glinting off his shades, apparently paying no attention to Herrin and Jack, was smiling out at the pool where teenage girls - like Anna - were swimming, their young limbs flashing whitely above the blue-green water.

"We had a murder here last week," Herrin said.

"I'm aware of that."

"Really?"

Jack shrugged. "I heard the talk."

"You shoulda heard more than talk."

"What do you mean?"

"The victim was killed...*slaughtered's* a better word...just outside your cabin."

"It was three or four cabins away. It happened the first night I checked in. Why didn't anybody talk to me about this then?"

"Somebody did."

"Yeah, took my name."

"We ran a check. You got an interesting back-ground."

Jack lifted his glass of Perrier off the metal table

beside him; he sipped. "Really?"

"Travel a lot, don't you, Mr. Wolff?"

"I'm kind of a man of leisure, yes, Lieutenant."

"How is you can afford that, Mr. Wolff?"

"I did it the good old-fashioned American way: I inherited money."

Herrin grinned, glanced back at the uniformed cop, who looked over his shoulder and grinned back. The kid was listening, after all.

"Inherited it from your late father."

"That's right," Jack said.

"He had interesting...connections, your late father."

"Oh. Is that what this is about?"

"He represented some violent people."

"And that leads you to think I had something to do with that woman's murder?"

"Did I say you did?"

Jack gulped. "Well, you sure as hell implied..."

"This woman was torn apart; did you know that? Like an animal did it. Her throat ripped out, bloody everywhere, some of her vital organs were...missing."

"Really."

"You don't seem impressed, Mr. Wolff. What would you say if I told you we found partially eaten human tissue in the bushes, not a stone's throw from your cabin?"

"I'd say you're barking up the wrong tree."

Herrin stood. His smile disappeared; his eyes disappeared into slits in the balloon of his mottled face. "Somebody's barking somewhere. Anyway.

You stay put, Mr. Wolff. We're running a complete check on you."

"What do you expect to turn up?"

"The FBI's Behavioral Unit has already told us about seven other murders, this summer, all around this lovely country of ours, that fit this same sick M.O. If, man of leisure that you are, you just happened to be in those places in the course of your journeying... well. You get the picture."

"You're looking in the wrong place, Lieutenant." Jack grinned wolfishly. "Do I look like a monster to you?"

Herrin studied him blankly, then laughed. "Not really. You look like a ladies' man who's drunk from the plastic surgery well one too many times. But hey - that's just my opinion."

And the beefy detective tucked his hands in his pockets and ambled away, the uniformed cop trailing, both of them ogling the pretty swimming girls.

Bastard! Jack thought.

He didn't like having the cops around. There was nothing keeping him here. After tonight, he'd be ready to move on, anyway.

He watched sweet young Anna stretch and yawn. Lovely mouth. Such full breasts.

Fuck that cop. Jack Wolff would howl tonight.

That evening, in the main lodge ballroom, a program of big band-style dancing followed an excellent buffet dinner. Despite the rare carved roast beef, and it did look good, Jack ate lightly; he didn't like to over-indulge when was planning the sort of sumptuous late-night snack Anna Mullins would provide.

And speaking of young Miss Mullins, she was not present, though her parents were. They didn't seem to be enjoying themselves. The mother and father danced almost every dance, but Mrs. Mullins was ragging her husband, and he was glumly taking it. No wonder daddy was boffing his little girl. With a bitch like mommy, and a piece of tail like daughter, who could blame him?

Jack made sure the parents were occupied with their dancing and nagging session and exited the ballroom. He felt the eyes of so many women on him; he knew he looked good enough to eat in his tux. But tonight, he'd be doing the eating...

The Mullins family had a large cabin. Jack didn't bother with the front door; he went to the bedroom window she had told him about, where he found the shutters shut. Her father really had locked her in good: daddy had wired the suckers shut.

He knocked on the shutters.

"I'm here!" he said.

"Hurry!" the girl said.

Above, the moon was hidden by clouds that were gliding by; it would show its face soon. That was good: Jack did his best work in the moonlight...

Jack cut himself on the wires and said, "Damn!" but he untwisted them, and opened the shutters, and the girl, dressed in the same halter top and lacy-trimmed shorts, stepped out of the window and into his arms. He held her for a moment, like Rhett Butler after sweeping Scarlet O'Hara into his grasp, but instead of carrying her up the stairs, or across a threshold, he strode toward the nearby bushes.

She seemed frightened. "Where are you going?"

"I have to have you, Anna," he said. "You can struggle if you want..."

She squealed and hugged him. "I don't want to struggle. I've been hoping you'd do this, ever since I first saw you..."

She reached her delicate face up and kissed him on the mouth; the kiss had that animal urgency that only a teenage girl can project. How sinfully sweet...

The soap smell of her was in his flaring nostrils as he carried her into the bushes, back to that hedgerow outdoor room where he would have her alone, under the stars.

"Rip my clothes off," she said. "Rip them!"

He did. Her pale flesh was so beautiful in the cloud-filtered moonlight, finding its way through the shade trees; her pubic triangle was white, the hair as gentle as baby down. She was so supple, so round; so young.

He clutched her breasts, squeezed them, wanting to hurt her, but she only cried out in joy, and hungrily, hurriedly, got out of his own clothes, popping tuxedo studs, losing them forever in the grass and not caring, and lowered himself over her.

How many conquests was this? Who could count...

Then her cry of joy became something else.

Something terrible.

And the flesh beneath his hands suddenly felt... downy?

He lifted part-way off her and looked down, squinting, trying to believe his eyes, but it was difficult...

The naked young woman on the ground beneath him, her flesh washed in the unadorned light of the full moon above, the clouds having fled, seemed to be undergoing a bizarre and yet beautiful transformation; the hair that grew and covered her body in gentle tufts was white, and even her face was covered with it, this tufted downy white fur, truly did make her a lovely platinum blonde all over, and when her mouth extended into a modified snout, the teeth were white, too, gleaming, sharp, long, like the claws that were suddenly where pink fingernails had been...

Her howl drowned out his scream, as Jack Wolff was reduced to a sorry pile of torn human flesh, the greenery around them splashed with blood, the young female animal bending over him, feasting on his flesh, tearing the vital organs from the gaping wound she had made from his neck to the one organ she had no interest in...

It took Jack Wolff a long time to die, but some would say not long enough. He had died without learning any of the lessons about life that most half-way decent people learn, with one exception perhaps.

He may have realized, in those last conscious moments, that a mere wolf is no match for a werewolf.

NOT A CREATURE
WAS STIRRING

The child was dead.

Homicide Captain Morgan Conway knelt over the slumped, crumpled form in its neat-as-a-pin blue-and-white snowsuit; he touched the boy's bruised face. The child was in a ditch, in a culvert, feet in, head out. Flakes of snow as big as half-dollars were drifting to the earth, and the countryside nearby was blanketed white like something off a Christmas card.

But in this ditch the snow mingled with cinders and soot and the boy looked as dirty as he did dead, even as snowflakes kissed his white face and dissolved into moisture.

Detective Cass Seymour, his hands sunk deep into his topcoat pockets, his breath smoking, stood next to Conway. His rumpled, freckled face was plainly mournful. He did not lean down to see the dead child better; he didn't seem to want to.

"About your boy's age," Seymour said.

Conway nodded. His eyes were slits in a face as blank as the blacktop road nearby. "About," he said.

"Tim's a little older."

"No," Conway said, and shook his head. His eyes were fixed on the small corpse. "This child is older than all of us."

"Huh?"

He stood. "You can't get older than dead."

Up on the blacktop, the ambulance awaited, its lights swiveling, casting streaks of blue light into a clear, cold night. Several squad cars were there, one city, one sheriff's department, as well as the farmer and his wife who'd spotted the little body, before dark.

"Fourth child," Seymour said, "in as many weeks. All boys. All about five, six years old."

Conway said nothing; he just stared at the boy.

"Strangled," Seymour went on, "with one powerful hand."

Conway sighed and began up the embankment.

"No apparent sexual assault, at least," Seymour said.

Conway nodded to the ambulance boys, who'd been waiting with their stretcher and tiny body bag. They went down to the culvert.

"The bastard's going to do this again, you know?" Seymour said.

"No, he isn't," Conway said.

Everybody called him the Fat Man, but his three-hundred pounds were remarkably solid on his six-foot frame. To glance at him, you'd take him for jolly; but there was cruelty in the Fat Man's eyes, and something else: something not wholly sane.

His features, however, were so benevolent, people often failed to notice - at first - the wrongness in his gaze. His hair was prematurely snow-white, thinning on top, long on the sides, tied back in a short ponytail; his beard was white, neatly trimmed. He had apple cheeks, touched with apple-red, a substantial yet rather pug nose, and a big, wide smile - albeit yellowed and sans eye-teeth, emphasizing the front teeth and canines.

He'd held many jobs during his forty-five years, hard, physical work, mostly: he was a veteran of foundries, shipyards, warehouses. He never lasted at any of them long because he inevitably either stole something, or hurt someone. For that reason, he'd had many names, various sets of fake, forged i.d.'s; and he'd lived everywhere, or at least in every major city in the States, including Hawaii and Alaska, and Canada, too.

He had the wanderlust, all right, but now as he was getting older, he was tiring of box-cars and flop-houses; for all the petty theft in which he'd engaged, for all the drunks he'd rolled, women he'd mugged, he had nothing to show for it. Years of hard work, and what had it gotten him?

He didn't drink, he didn't smoke - except occasional weed - and, other than enjoying a good meal, had no vices to speak of. Except for the little boys.

The Fat Man was no pervert, not in his eyes. The little boys were part of a scheme, a master plan. There was nothing deviate or sexual about it, as far as he was concerned. He'd always got worked up, when he did robberies; he'd always got stiff in his pants, when he invaded somebody else's home. Didn't everybody?

The wind, the snow, flecked his face as he stood on the street corner, ringing the bell. It was late morning in the Loop. Shoppers passed by and only occasionally stopped to toss coins or even more rarely paper money into his pot. People just didn't have the Christmas spirit this year, the Fat Man had come to realize; sometimes he didn't know what the world was coming to.

A little boy and his mother passed by, coming out of the big department store in front of which the Fat Man had set up his little tripod with pot; it didn't say "Salvation Army" on it, it didn't say anything at all, there was nothing to indicate any charity - but nobody noticed, or anyway cared. And some suckers did give. This boy's mother didn't. Rich bitch, in her fancy clothes; fur collar. An animal died for her to be fashionable and warm, the Fat Man thought disgustedly.

The little boy was perfect. The mother was obviously well-to-do. But today was wrong.

The Fat Man didn't know why, but he'd limited himself to Fridays. Every single one of them had been on a Friday; today was Saturday - he'd already done one, yesterday. And the funeral wasn't till Monday - so he might as well work the smaller con, today, and pick up a few dollars.

"Mommy," the little boy said, tugging his mother's arm, as he noticed the Fat Man. The little boy was about seven, a round-faced, bright-eyed child in a tiny camel's hair coat that must have cost a small fortune. "Mommy, Mommy!"

"What, dear?" The mother was in a hurry, but never in too much of a hurry to stop in her tracks and attend her spoiled brat. The Fat Man rang his bell, smiled, thinking about how people were scum.

"We should give some money," the little boy said. "It's Christmas and there's poor people in the world."

"Okay, dear," the mother said, digging in her purse.

She trotted impatiently over to the kettle where the Fat Man stood ringing his bell and tossed in a quarter. It rang against the metal. A rich bitch like that, and a lousy quarter. Jesus!

The mother then hauled the little boy away, down the street, getting lost in the falling snow and the swarm of holiday shoppers. His small face looked back brightly, and his little white smile was shy. "Bye, Santa - bye!"

"Ho ho ho!" said the Fat Man in the white-trimmed red suit, and his bell rang in the chill afternoon. "Ho ho ho!"

"We're glad you're willing to head up the task force, Conway," the weary, balding detective said. His name was Simmons, and he was a detective on the Bolingbrook force. He and half a dozen other detectives and two sheriff's deputies from adjacent counties were seated at a long conference table in the Homicide Squad's war room at Central Police Headquarters. Chief Paterson sat at the head of the table; Conway stood studying a map that had been tacked to the wall.

On the periphery stood the other members of the Major Crime Squad: Cass Seymour; Ann Greene; and Lee Brown. The two women were physically similar, attractive young women in rather severe dark suits designed to subdue their charms in favor of a business-like demeanor. Ann was in her early thirties, with a detached expression born of experience. Lee Brown was in her mid-twenties, an African American woman who, latest addition to the team that she was, was alert and eager.

But neither Ann nor Lee - nor the two men for that matter - were immune to the horror of this crime. Prolonged exposure to the seamy side of life - which Greene, Seymour and Conway had had, and then some - was no cushion for child murder. Lee Brown, when she went through the murder scene photos, had wept. Nobody held it against her.

"Gentlemen," Chief Paterson said to the visiting detectives, "I think we're all wise not to get bogged down in red tape and territorial rights. We've got a serial killer who has struck in three suburbs and in the city itself."

"He may be clever enough," Conway said, turning away from the map with its four pins stuck in it, at various points representing the murder sites, "to hope to muddy the waters by spreading the murders around, as it were."

"It's a potential bureaucratic nightmare," Simmons said, shaking his shiny head.

"Only if we let it be," Conway said, a forefinger gently raised.

"What I would suggest," Chief Paterson said, gesturing with open palms, reasonably, "is that you turn all the murders over to Conway and his team - and they'll interface with investigators in each of your cities, and counties, at the appropriate times."

One of the sheriff's deputies, a thin, dark man named Martins, said, "That doesn't sound like a task force to me." There was no irritation in his voice, but clearly toes had been stepped on.

"What *I* would suggest," Conway said, "is that an investigator from each department work out of our office. With us." He nodded toward Simmons. "When one of my people is investigating the crime in Bolingbrook, for example, you'll be along."

"What about the rest of us?" another detective asked. He was a heavy-set fellow named Schlemon, out of Naperville.

"You'll be here dealing with the various tips and confessions that are going to start pouring in," Conway said, "when the papers get wind of this cooperative effort."

Ann said, "We should encourage that, by the way - set up a Hot Line number."

"There's already a reward from the local Crimestoppers group," Seymour reminded them.

Conway nodded. "Are we in agreement, then? Can we proceed as a task force?"

There were nods and murmurs of agreement all around.

"We need a name," Simmons said.

Seymour snorted. "How about the 'Let's Nail the Psychopathic Son-of-a-Bitch Task Force'?"

There was a smattering of wry laughter.

"We'll make it the Christmas Killer Task Force," Conway said, with finality.

"Why?" Simmons asked.

"Because Christmas figures in," Conway said matter of factly. "Each of these children was with his mother, shopping at a mall or a major department store. They were separated, in various ways, and the child was lost in the Christmas crowds. Forever."

Everyone nodded. Several sighed.

"Besides," Conway said, with a tight smile that really wasn't a smile at all, "I intend to stop the psychopathic son of a bitch *before* Christmas gets here."

The Fat Man sat on the threadbare couch of his dingy two-room apartment and counted his money. Next to him on the couch, at his right, was the kettle; on his left was a leather pouch into which he was dropping the coins. At the moment he was thumbing through the greenbacks he'd collected in a long, cold day's work. Fifty-one bucks in bills; maybe another twenty in change. Cheap bastards.

He wore the red pants from the Santa Claus suit, and the upper part of him, including his enormous belly, was encased in the pink of long johns; his socks were black and holey. He was smoking a small pipe filled with hash. His apple cheeks beamed. Despite the small haul of the day, he knew he was getting richer.

When this was over, he'd have a hell of a stake. Maybe open-up a small business of some kind. An adult bookstore would be nice. Maybe he could fence stuff out of the back or start dealing dope. Leave all this petty theft behind and be a solid, respectable businessman.

He put a rubber band around the bills and rose slowly, the hash making him drowsy, and moved over to the tiny plastic tree on the television. Several strands of red and green lights winked on the little tree; some aluminum angel hair shimmered there. On the TV screen, the sound turned down, the news was on; an image of a car crash was replaced with that of the boy the Fat Man had most recently killed.

He placed the cash under the tree where many more rubber-banded wads of money lay - the proceeds of the expensive goods he'd been peddling to fences these past weeks. He stood rocking on tiny feet that seemed barely to support his weight, smiling, smoking, looking at his money.

He kept the cash hidden under a floorboard, when he went out; but when he was home, after a day's work, he carried the bills from their hiding place to the tree, where he arranged them carefully, like so many presents to himself.

How he hated Christmas. That had been the worst time, at his house. His father was a brute who drank and beat his underfed skinny son, and the three similarly underfed skinny daughters. The skinny little boy's mother was fat, and the drunken father hated her for it; she got beat worst of all.

There were no Christmas presents in that house. It was a house - or rather shack - where Santa Claus never came. Except for one year when Mama bought them a few toys, but Pop, when he found out, beat her for "spoiling the brats". Really, he beat her because buying the toys meant she was holding out money on him. Money he could've drunk up.

Not that Mama was a wonderful person. She caught the skinny little boy abusing himself, when he was eleven or twelve, and she beat him with a belt, worse than Papa ever did, almost. Told him sex was a sin, told him it was ugly. She was right about that. The skinny little boy, who had grown into the Fat Man, felt no particular attraction to men or women. His great pleasures in life came from eating, stealing, and hurting.

For several years now, he had parlayed his resemblance to Saint Nick into an effective Yuletide con, dressing up in the Santa suit and ringing the bell next to the kettle outside various department stores and within malls. He stayed on the move, working one place a day, sometimes two, so that nobody caught on.

He despised children, but had to pretend otherwise; they always came up to him and pestered him, calling him Santa, or accusing him of not being Santa, asking if he was the real Santa's helper, wanting to pull his beard and see if it was real - all that crap. He stood ringing his bell, wishing he could wring their necks.

Then, at the beginning of the season this year, just before Thanksgiving, outside a particularly posh department store, he noticed a mother dressed to the teeth, accompanying a nose-in-the-air brat wearing a brown leather coat, and the idea came in an instant.

Or at least, it came in the instant during which the brat's stuck-up expression melted upon seeing Santa Claus. The boy was probably six, and still believed.

"Santa!" he said, eyes Sugarplum-bright. "Santa - are you going to bring me my pony?"

"Ho ho ho," the Fat Man had said. "Ho ho ho!"

"The victims have a lot in common," Ann Greene said, pointing to pictures that were tacked to a bulletin board in the war room. Fortunately, these pictures of the boys were not death photos, though seeing the portraits - studio photography, all - was sad enough.

"Wealthy parents," Lee Brown said, nodding.

"Six years or under," Seymour said.

It was early Saturday evening, with Christmas a week and a day away, and the task force members from the suburbs had gone home. Only Conway and his team remained; they'd not been out in the field yet.

The long day had been spent going over the files on the four homicides. Forensic evidence was skimpy: a few strands of red cloth, a few more of white wool, had been found at two of the killings respectively. Each child had been strangled by a single powerful hand, presumably but not necessarily the hand of a man.

On Monday, the detectives would start talking to the parents of the victims and begin trying to retrace the steps of the last day of each child.

"We have white kids," Conway said, sitting on the edge of the table, "from all over the city." He ticked that fact off on a finger; proceeded to do the same for the facts that followed. "We have rich kids - or anyway kids whose parents are relatively well off. We have young kids - kindergarten or pre-school, but no toddlers. Always boys. Always out Christmas shopping with their mothers."

"Always on Friday," Seymour said.

"You can count on serial killers to be two things," Conway said.

"Sick," Ann said, finishing his thought for him, "and cyclical."

"Right," Conway said. "And as far as I'm concerned, the significance of Friday is limited."

"Limited to what?" Seymour asked.

"Limited to," Conway said, "we got till next Friday to catch him."

The Fat Man hadn't planned to do it more than once. But he hadn't planned to *like* it, either. When he strangled the first boy, he'd felt that familiar stiffening, followed by the warmth, the wetness of release.

He'd suffered guilt afterwards - not for the killing, but for the sexual emission. But the guilt passed, and as the Fat Man did not deny himself any pleasure, he began to think of doing it again.

When the first haul proved enormously lucrative, he decided to continue. The police would think they were dealing with a serial killer. They would not, the Fat Man knew (and it was a thought he relished), suspect that they were dealing with a criminal mastermind, a world-class thief.

"It will just take a moment," Conway told Bess.

Bess, his wife of many years, a lovely blonde with delicate features, smiled bravely and nodded.

From the back seat, Tim - their mid-life son, who was now ten years old - said, "Come on, Dad! They'll be sold out of 'Hatchet-Jaw' if we don't hurry!"

Conway turned and looked back at the boy. "Who says you're getting Hatchet-Jaw for Christmas?"

"Dad, it's such a cool game. You've played at the arcade with me! Scott has the home version, and it's really great - truly *awesome* graphics!"

"I'm not crazy about you spending so much time planted in front of these video games."

Bess reassured her son. "Maybe Santa Claus'll bring it to you."

"Santa Claus," the boy said, derisively. "Yeah. Right. Him and the Easter Bunny and the Tooth Fairy. They'll all chip in."

Conway shook his head, smiled, climbed out of the car and walked through a snowbank to a shoveled walk before an impressive, Colonial-style house. These folks had money, Conway thought; but today they were the poorest people on the planet.

He knocked.

A sad-eyed, red-haired woman of about forty, in black, answered. "Yes?"

"Are you Mrs. Jeffries?"

"No. Mrs. Jeffries is my sister. I'm afraid she's not seeing anyone right now."

He showed the woman his badge. "Is Mr. Jeffries here?"

"I'll get him. Step inside, would you, please?"

Conway stepped into the entry way.

Jeffries, a handsome, haunted-looking man in his thirties, approached and offered his hand. He wore a white shirt and a black tie.

"Mr. Conway," he said, obviously recognizing the detective from the TV news. "An honor to meet you."

The men shook hands.

"I was pleased to hear you'd taken charge of this investigation," Jeffries said. "Would you like to come in? Can we get you coffee...?"

"No, Mr. Jeffries. I had hoped to speak to your

wife, today, because...well, I know the funeral is tomorrow, and I thought, perhaps..."

Jeffries shook his head, smiled tightly. "I'm afraid Maggie isn't in any shape to...well, as you can imagine, she's taken this rather hard. Bobby was our only child, you know. And we can't have any mo...uh... anyway, she's blaming herself." He shook his head again, made a clicking sound in his cheek. "She's been sedated."

"I understand, Mr. Jeffries." He gave the man his card. "My work number and my home number are both on there. If you wish, call me this evening, and I'll come back. The sooner we can do this, the better."

Jeffries nodded. "I understand. Do you think you can catch this creature?"

"Yes."

"You sound confident."

"I am."

"Mr. Conway, my son was a good boy. A sweet boy. He never hurt a soul. How could anyone harm a sweet child like Bobby? What kind of sick son of a bitch could do that?"

"I don't know, Mr. Jeffries. I've been at this a long time, and I never cease to be surprised by the depths human beings, at their worst, can sink to."

Jeffries shook his head, stared at the floor.

Conway put a hand on the man's shoulder. "But you can't dwell on that. There are also heights that human beings rise to. Sometimes human beings can be as good as your Bobby was."

Jeffries smiled a little and nodded. "I know. I know. But Mr. Conway...at their worst, people can be...ghouls. We've had reporters hounding us. TV cameras in our front yard. I talked to the father of the little Reynolds boy, the boy who was killed last week. Do you know that the day of the funeral, somebody broke into their house and looted the place?"

"Unfortunately, that's common. Thieves watch the papers for funeral notices and hit the place while the family is away."

"Ghouls! Goddamn ghouls..." The man was shaking his fists.

"Take it easy, Mr. Jeffries."

"I...I'm all right, Mr. Conway."

"I'm a father, too. I understand. Can I give you a little advice?"

"Certainly, Mr. Conway."

"Quit holding it in. Start crying, now. You owe to yourself. And to Bobby."

Tears began streaming down the man's face and he nodded and swallowed. Conway went out.

At the mall, Bess went off by herself and Conway and Tim shopped together for the boy's mom, stopping at a cosmetic counter for perfume, then getting a salesgirl's help picking out clothes. Out in the central area, Conway was standing at the gift-wrapping booth, paying, when he suddenly realized Tim was no longer at his side. He looked over his shoulder and saw his son standing over by the fenced-in "lawn" of gold-flecked cotton-snow surrounding the throne where the mall's Santa sat. A line of kids was waiting; a little girl was on Santa's lap.

Tim didn't believe in Santa, anymore; hadn't for a couple of years. Nonetheless, the boy was standing looking at the man in red and white with the fake beard, looking at him yearningly. Ten years old, Conway thought, and the boy's already lost some of his innocence.

Still, Tim wasn't so old that he couldn't get caught up, for at least a moment, in the myth, in the spell, in the magic of Santa Claus. The thought made Conway smile.

Then it made him frown.

On Monday afternoon, the Fat Man went to the Jeffries house. He was dressed as Santa Claus. In his hand was a large tin can with the words "Help the Homeless". He went to several houses on the suburban street where the Jeffries family lived and collected donations. There weren't many homes on this street, however - Jeffries had dough, and he had the big house and the big lawn that that kind of money could buy.

This afternoon, the Fat Man knew, the Jeffries were at a big, expensive funeral. They were Catholic, according to the obit in the paper, and the boy (Robert, his name was) would receive a full Mass. Plenty of time to fill Santa's sack - and the back of Santa's battered panel truck, which he would pull into the garage once he'd swung open the door from within.

He would go in through a window in back (after he clipped the phone line - most alarm systems were tied in that way), fill his laundry bag with smaller valuables like jewelry, cash and art pieces, and figure out exactly what he was going to take of bigger items, before moving the truck inside.

What had made his plan so masterful was that he'd hit a number of other homes, on the days of funerals, in the last month, so that the fact that the families of the slain boys were among these robbery victims wouldn't seem significant.

But it had been those robberies, the ones of the parents of the dead boys, that had been the most profitable. Because he'd gone after little boys who were obviously from rich families. Like the one whose distracted mother had stopped at a perfume counter and didn't see her son making awed conversation with Santa, who'd stepped inside from the cold for a moment, from his charity-kettle stand. Or the one whose mother stepped into the ladies' room, leaving her boy to wait just outside; or the mother at the mall gift-wrapping booth who didn't notice her boy wandering away, his attention caught by a bell-ringing Santa; or the mother who was making a call in pay phone just inside the door of a department store, while her boy's attention was caught by Santa on the street corner nearby.

They'd all been wealthy, at least by the Fat Man's standards, and he liked hurting them. Hurting the children first, and then, like today, hurting the parents.

The window, which he broke with his gloved fist, opened onto the kitchen, but he soon moved into a large, plushly-furnished living room, dominated by a big, real evergreen whose lights twinkled and whose elaborate decorations were storybook perfect. Other Christmas touches made the room festive: here a holly wreath, there a Poinsettia plant; a nativity scene shared the mantel of the brick fireplace with framed family photos and three carefully draped, knit green stockings with names sewn in red thread: MOM, DAD, BOBBY. A fire crackled below. Odd. No one home, and a fire going...

"Get your hands up," a voice said. "Right now."

The voice was deep, and it meant business.

The Fat Man turned and saw a firm-jawed, slit-eyed guy in a black suit and red-and-black tie. He wore a yellow fedora and had a .357 mag in his fist. He looked like a kid's idea of a detective.

But the Fat Man knew this was no kid's fantasy: this was Morgan Conway himself, that homicide dick who made the damn news all the time.

The Fat Man had no weapons. He never carried a gun, and though he used a knife, had none with him. This was his day to steal, not to hurt. All he had to fight back with was himself, and a surprising quickness.

He flung the empty laundry bag at Conway, whipping it through the air, and it caught the detective's wrist, and the gun went flying toward the big tree, which seemed to swallow it. Then the Fat Man charged Conway, lowering his head, and running him down, like a car plowing into a pedestrian.

Conway was on his back with the enormous fat man in the Santa Claus suit on top of him. The man smelled bad, and his Santa Claus face was looking down at Conway with a contorted expression, which made for a bizarre effect: this guy was like the Santa Claus in the old-time Coca Cola ads, only decayed - several teeth missing, the rest yellow, the eyes hard and crazed and bloodshot.

And massive rough-gloved hands were sliding around Conway's throat.

Conway was pinned beneath the man, but one of his arms was free, and he slammed a fist into Santa's side, once, twice, and again, and again, but it seemed to have no effect, and as those fingers gripped and squeezed, and as Conway's world began to go red, he wondered if Cass, Ann and Lee - posted variously outside the house - had heard the clatter.

The detective summoned his will and his strength, and he directed a solid fist into the side of Santa's head, aiming for the man's ear - and striking the mark.

Santa howled, his weight shifted, his grip loosened, and Conway lifted and dumped the fat man off him, to one side, like a big sack of cement. He rolled to one side, and the fat man, recovering, came after him, but Conway swung a foot up and caught the bastard in the groin.

The fat man curled into himself, silently screaming.

He was one red ball, his pink balding skull presenting a target Conway couldn't resist. He slammed a fist into the skull, and the fat man toppled, backward, like a giant bowling pin.

There was no time to try to recover the gun; it was lost in the tree and the presents underneath. Conway fished his handcuffs from his suitcoat pocket and snapped one onto the wrist of the fallen fat man, who was on his back, his face distorted with rage.

But the other hand, balled into a fist the size of a softball, plowed into the side of Conway's face, knocking the kneeling Conway onto his side. The big man lumbered to his feet and, with both fists raised, moved like a tank toward Conway, who scrambled back, and he felt the heat of the fire on him, realized the fireplace was nearby, and his fingers found the fireplace utensils in their stand, his hand curled around an iron poker, and he swung the poker into the fat man's belly, cutting him in half.

Conway stood, and swung the poker like a golf club, catching the doubled-over fat man in the back of the neck, and the man plowed into the brick fireplace head-first. The fat man fell with a whump in a heap on the hearth.

Conway bent and pulled the arm with the cuffed wrist around behind the guy to meet his other wrist, but Santa came suddenly alive, and bucked Conway off.

The fat man was getting to his feet when Conway charged him, knocking him back onto the hearth; the fat man's head was inches away from the fire but he reached up maniacally and got his hands around Conway's neck again and started to squeeze. Hard. Conway's fingers fumbled for the poker, instead found its mate, a small shovel, and he swung the shovel back, and brought it down savagely, and flattened the fat man's face.

The hands fell away.

Conway, swallowing, got up. His breath was heaving. He stumbled back and got his balance and looked down at the fat man. The fat man's eyes were open wide, staring at nothing. The bones and cartilage of his nose had been shoved up into his brain. His white beard was spattered with blood; his mouth was a pulpy mess. He was deader than a Christmas goose.

Cass and Ann were inside, now; the fight, which had seemed to go on so long, had been only a minute or two at most.

"When we didn't hear from you by walkie," Ann told Conway, "we thought we better come in."

"Good decision," Conway said, still catching his breath.

Seymour was looking at the fat body sprawled on the hearth. "Looks like Santa here came down the chimney the hard way," he said.

Conway sat on the edge of a sofa. His face was touched with red here and there - his own blood and the fat man's. He sat there and looked at the Christmas tree. Its lights sparkled; angel hair shimmered; round shiny decorative balls of green and red reflected.

"Are you okay, boss?" Ann asked him, a gentle

hand on his shoulder.

Conway's battered, bloodied face, which had settled into a blank mask, broke into a smile. "Never better. How often do you get exactly what you want for Christmas?"

OPEN HOUSE

The trip was a bust, and my editor would likely glower at my expense account voucher, even though it was mostly made up of such extravagances as my $32.50-a-night motel room and this $8.54 breakfast (two scrambled eggs, hash browns, link sausage, toast, coffee) in Homewood, at a café downtown populated by farmers, merchants, insurance agents and other heartland salt of the earth.

I was in a corner booth, thinking that Mrs. Rorshak's boy Gavin, who had wanted to win the Pulitzer Prize since the age of seven, had somewhere gone astray. My reputation, such as it was, seemed built on ghosts, goblins, vampires, ghouls, and my investigations therein had mostly wound up spiked by nervous editors or as supermarket-tabloid fodder.

In my rumpled white suit with matching porkpie

hat, and striped tie loose around my collar, the only ghost haunting this little farm community seemed to be me – a specter straight out of *Front Page*, that ancient newspaper play that had spawned multiple movies as well as the eternal newshound cliche, of which I appeared the only (technically) living example.

"Mr. Rorshak?"

The voice was male, resonant, but quivery – nerves, not age.

I glanced up at its owner, a white-haired, slender man who (if his hair could be overlooked) seemed to be about thirty-five. He was dark – whether a tanning bed disciple or back from a vacation, I couldn't hazard a guess – which made his white eyebrows seem like peculiar apparitions in his face – fuzzy white caterpillars floating above small dark eyes.

Otherwise, he was fairly average – the sort of regular features you could forget by this afternoon. He wore a bright red blazer with a logo on its pocket – FAMILY REALTY – and his tie was a neatly knotted patriotic red-white-and-blue stripe.

"Do you mind if I sit down, sir?" he asked.

"It's your town," I said, gesturing with my fork. "I'm just passing through."

He sat. "You're something of a celebrity, Mr. Rorshak. We don't get many celebrities in Homewood."

I swallowed a bite of hash browns. "If writing for a tabloid and appearing on the occasional cable paranormal sleazefest qualifies me as a celebrity...well, then, I guess Homewood doesn't get many, no."

His eyes tightened. "I realize this trip was a disappointment."

"Does everybody in town know what I'm doing here? Or what I *was* doing here...Like I said, I'm on my way – "

"Please stay one more night."

I pushed my plate aside. I had only half-finished the meal but was completely through with Homewood.

"Look," I sighed, "some nutty gal at the community college lured me out here to watch for the ghost of some professor in the library, and...after two long nights camped out in the stacks, the scariest things were when we saw a janitor smoking a joint, and when Library Lady put her hand on my thigh and told me she was the reincarnation of Cleopatra."

"Do you have a lot of...false alarms?"

"More often than not. I'm a reporter whose specialty is the weird. And boy do the weird seek me out. Unfortunately, oddballs in and of themselves do not make for a good story."

"Do you...believe in these things you write about?"

"I've run into some unusual stuff, over the years. Some of my best stories never made it to the public's eyes and ears, however – between nervous publishers and government intervention, I've lost more games than I've won."

A white-caterpillar eyebrow skewed skyward. "But you *also* have been known to debunk."

I sipped black coffee, nodded. "That's a reporter's

best instinct...what's your name again?"

"Oh! I'm sorry. I'm Martin Crankheit. I manage – "

"Family Realty?"

He smiled, impressed; shook his head. "You *are* good," he said.

I didn't have the heart to remind him of the logo on his blazer pocket. "Anyway, Mr. Crankheit, my natural instinct is to question – to be skeptical. If you've followed my work at all, you'll know those who lure me into a staged 'phenomenon'...those who seek to take advantage of my reputation, such as it is, to put some scam over...well, they soon find themselves the subject of a scathing exposé."

He was shaking his head. "Well, I assure you my... situation is no scam, nothing staged."

This is where I should have yelled, "Check please."

But something about the earnestness of my white-haired, well-tanned new acquaintance caused me to ill-advisedly ask, "What situation is that, Mr. Crankheit?"

His eyes narrowed, his voice hushed. "It has to do with a house five miles out of town – a lovely old foursquare farm house. It's owned by distant relation of the late residents."

"*Recently* late?"

"Well – they died five years ago."

"They...all died?"

"Yes – father, mother, child. The house is large, almost a mansion, and should be worth a quarter of a million dollars...which in this part of the world is a considerable chunk of real-estate change."

I got out my notebook. "And there have been no other owners in those five years?"

Crankheit frowned. He flagged a waitress, ordered coffee, and said, "Family Realty is a new agency, Mr. Rorshak. Two others in town previously had this listing. I'm sort of...just starting out."

"I see."

"Actually, you don't. Family Realty's home office is in Jefferson, thirty miles due west. My father owns it and has spun off into half a dozen other small communities around the state. He's a wealthy man, my father...and I've been, well...not terribly ambitious."

"I see."

"Now perhaps you do. I struck off on my own and made a mess of things. I came back home, and my father has given me...I'd be lying if I said it was a second chance. More like fourth or fifth chance. But certainly, my last chance."

"You need to make a go of it here."

A vigorous nod. "Right. And this listing...this home...in addition to getting the agency a sizeable commission...would represent a conspicuous success, if I could move it."

"Because the other two agencies, the well-established agencies in Homewood, have failed."

He beamed. "Exactly, Mr. Rorshak."

"But *why* have they failed, Mr. Crankheit?"

His coffee came. He drank half of it before he found any more words.

"The family who lived in that house was called Larson. Mr. Larson was an older man – he had inherited Larson House, as the place is called, from his parents, a very successful farm family. Mr. Larson was ugly – that may sound harsh, but he had a bad skin condition as a young man that left his face utterly ravaged – a puffy landscape of pockmarks and scars, not helped by features that would have been unpleasant with a perfect complexion – cow eyes, a bulbous nose, and thick, fleshy lips."

"I'm glad I finished eating," I said.

"It's not an appetizing tale. Through young manhood, Niles Larson had worked on the family farm for his father, and they say his father was a stern taskmaster – did not want his boy to feel privileged, wanted him to earn his way. Frankly, I can understand this all too well – rather parallels my situation."

"When did Larson inherit?"

"He was about thirty. Despite the wealth of his family, he'd never enjoyed any fruits – certainly had been anything but spoiled. He'd never traveled, and despite a love for literature – he was a boy who read voraciously, it's said – he was not allowed to attend college. His father wanted Niles to be a real man, a man of the land, of the earth – a farmer. It's said that the boy's mother was doting, and that her love was the saving grace in his life. But she died of influenza at age twenty-nine, and from his early teenage years on, Niles was raised by the old man, a stern disciplinarian."

He waved the waitress down again for more coffee.

Then he continued: "The old man had a game leg from a thresher accident, and that presumably is how he came to fall down the long flight of stairs, to his death. There have always been rumors that Niles pushed his father, but no proof, and certainly no charges were brought."

"How old was he at this point?"

"Thirty-five, thirty-six. He inherited the farm, and half a dozen other farms that the father owned. He arranged to have the land worked by other hands, kept Larson House, but never again had a thing to do with farming, other than to collect checks. At age thirty-eight he went to the university and studied literature. At forty-two he began to travel the world. He loved the theater, and spent lots of time in New York, going to plays. He was fifty when he returned from one of these trips with a wife, a young actress."

"When was this?"

"Six or seven years ago. At first Susan kept to the house, and was subservient, submissive, a loving young bride. Later she made friends in town."

"What kind of friends?"

He shrugged elaborately. "Understand, Mr. Rorshak, that I am a recent resident here, myself. All of this is second hand..."

"That's all right. Go on."

"Well, Susan Larson got involved in community theater. She indicated that Niles had said he'd support her acting career, and that he'd promised they'd take a place in New York, and his wealth would help her achieve her goals."

"He'd be an angel to her theatrics? Fund productions...?"

"That had been Susan's understanding. But once he got her back to Homewood, he seemed to forget his promise. He joined the country club and displayed her on his arm, a beautiful young trophy wife. I don't think he was cruel, not physically, but he tried to forbid her from even amateur theatrics, which didn't go over well with the girl. She began to drink, and supposedly ran around on him – with the golf pro at the club, among others."

"Did Niles know about this?"

"I don't know. He was out of town quite a bit – he had become respectable, in his wealth, and served on the boards of several companies and was in particular active with his college. Susan rarely went on these trips with him. Friends of Susan claim that she frequently complained that Niles wanted a child, and she did not – the thought of a child from those 'grotesque genes' sickened her. But then, she got pregnant, after all. Some say her husband raped her, repeatedly, with procreation as the goal. At any rate, willing or not, with the pregnancy, everything came to a head."

"How so?"

Crankheit leaned forward, the small eyes becoming large, the caterpillars wriggling. "What follows is conjecture – worse than rumor. It's even...a legend...a myth."

"Go on."

"Susan had a little boy – Niles, Jr. A handsome child, as beautiful as his father was hideous. And Niles doted on the boy – apparently was determined not to treat him as despicably as his own father had him. But Susan's drinking continued, and they began to argue."

"Is that conjecture?"

"No – they argued in public. At the country club, in particular; they raged at each other – it was a public embarrassment. There are those who claim to have heard Susan scream at Niles that the boy was not his. Whose baby was it, then? But Susan laughed and said, it could have been any one of a dozen men – but not him, because she always used protection when he 'defiled' her. But with the 'beautiful boys' she slept with in Homewood, she never used protection – having a child with any one of them would be far preferable to bearing a 'gargoyle'."

"This argument was overheard."

"Yes. Of course, I got it second- and third-hand. So it may have been exaggerated."

I sat forward. "You said the whole family died..."

Crankheit drew a deep breath. He spoke softly, his tone low, but I didn't miss a word.

"That night...the night of the argument...Susan Larson bathed, as was her habit, before retiring. Her husband came in and drowned her in the tub."

"We know this for a fact?"

"Yes. Her body was actually laid out on her bed

– dry, in her nightclothes – but her face was frozen in a death scream, twisted like that horrible Munch painting...what is it called?"

"'The Scream,'" I said.

"And the autopsy showed that she had drowned – the water in her lungs was soapy."

"I wonder why he didn't just leave her in the tub," I mused.

"Because after he removed her," Crankheit said after a shudder, "he brought in his slumbering son... and drowned him, as well, leaving him there."

"Hell."

"Then, Niles either stumbled or threw himself down the stairs...the same stairway where his father had plunged to his death."

"And ever since," I said, "nobody's wanted to live in Larson House."

"That's not precisely the case," Crankheit said.

"Oh?"

"It's never really...got that far."

"I don't understand."

He shrugged. "The first Realtor who had the listing was preparing for an open house – he went in the night before, to spruce things up, make sure everything was shipshape. Turn the electricity on, put some refreshments in the refrigerator, and so on. Fairly typical."

"And?"

"And the next day when the first potential buyers arrived, no one greeted them. The door was open, so they went on in – a husband and wife in their late twenties, Yuppies coming up in the world. They found the Realtor on the floor in the living room – his face was frozen in the grimace of a scream."

"What did the police have to say?"

He sighed. "Well, let's start with the autopsy – the Realtor, a Mr. Donby, had drowned. He had soapy water in his lungs."

"What did the investigation reveal?"

"Nothing. Not a suspicious fingerprint in the house. They brought in a top crime analysis team, the best forensics in the Midwest...nothing."

"So much for the open house."

Crankheit flagged down the waitress again, asking for decaf on this third cup. I took my second cup of the real deal – thinking I could use the caffeine...

As he sipped, I said, "You mentioned a second Realtor took on the place? What happened there?"

"The same thing."

"What do you mean...the same thing?"

Another sigh, he closed his eyes. "Two years ago, after the house had sat for almost three years, another Realtor decided to give the place a try. It was a husband and wife team, a couple named Simmons, in their early thirties; they were kind of hot shots, I'm told, and bragged it up that they would find a buyer for this so-called haunted house."

I paused in my notetaking to sip my own coffee. "And they died, as well? Come on!"

"They went in the night before – same routine. The electricity and the water was turned on, and they put food and Hawaiian Punch in the fridge, and set about to generally spruce up the place – Mrs. Simmons may have started with the bathroom upstairs, where the murders had taken place."

"Why do you say she started there?"

"Well, because that's where she was found, in rubber gloves, with a can of Comet in one hand and a scrubber sponge in the other, sprawled in a silent death scream. Her husband was found on the floor in the library with a can of Pledge in one hand, a dust rag in the other, and his own scream grimace. Both were drowned – soapy water in their lungs."

"And the investigation...?"

"Nothing."

I shifted in my seat. "Meaning no offense, perhaps a small-town police department wasn't up to this crime."

"You're right, Mr. Rorshak – that's why the top serial-killer squad from the FBI was sent in, top CSIs, a profiler, chemicals, lasers, the works. They didn't find a fingerprint that didn't belong to the couple."

I chuckled drily. "And now you're getting ready for an open house?"

"Tomorrow morning." He swallowed, smiled nervously. "Unfortunately, I won't be able to make it, this evening...one of my people will be there. Jill Gannon, my best agent. She can meet you there...at seven?"

I reared back. "Hold on – what are you suggesting?"

"I'm suggesting you and Jill get ready for the open house. What I'd really like is for you two to spend several hours, well into the night if necessary."

"Oh, you would?"

Crankheit's expression was a mixture of earnestness and embarrassment. "Mr. Rorshak, if I can sell this so-called haunted house, my agency will top every list in the Homewood area...I'll be the talk of this little town, in a very good way...and my father will know I've really made a go of it, this time."

"Only...you don't want to be part of this experiment. You want to put this Jill...and *me*...on the line."

A nervous smile flickered, and he didn't quite look at me. "Jill volunteered – she'll have a gun with her. It's registered, and she knows how to use it. Whether you accompany her or not, she's going to be there. At seven."

"Why should *I* be there? At seven?"

The smile broadened. "Because it's a great story, Mr. Rorshak. Either way – you can debunk the myth of a ghost, or you can prove the existence of an afterlife... If that isn't Pulitzer material, I don't know what is!"

The guy had found my weak point.

"I've already stopped by your motel," he said, "and told the desk clerk that if you stay another night, the charge goes on my Visa."

"You're willing to make a $32.50 commitment like that, Mr. Crankheit? Wow."

"And I've left detailed directions to Larson House, plus a file folder of photocopies from the local paper's coverage of the original murders, and the two later ones. So you can familiarize yourself, further, with the facts."

"If I agree to this," I said, "either way, I'll want to interview you and Miss Gannon, tomorrow – with pictures."

"Fine. The publicity will be a bonus – we'll properly exorcize this demon."

I looked at him carefully. "Mr. Crankheit – who do *you* think was responsible for the murders of those Realtors? Donby, and the Simmons couple?"

"There are non-supernatural possibilities, and I'm a realist as well as a realtor, Mr. Rorshak...You'll find a story in the file I dropped off. About a year ago, a local man named Watkins – a friend of Niles Larson from back in high school, another farm boy – killed himself. He left a suicide note taking credit for the crimes."

"Oh. Well, that's an interesting small detail you left out."

"The problem is, Watkins – who was in his late fifties when he killed himself – had a long history of mental illness, of schizophrenia. He'd admitted to every murder in the Midwest, and was what the police call a – "

"Confessin' Sam," I said. "It's common everywhere."

"Right. Now, I happen to think Watkins probably did commit those crimes. Which is why I would risk sending Jill, and yourself, into that 'haunted' house."

I twitched a smile. "You just aren't willing to go."

He raised his hands in surrender. "I would, but my daughter has a ballet recital."

"Stop out after, why don't you?"

"I'll try to. I really will – are you saying you'll meet Jill at seven? It's a great story, Mr. Rorshak!"

"I'll be there. With you paying for my motel room, how can I resist another night in Homewood?"

"Here," the grinning Realtor said, and snatched up the check. "I'll take care of your breakfast, too!"

"Such a deal," I said.

And he was up and off, vanishing like a ghost – or anyway, a ghost that stopped at the cash register to pay for my tab and *then* vanished...

I spent the rest of the day in my motel room, going over the file of blurry photocopies that Crankheit had left at the desk.

The newspaper coverage didn't tell me much that the Realtor hadn't already. Several photos of the craggy-pussed Niles Larson lived up to the promise of one ugly mug. Several photos of Susan Larson revealed an undistinctive but pretty, young woman. Realtor Donby was a pudgy, smiling guy with glasses, his pleasant small-town photo-studio expression at odds with the description of his frozen scream at death. The Simmonses, an attractive brunette with a square-jawed blond hubby (in what appeared to be an anniversary photo), were a handsome but unremarkable-looking couple, projecting the bland personable vibe of their profession, and no hint of their grotesque end.

Many quotes from perhaps a dozen law enforce-
ment officers – local, state, and eventually federal –
started with assured statements of a case that would
be handily solved and devolved to admissions of
dead-ends but promises of open case files. The local
coverage of the Watkins' suicide almost hysterical-
ly hoped that this closed the murder cases that had
haunted Homewood in general and the old Larson
place specifically.

I took a nap and watched some TV. Whether I
watched the pay-for-view porn or not is not really
pertinent to this account. Shame on you people for
thinking so poorly of me. On the other hand, a reporter's life on the road is a lonely one...

But not as lonely as Larson House.

Nearly five miles out of town, down a blacktop
drive but minus a gate, Larson House sat on a slight
hillock – an unpretentious but massive square structure, two stories of tan brick with white trim (not
peeling – someone had maintained the place well)
on a raised basement, first floor approached by an
eight-step stairway with a porch the full-width of
the first story, the pyramidal roof broken by front
and side dormers.

The drive continued up into a graveled parking
area; at one time, one or more barns had likely abutted
the gravel square, and possibly animal pens, but those
were long gone. Niles Larson had put farming behind
him, except as a business others ran for him.

I parked and walked around to the steps and went up onto the porch. My hand was poised to knock when the door opened quickly enough to startle me – and at this point, ol' Gavin doesn't startle all that easily.

But as I caught my breath, I appreciated the view of my hostess – a slender woman in her late twenties whose red Family Realtor blazer with white pleated skirt and heavy black plastic-frame glasses could not disguise her beauty. She was blonde, shapely...and pretty, albeit in an unremarkable way. Like her boss Crankheit, she had nice features, even if you might forget them in a few hours.

Her eyes, however, a deep dark blue behind the glasses, were large and memorable. And her smile was instant, white, and lovely.

If I wasn't in love, exactly, I was at least smitten.

"Gavin Rorshak," I said, doffing the porkpie. "And you're Jill? Jill Gannon?"

"That's right, Mr. Rorshak." Her voice was a wonderful liquid alto. She stepped aside and gestured, that lovely smile still generating wattage. "Come in, come in."

I stepped inside. The place was beautifully furnished in a surprising 1930s art-deco fashion – surprising for two reasons: first, though the vintage of the dark-wood furnishings was certainly antique or at least collectible, they didn't match the turn-of-the-century plain-house style of the exterior. To the right was a dining room with striking '30s-modern furnishings, the long sleek table dressed with chrome candlesticks atop an oriental carpet worthy of Aladdin.

"The outside's American gothic," I said, scratching my head, "but this joint's strictly art deco."

"You should see the living room," Miss Gannon said, and guided me left, through an open archway into a square chamber where a sleek light-brown mohair sofa was flanked by tufted round-backed armchairs, with chrome and walnut furnishings spotted around a burnt-orange and brown room dotted with framed posters of Erté prints that seemed vintage. The far end had a white baby grand and a wall of books. I might have walked into a Park Avenue apartment circa 1935.

"Has your boss Crankheit had this stuff appraised?" I asked.

"Not to my knowledge," she said. "I know he thinks it's attractive, providing the place furnished."

"Furnished! This stuff is worth a small fortune. If the rest of the house is like this – "

"It is."

"Well, hell. The contents may be worth more than the house or the land!"

Miss Gannon shrugged. "That's not my department, Mr. Rorshak."

I gave her a long appraising look, getting past her attractiveness and appreciating her cool demeanor. "You're not afraid, are you?"

She laughed and the blonde locks bounced off red-blazered shoulders. "No. Why I should be?"

"Oh, I don't know – because the last two Realtors prepping for an open house here wound up...dead?"

She patted her purse. "I'm armed, Mr. Rorshak."

I cocked an eyebrow. "You really know how to use a gun, Miss Gannon?"

"Isn't it like a camera? Point and shoot?"

I laughed and shook my head. "Well, how are you doing, as far as getting ready for showing this place tomorrow?"

She gestured toward the rear. "I've been in the kitchen, mostly. I've got bottled water and five different kinds of soda in the fridge. No coffee yet, though I could make some."

"I'll have a Diet something."

She gave me a lovely smile. "Watching your figure, Mr. Rorshak?"

"I'd rather watch yours," I blurted. "Sorry...no harassment intended."

Her smile seemed genuine. "Don't worry about it."

"Hey, it was out of line. I'm old enough to be your father."

"I suppose...but the nice thing is – you're *not*."

Then she smiled fetchingly, and turned to head toward the kitchen, and as I pondered her words, the view was fine, her hips making the white pleated skirt do fun things as she walked.

The kitchen was a typical good-size farm kitchen, reworked into a modern white affair, the only deco touch silver curving knobs on the cupboards.

We sat at one end of a big black square lacquer-top table, and I had a Diet Coke while she poured herself a glass of water from an Evian bottle, but never got around to drinking it.

"Why *you* for this task, Mr. Rorshak?" she asked.

"Well, I'm a reporter. Didn't your boss tell you?"

"Of course, but why a desire to cover stories about...spooks?"

Shrugging, I hefted the can of Coke and sipped. "I kind of fell into this line. I was covering a straight crime-beat story and it got...weird. After that...well, everybody needs a specialty I guess."

Those big blue eyes had a sparkle of real interest. "And how often do you encounter something *really* weird? Something that isn't just...silly campfire stories?"

"About one out of ten or fifteen, I guess. People don't hear about the ones that don't go anywhere – of course, sometimes they don't hear about the ones that do."

She frowned. "Why's that?"

"When the truth is too disturbing, the powers-that-be have a habit of revising it – sort of, instant revisionist history."

"Why would they do that?"

"Public can handle a serial killer. But the thought that a real vampire might be among us? Or that a mummy from ancient Egypt might stagger around strangling people in this century? We can't have the populace panicking."

"You surely don't really believe in such things, Mr. Rorshak."

"My name is Gavin, and I'd just love to call you Jill."

The smile took on a pixie-ish quality. "Why don't you, then? Gavin, you're not saying you've really encountered such...such..."

"Creatures? I have. But other times such matters don't go unreported out of any kind of governmental concern for the public – it's sheer cover-up."

"How so?"

"Does Uncle Sam want voters to know that biological warfare research led to a zombie outbreak in Pennsylvania? Not hardly."

She was shaking her head and laughing. "I don't know whether you amuse me or interest me."

I grinned. "No law that says you can't be both." I leaned toward her. "Listen, on the long shot that there's some truth to this legend, or that maybe some whack-job out there has been killing Realtors over the years, and has just been waiting for the next opportunity..."

"Yes?"

"Why don't we look around this place, and get this over with? We're satisfied the kitchen is fine, right? So why don't go we check the house out, convince ourselves that all is well, then maybe...sit in the living for an hour or so and wait for nothing to happen...and maybe then we can leave this place to its memories, good and ill, and you'll let me buy you dinner somewhere in the sophisticated city called Homewood."

She shrugged. "Sounds like a plan."

The layout of the house was simple and typical of its era. We'd seen the downstairs with its large living room, and good-size kitchen and dining room;

and the upstairs was home to three bedrooms, one
obviously the master but the others generous as well.
The furnishings again were of the art moderne style,
with the master bedroom's blond suite including a
dressing table with rounded mirror where if any ghost
were haunting, by rights it would be Jean Harlow's.

The bathroom was large and the tub an old-fashioned big-as-a-Buick one, with claw feet, dating
back to farmhouse days and not touched by Niles
Larson's deco fetish. The walls were pale pink and
the porcelain gleamed.

"You cleaned up in here already," I said.

"Shouldn't I have?"

"Well...if you'll forgive me for taking this seriously,
if *any* room in this house has demons, this is the one."

She nodded, poised in the doorway, looking like
a refugee from a high-school show choir in her red
blazer. "The little boy was drowned here, right?"

"After the wife, yes."

She shivered as I joined her and ushered her away
from the cold pink room. "What a monster Niles
Larson was..."

"Or tortured soul," I said. "He'd loved that woman
and brought her here into this artistic world he'd revised out of his parent's farmhouse...and she betrayed
him, had a child by a lover. So, he killed her and the
kid. Not so hard to figure."

"Gavin! You don't *sympathize* with him, surely..."

"I always sympathize with monsters, Jill. How
else could I write my stories? I have to try to under-

stand these creatures...even as I deplore the cruelties they commit."

The staircase was wide and open; we could almost walk side by side, but she led the way.

"Sometimes that's what happens," I said.

"What is?" she said, and glanced back, almost losing her footing.

I took her arm, steadying her. "Easy – could be Niles's father's ghost haunting this joint, not his, y'know – didn't you ever wonder if the old boy's spirit didn't take his revenge on his son, and push *him* to his death that fateful night?"

Her eyes were huge. "Then you believe Niles killed his own father?"

"It's a possibility, is all."

Soon we were seated on that mohair sofa. The lighting was subdued, yellowish, from a pair of bronze nude-nymph lamps; I noted the far wall with its library of books, and if those were first edition Hemingways and F. Scott Fitzgeralds in dustjacket, over there, the Realtor had even more money coming his way, assuming Crankheit could start thinking outside the property box.

"What did you mean?" she asked. She was sitting fairly close to me, and her perfume was a lovely, faintly floral scent.

"Huh?"

"When you said, 'Sometimes that's what happens.'"

"Oh. Well, sometimes these legends grow up around horrible crimes – crimes so monstrous by human standards...killing a child, for example...that folklore steps in and substitutes monsters for men."

"But men can do monstrous things," she said.

"Oh, yes."

She hooked her arm in mine. "How long should we stay?"

"Getting creeped out, finally?"

"...Maybe. I was fine until I looked into that bathroom. I could just see that poor child under the water." She shivered again.

"You know what some of the parapsychology experts say, don't you, Jill? About such rooms? About houses like this one?"

"No – what?"

"That an act can be so terrible that the spirit of the one responsible for that act is condemned to remain here, on earth, in a sort of limbo...a prison fashioned from the very site of his crimes."

She swallowed. "You don't...you don't *really* think Niles Larson is haunting this place?"

"Well, if he is, that purse you're keeping close to you, with the gun in it? I don't think it'll do us much good."

She cuddled closer, and if you think saying what I did was intended to provoke such a response from this attractive young woman, you really must have a low opinion of me...accurate, but low...

"How...how much longer should we stay?" she asked.

I checked my watch. I'd been here about an hour

and a half. "Let's give it another thirty minutes. Honestly, I don't think there's anything to this, Jill."

"Are you sorry you came?"

"No! No..."

She kissed me.

I don't know about you, but I hadn't seen that coming!

But I didn't shirk my masculine responsibilities, and when she kissed me again, I responded in kind. Now, out of respect to the young lady, and to the reader's sensibilities, I will not report every detail that followed; suffice to say that we began to neck and pet like a couple of kids, and it was her idea, completely, entirely, I had not a damn thing to do with it, when she slipped out of the blazer and, okay, maybe I did unbutton her blouse but she eased out of the pleated skirt and got out of her panties, all on her own, and all I'll say about it is she had no inconsistencies of hair color.

Which is how I ended up naked myself on that mohair couch.

It happened so quickly that notions of safe sex didn't enter into it, and I won't deny that we made love but I'll be damned if I'll give you any specifics, other than to say she was on top and she was ethereally beautiful in that yellowish light in that art deco room...

We were in each other's arms, sprawled on that couch, breathing regular again, when the noises started upstairs.

She clutched me and I tried not to sound afraid when I said, "That's, uh...running water, isn't it? You can hear it in the pipes."

Her eyes showed white all around. "Who...who could be running water up there?"

"I don't know. Give me that gun."

"But Gavin!"

"Give it to me!"

She got into her purse, and dug for it, and handed it to me, a little .32 revolver.

"You wait here," I told her.

"The hell!"

There was no arguing with her, and neither of us had a stitch on as we made for those stairs and this time I led the way, stark naked, and I didn't envy Jill the view, but niceties were not the issue.

The issue was the sound of roaring, pounding water running, echoing through the pipes like Niagara, getting louder and louder...

When we got to the bathroom, standing there nude like bathers who'd been banished, we exchanged glances and gulps, because the sound was massive, churning, a watery howl as if every faucet in Homewood was running full blast, behind that single door.

"Go downstairs," I said to her. "Now."

She shook her head. "Open it. I have to see."

"Jill – go..."

"No! If you won't open it, I will!"

And she reached past me and opened the door and a wall of water rushed out, a tidal wave, a Tsunami, carrying me and presumably Jill, though I couldn't see her, away and down the hall, tossing me like a ragdoll, and I suppose you'd say I fell down the stairs, only I didn't feel any wood beneath me because there wasn't any, just water, a wall or rather a bed of liquid that carried me along and deposited me unceremoniously at the bottom of the stairway, and that wave rolled over me and consumed me and I had the taste of soapy water in my mouth, choking, when I blacked out.

Hands shook me awake, and a voice was shouting, "Rorshak! What the hell! *Rorshak!*"

And it wasn't Jill's voice, but a man's, and as I came to I recognized the voice as Crankheit's, which was easily enough accomplished because the darkly tanned, white-eyebrowed Realtor was leaning over me, his expression astounded and concerned.

Also, angry.

"What the hell is the idea?" he asked. Demanded.

I sat up.

Yup, I was jaybird naked, at the bottom of the stairs, but there was not a drop of water anywhere.

He helped me to my feet. "Where's Jill?"

"I don't know. Have you looked for her?"

"No! I just unlocked the front door, and you were sprawled bare-ass on the floor, here!"

Daylight was coming through windows, and that's when I realized I was standing naked in a house as bare as I was. Not a stick of furniture. I could see my clothes on the uncarpeted floor of what had been the living room but now was just an open chamber.

"Where the hell is all that art deco crap?" I asked.

White eyebrows knit. "What art deco crap?"

I tromped into the living room, the Realtor following me, and started putting my clothes on, quickly, like the lover of a wife whose husband was pulling in the driveway. "Crankheit, this house was filled with vintage art moderne furniture, and artwork, and valuable books and...where the hell did you take it to?"

Crankheit was looking at me like I was a madman – you know, a madman he'd discovered naked who was now raving and ranting while getting hurriedly dressed?

"Settle down, Rorshak – from what you're describing, I understand that's how Niles Larson furnished this house; but those things were sold years ago, by the estate."

"You weren't showing this as a *furnished* house?"

"No! Furniture like that belongs on the *Antiques Roadshow*, not in Homewood."

I was trying to make sense of that – and sense in Gavin Rorshak's world is different from your average bear's. All I could come up with this is: that pretty Realtor and I had found ghosts in this house after all, and those ghosts had been furniture! Including the sofa we'd...sat on.

"We have to find her," I said.

Crankheit followed me through the big empty house. But it wasn't until we looked somewhere I'd ignored yesterday that we found her...

...the dead naked woman.

Only it wasn't the woman I'd trysted with last night: this was a naked woman of about thirty-five, a little overweight, brunette, and whether she was attractive or not was hard to say, because her face was frozen in a Munch-ean scream.

"Is *that* Jill Gannon?" I asked him.

"My God...poor woman. Yes. Yes. Were you with her last night?"

"No."

"I thought – "

"I was with someone else."

"Who in hell?"

Shaking my head, I said, "I'm not sure, Mr. Crankheit. I'm not sure at all about what happened last night. It was like a...dream."

"More like a nightmare."

"No. A dream."

If I'd been completely honest with the guy, I would have added, *Wet dream...*

I wound up staying in Homewood for another two days. I was lucky I didn't have to stay longer, but the locals moved it through quick. Maybe it was getting old-hat to them...

Jill Gannon's clothing, black-rimmed glasses, and handbag with .32 revolver were never found. The brunette Realtor in the basement had been drowned – soapy water in her lungs, the coroner said.

I told my story and wasn't even questioned very

hard at the inquest. Maybe they thought I was just feathering my nest, coming up with a good yarn for my editor.

Or maybe they believed me.

A month later, I heard from Crankheit, who reported he'd asked and received permission from the owners to have the farmhouse torn down, so that he could sell the lot. With luck, the ghost in that house would not linger once the structure was demolished.

So what happened to me that night? Was I a middle-aged man who had some kind of hallucinatory sex fantasy?

Maybe.

Let's just say I don't believe Niles Larson ever was haunting that house; it was Susan, always Susan, the actress who wanted to keep people away from where she and her beloved child were last together. When I went back to the blurry photocopies Crankheit had provided me, I could see the resemblance between Susan Niles and the "Jill Gannon" she'd become. Perhaps the most disturbing thing was knowing that the real Jill Gannon had been dead in the cellar all the while, screaming a scream no one would ever hear.

Why my hostess had chosen not to kill me I put down to my native charm and rough-hewn good looks. Hadn't I been sent to Larson House, as the old phrase went, to lay a ghost?

Or did she lay me?

TRACES OF RED

The sky on this summer evening in the Catskills in 1954 was so deeply blue it might have been black, but the three-quarter moon and a scattering of diamond-like stars provided illumination. So did the light bulbs and Chinese lanterns decorating the wooden deck overlooking the lake. The handful of tables on the deck were empty; it wasn't the mosquitoes keeping the guests inside the lodge: it was that kid she'd hired, Walden Roberts. He was tearing it up again, doing a song-and-dance routine in Donald O'Connor style.

Leaning with her back against the wooden rail, the mosquitoes ignoring her, Maria Villarias wore a white scoop-necked short-sleeved blouse and a crimson, many-petticoated skirt filigreed with black lace. Her large brown, lavishly-lashed eyes, her high cheekbones, flawless tan complexion, her bruised lips, painted blood red, gave her the aura of a star; so did the way she held her head, chin up, eyes hooded, vaguely aloof.

But she was not a star.

With her flamenco dance routine, in which she showed off long shapely legs and a talent *Variety* had described as combining "the grace of a ballerina with the savagery of a panther," she *should* have been a star. *Could* have been, easily. She had turned down Ed Sullivan just two months before. But then she had turned down so many others, from Frank Daniels to Florence Ziegfeld.

To be a star was to attract attention. As much as she craved attention, there was something else she craved more - something without which her existence would cease. So, she satisfied her craving for attention, exercised her talent for dance, in small clubs in the Catskills and other hinterland areas, in America and Europe alike.

Always finding a new venue. After all, she dare not drink too often from the same well...

She looked about twenty-seven. She admitted to thirty-one. She had been thirty-five, when she came into the life, and now was much older. In fact, she had stopped keeping track of the years. She turned away from the lodge, to look out at the lake, quietly shimmering in the darkness, the sound of the kid - how old *was* he, seventeen? - teasing her with an impossibly knowing, "You'd Be So Nice to Come Home To."

What, was he born thirty-five? But then, she knew all about being frozen at one perpetual age. She gazed down at the water. No reflection looked back.

Thunderous applause - and these Jewish New Yorker crowds weren't always this generous - emanated from the wooden building to echo across the lake. He was good. In fact, he was great. And of course, he knew it, the cocky little bastard.

She smiled wryly to herself. That chip-on-the-shoulder confidence had been what attracted her, when she saw him in that bus-and-truck production of *Kit Carson* a few weeks before. He had been playing an Indian - a secondary bad guy - and had nonetheless stolen the show with self-assured overplaying. She had flirted with him backstage.

"You want to be an Indian all your life?" she'd asked, lighting up a cigarette, and handing it to him, slender boy with a cherubic face, his slightly bulbous nose betraying Italian roots, his souffle of a black pompadour disguising already thinning hair. His white tee-shirt and jeans were calculatedly casual.

"Lady, I may be an Indian today," he said, taking the cigarette, dragging from it, "but I'm a born *chief...* and I'm just passin' through this reservation."

"I hear you sing and dance, a little."

"Who told you that?"

"Your director. We're old friends."

"Well, he's dead wrong."

"Oh?"

"I don't sing and dance a little. I sing and dance a

lot. I sing and dance up a storm."

"Really? How are you on bongos?"

He grinned. It was an infectious, giving grin, far more likable a grin than a cocky kid like this ought to possess. "I played drums in a combo for three years."

"You don't look like the drummer type."

He shrugged. "I'm not. I play piano, mostly, but another kid in the combo was better on the keys, so I picked up the sticks."

"No!" she said dramatically. "Somebody was *better* than you at something?"

His grin turned one-sided. "I know. Hard to believe, isn't it?"

"What are they paying you?"

"I won't lie to you..."

"Not when the director's a friend of mine, you won't."

He laughed, blew out smoke. "Right. I'm getting forty-five a week."

"I'll give you fifty, plus room and board."

"What do I have to do?"

"Play bongos for me while I do my routine."

"What routine is that?"

She clicked her heels. "Flamenco."

"Nice. But when do I get to show *my* stuff?"

"Who says you do?"

He leaned back insolently against the wall, shrugged again. "I got a nice part in this production...if I can't do my own act, I might be better off stayin' put."

"You can come on after me," she said, "and do a few minutes."

His eyes widened. "Half an hour."

She smiled. Nodded. "Half an hour."

This was their second week at Sunnylake Resort, near Parksville, New York, and the management wanted to hold them over indefinitely, only they were already booked at Kline's Hillside Hotel next month. He wasn't showing her up - not exactly. She was good at what she did - in fact, she was better than good. But for a kid of seventeen to go out there and kill 'em like he did...it was something to see. After all these years in the business, she was suddenly an opening act.

Maria hadn't chosen him for anything except a bongo player and, possibly, a lover. She certainly hadn't targeted him for anything...else. What she liked about the Catskills was the elderly people: she could choose some old man (or woman), drain him of what little life he had in him, and leave him to some country coroner to declare dead of natural causes. Just another coronary on the corned-beef circuit, those twin tell-tale punctures lost in the folds of neck-flesh.

She almost never chose to bring someone over into her way of life, which was to say, way of death. One of the misnomers about what she was was that a single bite - even a fatal one - would create another creature of the night. No. To bring someone over, you had to wean them - it was a gradual process, an act of love committed again and again, slowly draining them of the life that was death until the death that was life began to blossom.

But she was growing fond of this boy; so very fond...

They didn't have rooms in the lodge, rather individual cabins; his was next door to hers, and when he'd walked her back after the show on their second night, she noticed the kid was breathing hard.

"Are you all right?"

"Yeah, yeah," he said. He was such a man, at seventeen, that his boyish grin seemed wrong, somehow. "It's just the breathless company I'm keeping."

"Oh, really?"

"You looked like a million bucks tonight. Man, you make Abbe Lane look like a piker."

That made her laugh; even his sweet talk had a Dead-End Kid flavor. She stopped and they stood beneath a tree; moonlight and stars peeked through, barely.

"No," he said, "really! I'd take out stock in Spanish lace if I had any bread."

"Bread?"

"Mazuma. Dough." He laughed. "You're not the hippest mouse on the circuit, are you?"

She bristled. "Must be my advanced age."

His smile lost its smart-ass quality and turned soft, even regretful. "Hey - I didn't mean to hurt your feelings. You're not so old."

"You'll never know."

"What are you, thirty? That's not old. That's... experienced."

"As opposed to a callow, inexperienced youth like yourself."

He moved closer to her, slipped an arm around her. "I'm not inexperienced. Callow, maybe..."

He kissed her and she was surprised by how tender it was, and how knowing. The kiss was slow, as if he were tasting her; his mouth was soft, sensual, almost feminine.

She put her arms around him and embraced the boy, kissed him back, let the kiss turn from warm to hot.

He was still locked in her arms and he didn't seem so cocky or so cool when he said, haltingly, "My place or yours?"

They used his, and though he was a slender youth, he took command of her; she was as muscular as she was shapely, and she could have overpowered him physically if she wished, but he had a strength of will she couldn't resist. She allowed him to take the superior position, and while his technique was less than polished, he was no virgin. He was giving her everything he had...as if she were the audience and the only ecstasy he was seeking was applause...

In the darkened cabin, their cigarettes were amber eyes as they lay staring at a ceiling that might or might not have been there.

"We make a pretty good team," he said, "don't you think?"

"Are you talking about bed, or stage?"

"Well, both apply - but I meant, show biz. You're

the beauty who sets 'em up for this little beast to bowl over."

She had to laugh. "You won't be sharing a stage long, not mine or anybody's."

"Don't be so sure. Lots of great duos around - Louis Prima and Keely Smith, Marge and Gower Champion..." Then, in an unerring Jerry Lewis voice, he said, "You could be my Deeeeean..."

Now she was laughing even harder. She hadn't laughed like this in years...perhaps decades...

"You're a *single* act if ever I saw one, Wally."

"Hey, don't call me that. Nobody calls me that."

"'Walden' seems a little formal, at the moment."

"My friends, my family, call me Dodd."

"What, is that your real name?"

"No. Just a nickname. Look, we should work something up together, besides me just bangin' the bongos. I can dance a little."

"I've noticed. I've never seen a singer with better stage moves. But that's not...dancing, really."

"Yeah? Get up! Get out of bed!"

"Are you breaking into song, Dodd?"

"Maybe." He yanked her out of bed. He hummed, "Dancing in the Dark," as he wheeled her around the tiny cabin in a gliding, only part-comic display of ballroom dancing. "And Lucy," he said, in a perfect Desi Arnaz, "wait'll you see my mambo..."

What an ear this kid had!

After a few moments, she stopped him. "You don't want to team up with an old broad like me."

"Sure, I do. I got this mommy fixation. You gotta get me through it." He nuzzled her bosom and she laughed, but then the laughter turned to something else and they were soon in bed again.

Every night, after their performance, they would go to his cabin and make love - often several times; the energy and abandon of a seventeen-year-old boy was exhilarating to Maria. She began to feel young herself. She began to think of things, to think in a way, she had abandoned so long ago.

And every night he was as insistent about forming an act with her, becoming a team, as he was an intensely attentive lover.

As they sat in the resort dining hall having breakfast on the third morning of their affair, Maria touched Dodd's hand and said, "Perhaps we could work a little something up."

"Fan-tastic!" he said, lighting up, the apple cheeks of his cherubic countenance looking to burst off his face. "You go on first, then I come up, do my bit, and you come back for the socko finish!"

She smiled and nodded.

That afternoon, between the lunch and dinner seatings, they took the dance floor in the dining room and began to rehearse; she showed him the steps of a fluid, sensual tango and he took to it instantly. The Dead-End Kid was suddenly Valentino.

She was giddy from how good it was as they had a

drink in the bar. "How can you be so show-business savvy at your tender age?"

He shrugged; he was sipping a Coke - they wouldn't serve him hard liquor. "My mom was a singer and dancer, before she married my father. In Chicago. Featured player in a Weber and Fields musical, and she and Frank Daniels were something of an item."

This startled her: she had known his mother!

"Paula Walden?" she asked.

"Yeah! How could you know that! That's way before even *your* time!"

She smirked. "Thanks so much."

"Sorry. Anyway, they called her..."

"The Girl with Three Voices. Yes. She was very good. So I was told."

He beamed. "Hey, you're a buff on this show biz stuff yourself."

"I'm 'hip' to it, yes. So, you got the bug from your mom?"

"Yeah - when other kids in the Bronx were playin' stickball, I was inside listening to Jolson and big band records. And I couldn't get enough of the movies. Practically lived there. That's what I want to be eventually, you know - an actor."

"You'd be good. I have a feeling...you could do anything."

Something strange came into his eyes - all his enthusiasm waned, just for an instant - and then a puppy-dog gleam returned.

"Yeah," he said, and took a last sip of Coke. "If I

can get it all in."

"You have all the time in the world, Dodd."

He was lighting up a cigarette. "I wish."

She asked him what he meant by that, but he only shrugged, and said, "How about a swim?"

"I don't much care for the sun," she said. "You go."

He leaned over the table and kissed her on the forehead and bounded off.

The sunny lake the lodge was named for did not appeal to her. Not that the sun was deadly to her and her kind...that was another folklore/movie misnomer...but it *was* unpleasant. Sensitive eyes, sensitive skin - so her people tended to come out at night...when it was easier to prey...and during the day kept inside, and in the shadows, and in the shade, and in shades.

She spent the afternoon in her cool air-conditioned cabin, listening to Frank Sinatra and Tony Bennett and Perry Como, among others, on a New York station. Dodd would sing rings around them, one day - he could almost do it now! But what did he mean, If I can work it all in?

From time to time she had taken lovers, but never one so young, never one who eased her loneliness to such a degree. The boy was fun to be with - he was funny, pleasant, the conceit largely tongue-in-cheek, full of surprises - and he was *so* talented.

You could spend centuries with this boy/man and never be bored.

But she would not, could not, do that to him - no. She knew that he craved the spotlight, and in this life, this endless prowling life, you had to recoil from fame like a Hollywood vampire in the sun.

She napped in her bed; he'd never slept with her here, and she wouldn't, couldn't let him. The soil she slept on would raise awkward questions. That much *wasn't* a Hollywood legend.

The audience sat hushed through their tango. Dodd wasn't really tall - probably five nine at most - but like so many good actors, he could seem to lengthen himself as he stood regally beside her, twirling her, dipping, swaying. His magnetism even inspired the little three-piece jazz combo - piano, bass and drums - and their Latin-tinged "Tangerine" seemed like a full orchestra.

Or maybe she was just in the boy's spell.

She wasn't alone: the audience went wild with applause as the couple took their bow.

His boyish, apple-cheeked grin glowed, as he lighted up first her cigarette, then his, out on the deck. The little trio was still playing, and he took her in his arms and they danced for no audience but themselves.

"Told you so," he said. "We do make a good team."

"Yes, we do."

"We should get an audition with an agent."

"That's not always easy."

"It is when you're good."

Later, in his cabin, she noticed several bottles of medicine on his bureau. He was in the bathroom as she was examining their labels: Sulfa. She frowned and glanced up at the bureau mirror, where she gave no reflection; another rare truth from the Hollywood myth...

She quickly turned off the light and slipped between the sheets; the room was nicely cool from the air-conditioning. The boy - his build slender, masculine, not overly muscular - walked naked from the bathroom where the light remained on, making him a silhouette.

"You're so beautiful," he told her, and lowered himself over her like Bela Lugosi taking a victim; the lovemaking session that followed began gentle but built to a frenzy. The heady rush of the smashing success of their act tonight had carried over into the bedroom. When he finished, he rolled and off and was breathing hard. Very hard.

"Are you all right?"

He nodded, swallowing. "You're just...you're just a lot of woman."

She got cigarettes going for both of them; he took his but didn't drag from it for a while.

"We *were* good tonight," she said.

"We killed them. We were great."

"I'm good, Dodd...but you're a star."

"Thanks, but you know what they say about the tango: it takes two. We should get an agent, we should..."

She sat up; sat on the edge of the bed. Slumped.

"Dodd...I..."

His hand was soothing on her shoulder. "What? What is it?"

"I'm so much older..."

"Aw hell! Forget it. What, are you thinking, when I'm forty, he'll be twenty, that bullshit? Don't sweat it."

"What do you mean?"

He didn't answer.

She looked back at him and he was smoking now; he had his wind back, but even in the dim light filtering in through sheer curtains she could tell he'd turned morose. His euphoria - both showbiz and sexual - had ebbed.

"Dodd...if you want me to be your partner, you have to be honest with me."

He said nothing for a while. Then, without looking at her, he said, "I had rheumatic fever as a kid. I had it bad. That's all."

"The sulfa medication...?"

He shrugged, nodded. "The docs told my parents, when I was eight, it'd be a miracle if I saw sixteen. That's why I spent so much time inside, listening to records. Well, hell - I beat the odds already, ain't I?"

"Oh, Dodd..."

"Hey, no big deal. If I can hang on into my mid-twenties, I can maybe live a normal life. Like to say, thirty-five."

Tears welling, she touched his arm. "Dodd...I'll be partners with you."

His smile tore her heart.

"You will, Maria?"

"Of course, I will."

She snuggled against him, with a hand on his chest, feeling the pounding of his poor young, ravaged heart. A smile tickled her lips. Oh, the gift she would give him.

But not tonight. Tonight, was for other things - particularly, a celebration of their dance.

Two to tango indeed.

Two weeks later, on the second-to-last night of their Sunnylake engagement, after the last show, Maria and Dodd were walking across the gravelled parking lot toward his cabin when a gruff voice called out: "Hey, kid! Hey, Cassotto!"

Dodd stopped, and she did, too, wondering what this was about as two heavy-set men in baggy suits and porkpie hats came lumbering toward them. They looked like gangsters, not Catskills tourists.

"Hold it up a second!" one of the men called.

Dodd stood waiting patiently, his mouth a thin line.

"Do you *know* these men?" she whispered.

"No. And yes."

"What does *that* mean?"

But he didn't answer, and then the two men were standing before them, big as buildings; one was slightly bigger, actually, and the smaller one, who had a surprisingly pleasant face, stood jingling change in his pocket as he spoke.

"You were good tonight, kid."

"Thank you."

"Mr. C sends his regards."

This enigmatic statement did not seem lost on Dodd.

"Well," he said curtly, "send him mine. Now, we're busy..."

"You know, Mr. C's been hearing good things about you. He knows this is a rough business, show business."

"Thank him for his concern. If you gents will excuse us..."

The bigger one, whose distorted features indicated a long-ago career in boxing, put a hand on Dodd's arm. "Be polite, kid."

Dodd pulled his arm away. "Look - I don't want anything to do with guys like you. *Capeesh?*"

The pleasant-faced guy said, "There's a lot of ways Mr. C can help you. We have a lot of show business connections. We have agents, we have a lot of clubs. Vegas. Tahoe. So much. The man only wants to help."

"I don't need *any* help from you or your kind."

"Your father, he and Mr. C were pals. He was your pop's best man at the wedding. Your sister's godfather..."

"He's a lota people's godfather," Dodd said, sneering. "My 'pop' died before I was born, and where was your Mr. C then, when we were broke, and starving?"

The smaller one put his hand on Dodd's suitcoat, clenched its cloth in his fist. "That's no attitude. That's no way to talk."

Dodd yanked the hood's hand away and said, "Go fuck yourselves! Get lost!"

And he shoved the guy away.

The larger one with the pug-ugly puss came moving forward, but the pleasant-faced one held him back, his genial features pulled into a tight, distorted smiling mask.

"No. That's okay. Let the kid go. This attitude of his...it'll catch up with him."

And they turned and went, kicking up gravel, the ex-fighter glaring back a couple of times. It wasn't pretty.

Maria clutched the boy's arm. "How could you talk to them like that?"

"They're trash. And they're stupid. They won't touch me, or their precious 'Mr. C' will slap 'em around."

They were walking toward the cabin now, swallowed up in the trees; a slight breeze off the lake was ruffling the leaves, which seemed to whisper to them. But Dodd wasn't listening. His face was cold, his eyes tight with rage.

"Who is this 'Mr. C,' Dodd?"

"Frank Costello."

"Frank Cos...he's the biggest gangster in the country!"

"Yeah, I guess." They were at his cabin door. "You coming in?"

"Dodd, what..."

His voice was hushed but charged with emotion. "Look, my pop, Sam Cassotto, died in prison. That's my roots, understand? That's the lowlife kind of life I want out of. I'm not selling my soul to those bastards. I don't care *what* they can do for me. You coming in?"

She nodded.

They did not make love. They wordlessly agreed that after the unpleasant confrontation, neither was in the mood; they didn't even talk. They lay next to each other, though, close, sharing warmth. It gave her an almost...married feeling. She now knew she needed him - needed the companionship, the affection, the meaning he gave her - as much as she needed that precious red fluid.

She could go for weeks without it, but now the hunger, that strange, special, all-pervasive hunger, was upon her. She would have to bring the boy over into her way of life tonight...or find someone else, to tide her over until the time *was* right.

It might have been right, tonight, if those gangsters hadn't turned the evening sour.

She got out of bed and was reaching for her slip when he touched her arm. "Can't you stay the night?"

"No. I...have trouble sleeping in a strange bed."

Now the brooding seemed to have passed. "This bed can't seem *too* strange to you, at this point."

She smiled, shook her head. "I have to go."

Soon she was on her own bed, nestled in the soil-lined sheet, but sleep would not come. *What would he say if she told him*? What if he spurned her gift?

But why would he? He was under a sentence of death, a clock ticking away precious moments, a clock that could stop with any beat of his damaged heart. And the world would be denied that talent, that amazing talent...

She heard something outside - her hearing was as sensitive as her eyesight - and she rose, brushing the dirt off her bare skin, going to the window. One of the gangsters - the pleasant-faced one - was standing outside Dodd's cabin door; the sounds of scuffling from within the cabin indicated the other one, the battered boxer, was inside...

She opened the window, and with her razor-sharp hearing made out: "Teach you some fuckin' manners, you punk bastard..."

Shape-changing required concentration and focused energy and usually she meditated for as long as half an hour before attempting it. But tonight, as Maria stood naked in her room, eyes squeezed closed, she summoned all her strength - physical and emotional - and it took place in little more than a minute.

She flew out the window, wings flapping, and the pleasant-faced gangster didn't even have time to shout before the fangs had sunk deep into his jugular; muted by shock and fright, he fell wriggling to the ground, the black vampire bat drinking, until the wriggling stopped.

Within the cabin, the one-time boxer was too busy

beating the boy to notice or hear the slight commotion beyond the closed door. The windows were closed, too, so she had to shape-change again, which she did just as quickly, and pushed open the door, strode into the cabin naked as a newborn child, wearing only traces of red on her face.

Dodd was unconscious, on the floor, bruised, bleeding, in only his shorts, and the one-time boxer turned with a snarling expression which faded into pleasant surprise, at seeing a beautiful naked woman before him, moving toward him with open, welcoming arms. But the pleasant surprise was momentary.

In his life of violence, he had apparently never before seen the yellow eyes and extended fangs of someone like her...

Her face was buried in his neck and his jugular vein was punctured and his scream cut very short; she almost wished he had maintained consciousness longer, so he might have suffered more.

She hauled the other body inside and, behind the closed door, drank more, draining both men of as much blood as possible; replenished like this, she could go for weeks without striking again. She really could find the right time to tell Dodd...

"Oh my God...Maria! What the hell..."

Dodd had come around.

And he had opened his eyes on what must have been to him a terrible tableau. He didn't understand yet.

She would make him understand.

"They shouldn't have hurt you," she said, rising from her crouch over one of the corpses; her mouth was red and wet.

His eyes were wide. "You're a...a...you can't be!"

"I hate the word. It's so...Hollywood."

His expression was the same one he wore when one of their back-up musicians played a clinker at rehearsal.

"Vam...pire?"

She nodded. "I'll live forever, if I choose." She held her hand out to him. "You can, too..."

He was looking at the two bodies, backing up onto the bed, scrambling up against the backboard. "You killed them! You crazy broad...you killed them!"

"I did. But the way I did it, they won't be joining us."

He blinked. "Us?"

She held her arms out to him welcomingly; she was naked before him, slightly washed in ivory from moonlight filtering through a window.

"I can bring you over to my side," she said, sitting on the edge of the bed. "I would never do to you what I did to them. It would be slow...gradual...like a kiss...a deep, soulful kiss...I would penetrate you, as you have penetrated me..."

"I'm dreamin' this. I'm goddamn *dreamin'* this!"

"No, Dodd...immortality can be yours. You can live forever. You can accomplish everything you've dreamed of, and more..."

He was confused, afraid, that much was obvious;

but he also seemed angry. "I don't need your help to do it, lady!"

"No more sulfa medicine, no more wondering when the time might run out..."

"When it runs out, it runs out! But I'm doin' it *my* way, understand? Mine! I didn't need *their* help, and I sure as hell don't need, or *want*, yours!"

She hesitated. "I can't do it if you don't want me to. I would never do that to you."

He touched his forehead with the fingers of one hand, as if he were reeling and trying to keep his balance; he was breathing hard. "Crazy broad..."

"I want you to *want* this..."

"All I want is to wake up! For this nightmare to be over!"

She slipped off the bed. She felt as if a dark cloak had been thrown over her; that cloak was loneliness.

"Then," she said, "it is."

She stared deeply into his eyes, locking his eyes with hers, until his lids began to droop, then close completely, and she lay him back gently against a pillow, where he snored contentedly.

And as if she were dragging trash bags out to the curb, she hauled the two dead hoods out of the cabin, each by an arm, and disappeared into the woods.

The next morning, two corpses – dumped in a gangland slaying, and set upon by wild animals (so the police and papers seemed to agree) - were discovered by hiking vacationers.

Maria Villarias had left Sunnylake during the night, without checking out, her room empty.

Her young partner was left to fulfill the dates on their small tour as a solo artist.

Six years later, in a dressing room at the Copacabana nightclub in New York City, a slender, dark-haired young nightclub singer checked his black tie in the bulb-lined mirror.

"How's it look?" he asked, smoothing his tuxedo front.

"Oh, it's a gas," the girl said. She was sixteen, blonde, blue-eyed, dimpled, the petticoated president of his fan club in the Bronx.

He smiled at her strain to sound hip. He turned in the seat and said, "Now, honey, what can I tell you?"

She was writing a story for the fan club newsletter.

"Is it exciting to be playing a big club like the Copa?"

"Sure is."

"Does it make you feel like Frank Sinatra?"

"No. I don't wanna be Frank Sinatra, honey."

"Really?"

"I just wanna be the biggest me I can be. I intend to be a legend before I'm twenty-five."

"You only have two years to go."

"Well, dear, the clock *is* ticking."

She was scribbling furiously.

"Anything else, dear?"

"Yes...why do you have a tank of oxygen in your dressing room?"

"I work hard, dear. Need a little pick me-up after the show. Milk and cookies. Gallon of bourbon. A little oxygen."

He watched his humor as it sailed over the girl's head and into the ether.

She chewed her pencil eraser. "Well...can I ask you something kind of serious?"

"Sure, darlin'."

"Why do you sing about death so much? I mean... 'Artificial Flowers', for example, it's so sad. A little flower girl dies. And in 'Clementine', that poor fat girl drowns."

"I'm spoofin' him, dear. The grim reaper man. Sort of thumbin' my nose at him."

"Oh," she said, clearly not understanding.

The muffled sound of a big band kicking in interrupted the interview.

He rose. "That's my cue. There's a table for you at ringside. See you there."

"Bye, Bobby!"

She watched him eagerly from ringside, but another woman was watching, too, wrapped in mink, in a low-cut red dress, black hair flowing to white shoulders. This was a woman who would have dearly loved to stop backstage and see the young singer, after the show, but didn't dare. She could only watch him from afar, from the back of the room. Watch his fingers pop, his shoulders hunch, his body sway. Watch him achieve his own immortality, his own legend, and wonder if he ever thought of her.

"And there's never," Bobby Darin sang, upper lip curling, "never a trace of red..."

Well, she thought, with a tiny smile, *almost never.*

AUTHOR'S NOTE: This story is suggested by several events in the life of Bobby Darin (1936-1973); as a Darin fan since childhood, I have absorbed countless articles and interviews about the singer, but wish to credit specifically Al Di Orio's fine biography, *Borrowed Time* (1981).

ROCK 'N' ROLL
WILL NEVER DIE

Zombies staggered toward him from either side, but Peter Lee—resplendent in leopard spandex, his bare chest lean but rippling with muscle, his golden hair brushing his shoulders, a pentagram medallion swaying from his throat—showed no fear.

The sound of his thin, high voice—loud as an air-raid siren—rent the air as he banished them: "Go to *hell!* Go to *hell!* Go to *heeeeh-laaaaaaa!*"

Behind him on individual platforms, the black-spandex-clad, rather anonymous-looking musicians of his backup band, Coven, their features obscured behind Satan-red facial makeup, hammered the droning final chord; the drummer on this central, highest of platforms unleashed a torrent of rhythm, his hands a blurring flurry as he went around his endless drum kit.

The audience was on its feet, screaming, chanting,

"*Pee*-ter, *Pee-ter, Pee-ter,*"fists waving, horned-finger symbols thrusting.

On stage, Peter Lee—shrilly repeating the final phrase (and title) of his hit song "Go to Hell" into a headset microphone that made him look rather like a satanic rock 'n' roll air-traffic controller—ran to the stack of Marshall amps, climbed them to where the Uzi was waiting.

Even with the organized cacophony of the band's final chord, and Peter's own earsplittingly amplified voice, the sound of the Uzi was a thunderous, frightening thing. In the smallish rock star's hands, the Uzi smoked, spat empty shells, and rained apparent death on the zombies staggering from either wing of the stage.

The Uzi's metallic chatter and the sight of the zombies twisting and turning, doing a death dance to the metal music, blood squibs exploding lavishly, splashing the stage, the musicians, the amps, the hanging skull props, and the first several gleeful rows, served to fuel the audience's fire. They imitated the death dance of the zombies, pouring into the aisles, knocking into each other until some of the blood on the crowd wasn't just from the squibs, pounding each other in this variation of slam-dancing that had grown up spontaneously on the tour for Peter Lee and Coven's first album, *Hell Hounds.*

College radio had loved them once—*Spin* called *Hell Hounds* "a dope parody of speed metal laced with Hammer horror-flick imagery." *Rolling Stone* had coined the term splatter-rock to describe Peter Lee's blood-drenched horror-spectacle rock shows, adding, "Lee makes Alice Cooper look like Alice in Wonderland."

But when *Hell Hounds* went to number one, particularly after it went platinum, the critics changed their tune; five years and five albums later, *Spin* was regularly deriding them ("bloody boring") and *Rolling Stone* had called *Into the Abyss* "sheer embarrassment—unintentional self-parody from the self-styled Splatter-Rockmeister".

The crowds, however, still loved Peter Lee—he sold out arenas and auditoriums in every major city in the United States, and Lee had done huge European and Japanese tours as well. His popularity was at its peak, and tonight's Chicago show made Peter Lee—his tanned body splattered with stage blood as he strutted triumphantly off into the wings, waving a fist in the air as he went—feel immortal.

In the dressing room, his stage makeup was washed away by a local makeup artist, a prissy boy in a lacy white shirt.

"Hey!" Peter said. "Watch it!"

"Watch what?"

"Quit bumping up against me. Just take off the fuckin' makeup. That better be cold cream you're wiping on me."

"Bitch," the makeup artist said, and continued.

When he was alone, after he'd showered and got into his street clothes (jeans and a vintage Stones

Tee-shirt), Peter stared at himself in the makeup mirror. He was only twenty-six, but the lines around his eyes and mouth made him look a decade older. Too much booze. Too much coke. He shuddered, lighting up a Camel.

Thank God for the Betty Ford Clinic, he thought. Now his only vice (aside from the Camel between his lips) was the one no doubt lining up, waiting outside the dressing room. If he wanted to last in rock 'n' roll, he had to take care of himself; no more substance abuse, and between tours he'd have to keep up the daily workouts with his trainer.

Nobody lived forever, not even in rock 'n' roll, but Peter Lee wanted to outlast his contemporaries. Five years at the top was an eternity in this business; but he was determined to join that small circle—Jagger, McCartney, Elton John—who remained superstars into their forties and even fifties.

His road manager, Edward, a dissipated, bloated-looking, thirty-five-year-old Britisher in a black satin shirt and white leather tie and black leather trousers, poked his face in.

"They're waitin', luv," Edward said.

"How many?"

"Joey screened 'em down to half a dozen. Choice ones." But Edward's voice betrayed boredom. This ritual took place every night after the show.

"Show 'em in."

The groupies crowded into the dressing room; the scent of perfume and pot and perspiration made a heady cocktail for the nostrils that sickened and excited Peter. He never tired of the smell of them, or the look. Skinny, long-haired Joey, his personal assistant, knew Peter's type: slender, dark-haired, not too busty, not too flat, no silicone. Every night when the little group assembled, whatever the city, whatever the country, they might have been sisters, giggling, squealing with delight, their albums in hand, or their eight-by-ten glossies or possibly a *Rolling Stone* or *Spin* cover clutched in slender, black-nailed fingers.

Even the clothing was similar. Peter had told an interviewer with *Sassy* magazine what his ideal woman wore—torn jeans, a leather jacket, and a halter top—and ever since, that had been the groupie army's uniform; they were lined up, this latest little battalion, beaming before him with the scarlet lipstick glistening on full lips, the heavy eye makeup, the pale powdered complexions, all reflecting his public pronouncements of feminine perfection.

Willowy young women in black-leather biker jackets, Samantha Fox torn jeans (not just their knees, but portions of thigh and ass showing through the fashionably torn places), cupcake breasts high and barely covered by bandanna halter tops.

"You are so cool," they would say. Funny, after all these years that word was still around: "Cool."

And his response still worked just as well: "You look so hot."

They would flush with pride and excitement;

every night it was the same, as he moved in and around and through them, signing their albums and pictures, rubbing against them, looking them over, choosing a victim.

Usually it was just as simple as picking the prettiest one; there was always a prettiest one.

Tonight, however, it was different.

One of the young women stood just a little taller; that was the one real difference between her and the other leather-jacketed, tom-jeaned, bandanna-haltered girls. That was the only thing that truly set her apart.

Except for her eyes.

Huge eyes, deeply brown, heavy mascara only emphasizing incredible long, real lashes. Her eyes—fathomless eyes —pierced him, held him. Hypnotized him.

"You are so hot," she said to him coolly.

"What's your name?" he asked her, about to sign her *Hellgate* album, Peter's latest.

"Marya," she said.

"Like in *Dracula's Daughter,*" he said.

"What can I say?" She smiled; her teeth were sparkling white. "My mother loved horror movies."

Their eyes locked; he felt dizzy.

"Marya," he whispered, "can you stick around?"

"Thought you'd never ask..."

Joey rounded up the other girls, who were to be ushered into the dressing room of Coven for more autographs and, for those girls who were interested, other fun and games. Passing along his rejects was a crumb Peter regularly tossed his bandmates.

When Peter and Marya were alone, the groupie found the zipper of his fly and teasingly lowered and raised it.

"Now?" she purred.

"When else?"

"I thought you might ask me back to your hotel."

"I—I'm wasted, babe. I gotta crash."

"I understand. Are you too tired to...?"

"No!" He unzipped himself and fished out his already engorged dick. He was throbbing. There was something special about her. Something beyond sexual... Not a bad line for a song, he noted, storing it away: *something beyond sexual...*

"I'll just turn out the light," she said, and moved fluidly to the door.

Streetlight was filtering in through a wire-mesh window, so he could see her return to him, moving like a shadow in the blue near-dark, to lower herself to her knees, take his member between her cool hands, and place her warm, bruised lips around its head. Her big eyes stared up hypnotically at him as she slowly, sensually swallowed the sword of his dick, right down to the pubic bone, nuzzling her pretty nose in his hair, making a sound that was part purr, part growl.

It sometimes took him forever to come. As blasé as he had become about this act (and fucking was worse, fucking barely interested him anymore) he sometimes had to work these poor little groupies till their hair was dripping unbecomingly with sweat and their eyes were filled with discomfort and their jaws ached; he would reward their dedication with the usual spuzzle in the yap, and the less experienced of them sometimes choked, which was their problem, he figured. If they didn't have any more self-respect than to go around sucking some stranger's cock, who gave a fuck if they choked and died?

But this was different. Marya was no inexperienced kid, halting, fumbling, awkward, treating a man's dick with the delicacy of a glutton gobbling a bratwurst. No—this young woman could take him all the way down into her throat, and the lubrication was incredible, the warmth, the satiny smoothness of it, jarred only slightly by an occasional nick of her teeth.

Less than a minute had passed when her rhythmic bobbing motion increased speed, sucking, sucking, sucking the soul out of him, and he exploded in her mouth, and she kept sucking, but slowly now, gently, bringing him to an easy, semi-limp finish, smiling up at him with a naughty white-smeared smile, which she greedily licked at, her pointy pink tongue getting every drop of him, savoring every morsel.

The last girl had choked and spat him out and damn near puked. Real fucking romantic.

But this Marya...she was still staring up at him dreamily with wide, brown, hypnotic eyes, swaying as she pumped him gently, licking at every last droplet she could milk.

He helped her to her feet and held her in his arms; he didn't want to kiss her—that would be gross. But he wanted to hold her, an emotional gesture that wasn't just rare, it was a first. These groupies were human Kleenex for him to beat off into. This young woman was... she was something very different, very special.

"Maybe you *could* come to the hotel with me," he said.

"Not this time," she said, and smiled in a sweet-nasty way, her big eyes slitted seductively; she pecked him on the cheek.

Then she was gone, flicking on the light as she left, and he was standing there with his dick hanging out.

He was tucking it away when Joey ducked back in.

"That's a sweet little piece," Joey said, raising an eyebrow.

"You get a good look at her?" Peter asked.

"Yeah, sure. So?"

"So if you ever spot her again at one of my shows, bring her around after."

"But you never use the same bitch twice."

"Rules are made to be broken," Peter said, quoting the opening line of one his biggest hits.

"Fuckin' A," Joey said, with an upward thumb gesture, and went back out.

Peter slipped into his studded leather jacket and waited for the security guys to come around to usher him to his limo in the alley. By now, he would normally have forgotten the face, form, and most certainly the name of the groupie who'd been granted his nightly gift.

But tonight, all he could see in his mind's eye was

Marya: her face, her semen-streaked smile, the mesmerizing gaze of those big, long-lashed brown eyes.

"What am I," he said to himself, "in love?"

And laughed harshly.

But it caught in his throat, and he choked for a second, like those poor groupies did so often.

The next night, in Peoria, he rushed backstage for his shower and was toweling off when Joey came round. "Is she here?" Peter asked.

"Who?"

"Marya! The girl from last night!"

"Oh. No. But tonight you got a sweet little corn-fed crop to choose from—"

"Forget it," Peter said, and threw his towel on the makeup table. "Just fuckin' forget it."

Joey looked at him like he was nuts, shrugged, and went out.

Peter was morose when he slipped into the bubbling whirlpool in his suite at the Marriott. Tired as he was from tonight's performance, he remained tense; even the churning water, the hot sprays, couldn't unloosen his knotted muscles. He thought about the liquor in the minibar in the outer room and considered falling off the wagon, just this once, just tonight, just to relax...

"Hope you don't mind," a sultry voice purred.

He looked over his shoulder; through the fog of steam he saw her there—an apparition? A mirage? Had he fallen asleep in the hot tub, and was he even now drowning below its cauldronlike surface?

She was naked, a slender, faintly muscular, high-breasted vision, pale as a ghost, the darkness of her trimmed pubic triangle a stark focal point; her similarly dark, pixie-cut hair framed a face whose features were indistinct, but for the large brown eyes and the mischievous scarlet slash of her smile.

"Marya..." He was smiling like a kid on Christmas morning, only this gift was already unwrapped.

She slithered into the hot tub, leaned luxuriously back against the edge opposite him, her peach-like breasts bobbing on the bubbling surface.

"How did you get in here?" he asked breathlessly.

"Does it matter? Maybe I flew in the window."

"I didn't think you were at the gig tonight."

"I wasn't. Couldn't get tickets. But anyway, it wasn't your *show* I wanted to see...it was you."

She glided over and wrapped her lithe body around him, enveloping him, her mouth on his, tongue searching greedily.

Her breath was hot on his face. "I hope you didn't give it away to one of those little groupies tonight."

"No...I was hoping to see you."

"Saving up for me?" Her smile dimpled one cheek. "I thought you might."

Then she disappeared below the surface of the foaming water, and her lips locked onto him under there, and she began working him...

It was ecstasy, but it was going on and on, and she wasn't coming up, and he pulled her to the surface. "Are you crazy? Do you want to drown?"

"I could never drown drinking you, Peter." She brushed back her wet black hair; her face streamed with droplets of water. She was radiant. Glowing. "You give me life."

And she disappeared below the surface and sucked him and sucked him, and he felt himself gushing into the warmth of her oral embrace.

She rose from beneath the water, shaking her head regally, her smile luminous.

He felt drained.

But he finally felt relaxed, too.

She stayed the night, and they slept a little, and she sucked him dry two more times; and they talked.

Pillows propped behind her, her pert breasts standing up though the nipples were flattened, she asked, "Have you always been fascinated by death? And horror?"

"I suppose," he said. "But not the real thing. You never met anybody more squeamish."

Her smile turned crinkly. "No kidding? The rock star who's famous for rock-concert bloodbaths?"

He laughed a little. "I'm afraid so. Maybe that's why I was so attracted to horror movies. I remember seeing a bad car accident when I was a little kid. Dead people scattered around on the highway...bloody limbs..." He shuddered.

"How did you happen to see that? Was your family just driving by?"

"No. My father was a driver's ed teacher. He thought...he thought I should learn at an early age about the dangers of the highway. Some of my earliest memories are those gruesome driver's ed movies—remember those?"

"Sure! Highway carnage! We always looked forward to 'em."

"I liked them, too. Every kid likes stuff like that. But my dad thought I ought to see the real thing, so when there was this bad accident out on the highway, he took me there."

She winced. "Jeez. How old were you?"

"Eight. Nine, maybe. A fat lady was pinned in one of the cars, wedged inside the front seat, arms flailing up out of the broken windshield, and she was covered with blood and she was screaming..." He shook his head, trying to banish the image. "It was awful. Ever since then, even the slightest cut, just the sight of blood, sickens me."

"Amazing. But your shows splatter the front several rows of your audiences with blood every night! It's worse than a Gallagher concert!"

"Stage blood," he noted. "I've always been able to separate fantasy from reality, Marya. Fantasy is safe. Reality isn't."

"So that explains the fascination with horror."

"Right. I read *Famous Monsters* and *Fangoria* as a kid. Listened to Alice Cooper and Black Sabbath records. Bought reprints of fifties horror comics. Collected videotapes of the Universal and Hammer horror movies."

"That's why you changed your name."

He grinned at her. "You are good—where'd you get that, the *Sassy* interview? Yeah, 'Peter' for Peter Cushing and 'Lee' for Christopher Lee."

"Your favorite Hammer horror stars."

"Besides, my real name just doesn't cut it."

She smiled wickedly, folding her arms across the pert breasts. "Oh, I don't know...I think Daryl Beesley has a certain ring."

He laughed once. "The ring of nerddom."

"You? A nerd? Never."

He didn't know what it was about her—the luminous eyes, perhaps—that made him open up so; he never talked about himself like this to anybody, particularly not a woman. Particularly not some cock-sucking groupie, which a part of his mind kept reminding him she was...

But he heard himself saying, "I was the nerd to end all nerds. A four-eyed, friendless, comic-book-collecting geek."

"What happened?"

"I went off to college on a scholarship, to Athens, Georgia. I dropped out of school the second semester, 'cause by that time the band was formed, and we were making some noise. I developed a whole new persona...and we got signed to a record deal, or rather I got signed."

"The band you were playing with wasn't Coven?"

"No. The record company wasn't interested in them, just me. We put together a band consisting of mostly session guys, though they had to have decent stage presence. The focus has never been on the band—just on me."

"Where it belongs."

"Well, I do all the songwriting, I front it...they're just paid employees. If one of them starts getting too much press or too much attention or his head starts getting big"—he drew a finger across his throat—"off with it."

"That's why there's been so much turnover in the band, then."

"Right. Marya, in show business you got to watch people every minute. It's full of bloodsuckers. Fucking leeches!"

Her smile turned teasing. "You don't like blood-suckers?"

"No."

"Maybe that's because you don't understand a simple scientific fact."

"Such as?"

She smiled wryly. "Semen and blood are identical, chemically speaking."

"No kidding?"

"No kidding. So maybe you don't want me around, if I'm going to be doing this..."

And she drew back the covers and buried her head in his crotch.

A few minutes later she was looking up at him, licking white droplets, catching every one, saying, "From that goofy grin on your face, I'd say you've decided to make an exception in my case..."

When he woke up the next morning, she was gone. He found her note by the open window, the slip of paper rippling in the fall breeze, held down only by a gold ring with a black stone.

"Obsidian," her note explained. "The stone of the night. Think of me then. This gift is in thanks for the love gifts you've given me. Your scream queen, Marya."

He put the ring on the fourth finger of his left hand; a perfect fit. He could see himself in the shiny stone.

When he went east with the tour, Peter didn't expect to see Marya again, and for a time he didn't. He tried to resume his practice of nightly anonymous groupie blowjobs, but at first it took him forever to come, and finally he couldn't get it up at all. She had ruined him. Marya, with her come-hungry mouth sucking like a warm, moist vacuum and those huge hypnotic eyes staring up slavishly at him, made these girls seem like the amateur night they were.

It turned him surly, and backstage in Pittsburgh, when he arrived early at sound check, he caught two of his roadies in his dressing room in faggot flagrante delicto.

Billy had his pants around his knees, and Arnie was on his knees in front of him.

"Jesus!" Peter exploded. "In my own goddamn dressing room! You're fired! Both of you! Fucking fired!"

Embarrassed and humiliated, these two who Peter had figured for your normal macho males fled his dressing room in shame and near tears. It made him sick.

Edward tried to reason with him. "You can't fire them over this, luv. It's terribly . . . politically incorrect."

"Yeah, right—like my show is on the Political Correctness A-List already!"

"Luv...it's none of our business what these lads do in private."

"Well, their privates were doing it in my dressing room, so they're fuckin' fired! And don't talk about unions to me, either! Get rid of them—pay 'em off."

"Honestly, Peter. Your homophobic attitudes are so...backward."

"Get rid of them, Edward, or I get rid of you next."

"Anything you say, luv."

The show was sluggish that night; there were missed cues, some squealing feedback, forgotten lyrics. Some of it was him, some of it was his off night rubbing off on everybody else. Backstage, he lit into his techies, then headed for the dressing room and showered and sat naked at his makeup mirror, staring at a face that seemed goddamn old to him.

Joey peeked in.

"Don't you fucking knock anymore?" Peter spat.

"Sorry. I, uh, got somethin' for you."

"I told you. Next time I'm in the mood, I'll tell *you.* I'm bored with these hollow-cheeked little whores. Got it?"

"You're not bored with this one, Pete."

"Go the fuck away, Joey."

"It's her. Your dream date."

"Marya?"

Joey smirked and nodded, his greasy shaggy hair swaying.

"Give me two seconds, then show her in."

He slipped into his jeans and stood waiting.

She wasn't wearing the groupie uniform tonight. She wore a black zip-up-the-front jumpsuit that clung to her like skin; her pixie hair was moussed up, her scarlet lips pulled back over brilliant white teeth.

"You need me tonight, don't you, Daryl?"

He grinned at her. "If anybody else called me that..."

"You'd kill 'em? A squeamish nerd like you?" She turned off the light switch. "C'mere, big boy..."

He went to her and they kissed; then she slipped to her knees, found his zipper, and this time he had no trouble getting up, or painting the inside of her throat white, either.

In his hotel suite, they lounged in another whirl-pool, the air pleasantly steamy, foggy, his arm around her.

He bit at her ear playfully. "Didn't expect to see you on the East Coast."

"Some of us star-fuckers get around."

"Don't say that."

"What?"

"I don't like to think of you with other guys."

She shrugged. "I don't mind you being with other girls. Or women. Or even guys."

"Don't say that!"

"What?"

"Guys." He shuddered. "I just had to bounce a couple of gay boys."

"Ah...you mustn't be prejudiced. It's just another alternative lifestyle. It doesn't make you *bad,* when you have an alternative lifestyle. You're not exactly *Saturday Evening Post* material yourself."

"I don't want to talk about it. It's unnatural."

"Is it unnatural when I do this?"

And she bobbed her head beneath the surface of the churning water and found him and sucked him again; he didn't think he had anything left in him, and he ached as he spewed into her. She came up and seemed to be savoring him, rolling him around inside her mouth.

"Nothing unnatural. It's sweet," she said, pink tongue licking white dabs off scarlet lips. "Well, actually...salty." And she giggled.

This turn of conversation disturbed him, and he crawled from the hot tub, found his towel, dried off, and headed for the bedroom. She snuggled naked against him.

"You're still wearing my ring," she said.

"Never take it off."

"You'd think you were in love or something."

"Maybe I am."

She looked at him, touched his face gently with black-nailed fingertips. "What do you want most?"

"What do you mean?"

"In life. What do you want most?"

"To stay young, I guess."

"To live forever?"

He laughed shortly. "Sure. Like they say, rock 'n' roll will never die. Unfortunately, a hell of a lot of rock stars *do.* And most of the rest of them would be better off if they would."

"What do you mean?"

"I mean, rock's a young man's game. Didn't you ever notice I don't do drugs or booze? You think that's 'cause I'm clean-cut? What did you say before—a *Saturday Evening Post* kind of guy? Is that what you see?"

"Not really."

"Right. I abstain, and I work out with weights, just trying to beat this fucking age thing."

"But you've had a wonderful ride. How long is it since *Hell Hounds?* Four years?"

"Five."

"That's a long time at the top, in your business."

"Tell me about it. The thing is, I've got the chops, both performing *and* songwriting, to stay at the top indefinitely. But to the next group of kids coming up, I'm going to start seeming like an old fucking geezer. Particularly if I *look* like one."

"Have you considered plastic surgery?"

"Do I look that bad already?"

She smiled gently. "No. But when the time comes... why not?"

"Go under the knife? Have you forgotten how

squeamish I am? I hate the sight of blood—particularly my own!"

"They'd put you under."

"I'd freak. I'd completely freak. Or I might wind *up* a freak, like that queen Michael Jackson. They've carved enough off him to make it the Jackson Six."

"Poor Peter," she said, stroking his face. "Poor, poor Peter."

He looked at her to see if she was making fun; but there was no irony in her expression or her tone.

"Maybe there's a way, my sweet," he thought he heard her say before he drifted off to sleep.

When he woke to sunlight streaking between hotel-room shades, he found her gone again. No note this time. No gift...other than the lingering memory of her.

On the rest of the East Coast leg of the tour, no sign of her. He began, after shows and into the night, getting the shakes, the likes of which he hadn't had since the Betty Ford Clinic.

At his hotel room in Newark, the private detective he'd hired in New York two weeks before came around with a hangdog expression. He was a balding, mustached man in his fifties with a paunch and a cigar; the only thing private-eye-ish about him was the rumpled trench coat.

"I couldn't get much of anything on her," he said, sitting on a couch in the outer room. "Other than what you already know."

"What do you mean?" Peter asked from the minibar, where he was opening a bottle of nonalcoholic beer.

"Her description and her name, well, she's well known backstage at most rock shows. If there's a dick in rock 'n' roll she hasn't sucked, I'd like to see it. So to speak."

Peter hated to hear that. Hated to! "You couldn't trace her?"

"Hell, man—you don't even know what town she's from! You first ran into her in Chicago, and I did some rudimentary checks there, but that's a big pond to locate a little fish in—if it's even her pond!"

"I know, I know."

"One thing odd, though."

"What's that?"

"I was checking out this auditorium in Jersey City, and there was this oldies show. The night before, they'd had Guns 'n' Assholes or somebody, you know—the latest dipshits on the block. No offense, but rock 'n' roll has sucked since the Beatles broke up."

"Was there a point you meant to make?"

"Oh, yeah! The afternoon I was poking around there, they were getting ready for an oldies show. Some guy with one of those old British acts—Kinks or Gerry and the Pacemakers or Herman's Hermits or somebody—overheard me talking to the stage manager. He said he knew Marya Morrison from the old days."

"What?"

"Said there was a chickie named Marya Morrison who did the groupie circuit back in the sixties. She was one of the original Plaster Casters...you know, hippie chicks who would dip a guy's dick in plaster of Paris and make themselves a swell souvenir."

"Marya couldn't be that old. That's ridiculous."

He shrugged. "Maybe it's her mom. Anyway, this chick back in the sixties was also named Marya Morrison and she was described by this Brit as being able to 'suck the chrome off a Bentley'."

"Just a coincidence."

"Probably. Anyway, you've used up your retainer. You want me to keep digging?"

"Think you can find anything else?"

"Probably not—but I'm always willing to take a client's money."

"Thanks, but no thanks."

Peter showed the detective out and went back to his near-beer. He sat sipping the flavorless stuff, doing the math in his mind: If Marya was, say, sixteen in 1968, she'd be in her forties today . .. was that possible?

No, he told himself. He thought of her smooth, pale, flawless skin: *No.*

The last show of the tour was at the Coliseum in L.A., and the house was packed; he spotted Marya in the front row and it sparked the most enthusiastic performance he'd mustered in weeks. The zombie finale had been expanded for this venue, and the blood-splattering of his Uzi send-off sent the front rows into a frenzy. They swayed and shrieked down there, splashed with red, although among them Marya was more composed, smiling mysteriously, her huge hypnotic eyes locked on him like brown lasers.

Backstage, in his dressing room, they showered together—she had to get the red stage blood off herself, after all—and she got down on her knees in the shadowed stall, but for once her magic didn't work.

She followed him, dripping wet, out of the shower; he toweled off, his back to her. He glanced in the mirror, didn't see her, and turned suddenly.

"Where'd you go?" he said.

"I'm right here." She moved to him, took the towel, and dried herself, gazing at him soulfully. "What is it? What's wrong?"

"Nothing."

"It's something. Tell me, Peter."

He shook his head. "I can't stand the thought of it...you with other men."

She touched his face, petted him with the backs of her knuckles. "There are no other men but you, Peter."

"Do you mean that?"

"Of course, I do. Take me home with you?"

He took her to his place in the Hollywood hills, and they swam in the moonlight in his pool, naked, free. In his outdoor hot tub, the stars above them, they kissed, held each other.

"I've never even made love to you," he said.

"Sure, you have."

"I've never been inside you."

"You've been inside me many times."

"In your mouth. But not...*inside.*"

She shrugged a little, smiled a wry half-smile. "I

figured you were...afraid of AIDS. A blow-job from a groupie isn't as risky as fucking her."

"Don't!"

"What?"

"You make it sound so harsh. So awful. I love you, Marya. I want to spend my life with you. I'd spend eternity with you, if I could."

Her wry expression faded, and something yearning and even tragic seemed to cross her perfect features, her pale face.

"Do you mean that?"

"You know I do."

He made love to her on the silk sheets of his round bed, driving himself into her, savagely, tenderly, and she was silken inside, she was wonderful, but at the moment of climax, with her on top, she ducked down and drank his seed greedily, using her hands to gather what her lips had missed, licking it off her fingertips, her tongue searching, seeking every morsel of it, until her smiling face was wet with only her saliva.

"You are an oral little thing," he said with a half-smile and raised eyebrow.

"Hope you don't mind," she said.

"How old are you?"

"What?"

"How old are you?"

"Old enough."

He was dreaming about the accident, the one his father had taken him to, dreaming of the fat woman trapped in the car, trying to squeeze out of the broken glass; there was blood everywhere, and the sound of pain, screams of agony, but suddenly the woman in the car wasn't obese, not grotesque in any way: She was Marya, and he could see himself in the dream, going to her, helping her out of the twisted wreckage, pulling her up through the broken glass of the windshield; but as he took her into his arms and she put her arms around his, his neck grazed the broken glass and he felt the puncture, and the spurt, the spurt of blood. Then he was underwater, and Marya was locked in his arms, entwined with him, he was in her, and he came and came and came, in an endless orgasm as vast as the sea that enveloped them....

He woke and she was still in his arms, but in bed with him, her face buried in his neck; it had been a dream.

Only his neck felt wet, and it hurt, as if the puncture had really happened.

He lifted her off him and her scarlet mouth was running with red, and her brilliant white teeth were dipped with red, her canines extended and razor-sharp. Her eyes had an animal gleam. The sound from her throat was not a purr, but it was catlike, all right...

Then he gasped and passed out.

When he woke with a start, before dawn, she was not in bed beside him.

Two such strange dreams—a dream within a dream. Very Brian De Palma, he thought. He rose but felt weak, his legs wobbly. Naked, he stumbled to the bathroom.

He threw water on his face, then noticed that his neck—where he had dreamed the glass punctured him—ached; he touched it with his fingertips and felt the two wounds.

But when he went to look in the mirror, he could not see his own reflection.

He backed up, looking at his hands, looking down at himself; the gold ring's shiny obsidian stone stared back at him blankly. Was he still dreaming?

"You're not dreaming, Peter," her voice said behind him.

But her image was not in the mirror either.

When he turned, she was standing behind him in the large marble bathroom. She wore a black negligee. Her high breasts, her long legs, her slender shape looked unreal, dreamlike in their perfect beauty.

"Come with me," she said, and extended a hand to him.

Negligee fluttering in the gentle wind, she walked him out into the night—actually, the early morning hours—and they stood looking down at the lights of Hollywood. The night was a glittering thing, jewels scattered on black velvet.

"You asked my age," she said. "I'm sixty-five."

"What?"

"I was a bobby-soxer when I drank from Frankie. I wore a poodle skirt when I took the King's love potion. I was a hippie chick when—"

"Stop! This is insane!"

She stroked his face, smiled sweetly. "Peter, in all

those years, you're the first man I've wanted to share eternity with. You're the first man worthy of the gift."

"Gift?"

"You'll be a star forever, now. You're like me."

"And what are *you?*"

She looked away, as if shy. "A nervous girl who was seduced many years ago by an older man. A squeamish girl who can't stand the sight of blood. I was a virgin until last night."

"Virgin?"

"I've never bitten a neck before. The cruelty of it, the thought of blood...I've nourished myself by dropping to my knees, accordingly. The chemical content of semen and blood are identical—remember?"

"I'm supposed to believe that you're a—a vampire?"

"And so are you. And we're a team now. Forever. You don't have to worry about aging. You may have to change your persona as the years go by. Music will change on us, as it always does. But you'll make adjustments—as I have."

"I'm a vampire," he said derisively. "Right."

"Did you see yourself in the mirror? You're a horror fan, Peter: Think about it. No—we're together now. But you'll have to be...understanding. As will I."

He pulled away from her. "What the hell are you talking about?"

"The chemical makeup of your semen has changed, Peter. It's as dead as you are. I need to seek sustenance elsewhere. We can make love, but we can't feed each other."

"This is fucking nonsense. Are you high? Ohhh! Owww...what's wrong with me?"

"It's dawn! Quick. Inside!"

The burning pain wracking him convinced him, at least for the moment, of what she was saying.

"To the basement!" she said.

"This is California! There is no basement."

Soon they were cowering in a closet. Light came in from under and around the door, but not sunlight. Head spinning, he wondered if the dream—this nightmare—would ever end.

"If you are to survive," she told him as she huddled in one corner, he in the other, "you'll have to overcome one of your aversions."

"What the hell do you mean?"

"Either you overcome your squeamishness about blood," she said, "and seek your supper like most vampires..."

"Or?"

"Or you'll have to get it like I do. I'm sorry, my sweet. You'll have to..." She made an O of her mouth.

"Never!"

"You don't have to decide just yet," she said, and she moved close, snuggled next to him. "You won't have to come out of the closet till nightfall."

INTERSTATE 666

Have you heard this one?

It's another of those stories about Interstate 666, which is only one of the nicknames bestowed on I-66 over the years. Maybe you know it as Bad Luck Highway, the Devil's Turnpike, or possibly the Highway to Hell...

Anyway, on a lonely turn-off just off the I-66, back in '66, three cheerleaders found themselves with a flat tire on the way to the big game. It was a cold fall night, but all three girls wore their little, short-skirted, red-and-white cheerleader costumes. Ronni, a cute brunette, had borrowed the shiny red Mustang from her boyfriend, Larry; but it was the equally cute La-Vonne, the cheerleading squad's only Afro-American member, who took charge, opening the trunk.

Betty, blonde and, yes, very cute, seemed on the

verge of panic. "What are we gonna do, Ronni?"

"What else, bubblehead? Change the tire! Haven't you ever changed a g.d. tire before?"

Betty's blonde locks bounced as she shook her head, no. "I don't have Driver's Ed till *next* semester."

LaVonne was looking down into an empty trunk. "Have *you* ever changed a tire, Ronni?"

"*Of course,* I've changed a tire..."

LaVonne shook her head, no, and her Afro bobbled. "Not on this car, girl. There's no spare - damn! We're already runnin' late." She frowned at Ronni. "If only we hadn't had to drop your little sister off..."

Ronni put her fists on her hips, like Superman. "Oh, I suppose it's *my* g.d. fault that babysitter lives out in the boonies!"

"Are we gonna miss the big game?" Betty asked, her eyes wide, and as if in answer, the whine of brakes caught the three girls' attention, headlights suddenly illuminating them as a semi bore down on them.

"Here's somebody who can help us!" Betty cried in relief, as the truck pulled over, bringing itself to a gear-grinding stop.

"We'll hitch a ride to I-66 Truck stop," Ronni said. "It's close. We can have the g.d. car towed."

"And maybe catch a ride to the game!" Betty added.

"Go if you wanna," LaVonne said. "I'll stay with the wheels - I'm not sure I *believe* that good ol' boy's smile..."

And the burly trucker, climbing down out of his cab, did wear a grin that was maybe a little too wide.

He also wore a Peterbilt cap and a lumberjack shirt, his gait a trifle bowlegged, his paunch hanging over his belt like a smuggled watermelon. As he planted himself before the awkwardly grouped girls, the cold night wind brought the odor of chewing tobacco to their nostrils.

"You young ladies in distress?" he asked, his voice gruff but his manner affable.

Betty touched her chest. "We have a flat."

He raised his eyebrows. "Uh, yeah...got a jack? Be glad to help..."

"We have a jack," Ronni said, "but no spare."

His grin got even wider. "I don't think one'a *my* spare's gonna fit this cherry little buggy... Why don't you kids pile on into my cab? Truck stop's just a hop, skip and a jump...getcha some help."

"That's white of you, mister," LaVonne said. "But I'll just wait here."

Somewhere an owl hooted.

He shrugged. "If you like... So I guess they musta caught that Hook character, huh?"

Betty swallowed. "Hook character?"

"Didn't you hear about it?" He shook his head, made a *tch tch* sound. "That insane feller with the hook, in the papers last year? He busted outa the nut-house last night. Couple kids parking, over by Mad Crick, kinda goin' at it hot and heavy, when they hear a *scratchin'* at the door..."

Betty hugged Ronni's arm. Each girl could hear her own heartbeat.

"So they take off like a bat outa hell!" he said, and the girls jumped a little. "And when this fella drops his little gal off t'home, and goes 'round to open the door for her - a *bloody hook* was caught on the door handle!"

Betty gasped. "That's horrible!"

The trucker shrugged. "*Horrible* thing is, they got the hook, but not the guy that used to be attached to it."

"I heard about him," Ronni said thoughtfully. "He...he's a g.d. *molester,* isn't he?"

"Oh yeah," the trucker said casually. "And a homicidal maniac." Then he smiled yellowly at LaVonne. "But I'm sure you gals'll be just fine here, 'long the roadside...Maybe you should all three stay, and I'll just stop at the stop, and send the wrecker - "

"No!" LaVonne said. "We'll all go with you."

But as the girls followed the trucker to his vehicle, LaVonne brought up the rear, so that nobody could see the tire iron tucked behind her back.

They rode about half a mile in silence, all crowded in the cab with the burly trucker, light from the dash casting an eerie glow, the vehicle lurching as he shifted gears, and soon they were on the interstate.

"You know," he said finally, "I'm doin' you little gals a big ole favor, what with the Hook at large and all."

"We're really grateful," Betty said.

"Yeah, thanks a lot," Ronni said, pointing to an exit as they rolled past. "But isn't that the turn-off?"

"Oh damn!" he said. "Pardon my French. Well, we can turn off up at the rest stop - we can use the phone from there..."

"I guess that would be all right," Ronni said.

He grinned over at them, and the affability had been replaced by something lascivious. "We can pull off to one side, nice and private..." He gestured behind him with a thumb. "...and I can show you gals where I *sleep* and things."

"No, thanks," LaVonne said.

He took one hand off the wheel and reached inside his jacket, as casually as if he were plucking a pack of cigarettes from a pocket; but what his hand came back with was a gun, a little revolver.

As the girls recoiled in fear, he said, "Kids today! You girls are gonna show me some goddamn gratitude. I saved your pretty asses!"

LaVonne sat forward, turning toward their "savior."

"See, I always had me this fantasy about cheerleaders," he was saying, his lips glistening with saliva in the dashboard glow, "me and three sweet young things, goin' rah rah rah on my sis boom bah..."

That was when LaVonne whapped him across the chest with the tire iron.

His yelp of pain accompanied a reflexive jerk of the wheel and the huge semi rammed into a bridge abutment, the sound of the girls' screams and breaking glass and tearing metal soon engulfed by an explosion as gas ignited and an orange fireball blossomed in the night.

"But," Dr. Janet Vanguard said, "the Tale of the Stranded Cheerleaders does not end there..."

Vanguard paced slowly before the blackboard as the small classroom of college students listened in rapt attention. She was thirty-five, her long dark hair pinned back, her glasses wireframed and functional, her gray tailored suit with blouse conservative; but none of these efforts to downplay her natural beauty were entirely successful. Behind the glasses were large dark eyes, and she had the high cheekbones, clear skin and slender shape of a fashion model.

She acknowledged a male student seated toward the front. "Yes, Steven?"

"Dr. Vanguard, we all know the Hook story is one of the oldest Urban Legends around. Has it *always* been a part of the Stranded Cheerleaders story?"

"Good point, Steven," Vanguard said, and sat on the edge of her desk, unaware she was further undercutting her efforts to maintain a cool professorial image by showing off perfectly formed nyloned limbs. "No, the first logged occurrence of the Hook legend converging with the Stranded Cheerleaders' Revenge is '81 - whereas the Cheerleaders tale in its purest form dates to '66, a year that has clung to the legend because of its echoing of the 'true' story's locale, Interstate 66...or I should say, 666."

There were smiles around the room as she continued.

"In virtually every variant of the legend, the story

picks up exactly one year later, to the night. Two truckers are in a truck stop parking lot, and one of them is drunk and getting drunker, swigging from a brown-bagged bottle. His friend suggests he's hitting the booze a little hard, and the drunken trucker takes offense. The drunken trucker is then seen, by his friend, lured into the back of a truck by three beautiful young girls in cocktail attire - in the earliest versions of the tale, the girls are wearing Playboy Bunny costumes."

"And I suppose," Steven offered, "one girl is brunette, another blonde, another black."

"Exactly," Vanguard said with a smile. "The drunken trucker disappears into the back of a semi which his friend takes for a bordello on wheels. The next morning, the drunken trucker is found in a ditch - stone dead. And when an autopsy is performed, he's found to have no blood in his veins...but pure, one hundred percent alcohol."

The ironic ending of the tale elicited more smiles, and few nervous laughs.

"Dr. Vanguard," Steven said, "in your book, you list no less than twenty-five variations on the trucker's demise - including several where the victim isn't even a trucker, but some unlucky male traveler."

Vanguard raised a gentle finger. "Unlucky *horny* male traveler..."

And that prompted more smiles and gentle laughs.

"Actually, Steven," Vanguard said, "that can be viewed as simple variants on a theme. Or we may be talking about multiple victims. You see, the Stranded Cheerleaders are said to reappear every year, on the anniversary of their tragedy, to lure men with a promise of erotic fantasy fulfilled by a horrible, ironic death..."

The busty blonde cheerleader was shaking her pom poms (among other things) to a Z.Z. Top tune as appreciative males looked on. On another stage, a stacked black cowgirl was twirling a lasso (and the tassels on her breasts), while on the final of the three stages, a brunette was slipping out of her negligee down to pasties and G-string undies that you didn't find at Victoria's Secret.

Around the stages of the glittering chrome-trimmed mirrored strip club sat hooting, horny guys, white- and blue-collar alike, stopping in after work for the chance to stuff dollar bills in the G-strings of the dancers. Along the mirrored walls were tables of the more pas- sive observers, including an afternoon bachelor party in progress, four guys in their early twenties who still looked like the frat brothers they'd not so long ago been.

The one who seemed to be having the least fun was the man of the hour, Jason Peterson. The dark-haired boyishly handsome young man seemed alternately bored and ill-at-ease.

His friends - Al, Bobby and Bill - were doing their best to get him with the program.

Al, tall, skinny, leering at the cheerleader, said,

"Jay, why don't you get your ass up there, ringside, and jumpstart your dick?!"

Bobby, chubby, curly-haired, said, "Come on, Jason - when did you shrivel up and die? You used to be such a *hound!*"

"I'm sorry, guys," Jason said, shrugging, sipping his Coke, "I'm just not into it."

"You used to be into *anything* female and friendly," Bill said. Bill was a little older than his pals, a broad-shouldered ex-jock with thinning blond hair.

"Hey, I always had my standards," Jason said, then pointed a finger at Bill. "You, on the other hand, would schtup mud."

Bobby leaned in conspiratorially. "See that little cheerleader?"

"I think I can just barely make her out from here," Jason said.

"Barely is right," Bobby grinned. "I slipped her fifty bucks for a table dance. For you. Sort of a going away present for your balls."

Bill let go with a slow whistle. "You know what kinda table dance you get in this joint for fifty bucks? I hope you wore your rubber jockey shorts."

"This is truly a Hallmark moment, guys," Jason said. "Bobby, you better collect on that, yourself."

Bobby, getting up, threw Jason a disgusted wave. "Some bachelor party!"

Bill rose and said to Bobby, "I'm with you, man! Jeez, you'd think the condemned man woulda wanted his last meal!"

And the two went over to find themselves seats at center stage ringside, hooting and whistling as they went.

Al said, "I remember when you used to live in places like this."

"That was before Jenny," Jason said.

Al's sigh was wistfully nostalgic. "You used to say your idea of heaven would be a titty bar where you were the only customer."

"You're right. I also used to be thirteen. Some of us get older."

"What, and wiser? She's really changed you."

"Maybe I changed myself."

"Hey," Al said, sitting back in his chair, "girls don't come any nicer than Jenny, or better-lookin'... but Jason, she's so...so..."

"Nice?"

Al held his palms up. "Hey, if you wanna marry some preacher's daughter, some Young Republican Stepford Bride, that's your problem. But I'll tell you one thing - *I* wouldn't buy a car without at least drivin' it around the block a few times."

"Is it too late to get another Best Man?"

"That hurts...So - you and Jenny are leavin' tonight? Driving to her folks?"

"Yeah. We'll probably stop for the night someplace on I-66."

"Separate rooms, of course."

Jason got up; he'd had enough needling, good-natured or not. "Listen, I'll see you this weekend. Tell the guys thanks."

"Yeah, sure," Al said, toasting him with a beer glass, then adding cheerfully, "See you in hell."

As he left, Jason noticed Bobby sitting in a chair over by a wall, with that cheerleader sitting in his lap, grinding herself into him. Jason shook his head and escaped from the smell of cheap perfume and smoke into the fresh late-afternoon air.

Dr. Vanguard used a corner of her classroom as an office, just one of the indignities of teaching at such a small college. She was correcting papers when a door slam startled her and she looked up to see an incongruous figure step into the classroom, closing the door on Vanguard and himself.

While neither tall nor strapping, his was an imposing presence; his well-worn apparel – work boots, jeans, work gloves, lumberjack shirt and stocking cap - suggested a trucker or perhaps construction worker. But his eyepatch and scruffy beard lent him a sinister, sailor-ish aura.

"Thought we might want some privacy," he said, his voice a throaty growl.

She half-stood at her desk, working to keep the alarm out of her voice. "Who the hell are you? What do you want?"

He removed his cap; his head was Yul Brynner bald. "Few moments of your time, ma'am."

"Open that door," she said, pointing, "or I promise

you a scream that'll wake the dead *and* bring campus security running..."

"We need to speak of things that only you and I can understand, ma'am." And he began to move toward her, dragging his left leg as he came; his left arm remained motionless at his side. "You have nothing to fear from me, Doctor. Might I sit?"

"What do you and *I* have to 'speak of'?"

"A mutual interest. Even an obsession."

She was interested despite herself, and heard herself saying, "Sit."

He did. "Might I ask what a famous person like yourself is doing at an insignificant institution like this one?"

Rather stiffly, she said, "My specialty is not in much demand, except for the very top people."

"Folklore," he said. "With an emphasis on urban legends. But you *are* one of the 'top people' - your book *The Stranded Cheerleaders' Revenge* got you on Leno and Letterman."

"That was five years ago," she said, annoyance rising. "Who the hell *are* you?"

"Jack Talion," he said. "Retired teamster." With his thick-knuckled callused right hand, he patted his useless left arm. "Been on disability some time, now."

"How fascinating. Is there a point to this?"

"That big university out east - why did they fire you?"

"Petty campus politics and jealousy."

He nodded. "*Because* you got on Leno and Letterman, and the bestseller lists. But what was their *excuse*?"

She shrugged. "My views were at odds with the conventional wisdom of the field..."

"You believe urban legends are rooted in fact. That if proper, in-depth research were done, you could find 'the core of truth at the heart of the beast'."

Her big eyes got bigger. "My words exactly. How -"

"They were reported in the *American Folklorist Journal*."

She smirked, shifted in her chair. "No offense, Mr. Talion, but you don't look the type to follow scholarly journals. What is your interest in this subject?"

His eyes seemed almost to glow. "Personal. You see - I was the only one of their victims to survive."

She frowned. "Only victim to survive...*whose* victim?"

"Those bitches from hell," he said, coldly matter of fact. "Those succubus cheerleaders that got you your fifteen minutes of fame. Here...look at these..."

And from under his navy coat, he withdrew a manila folder, and handed it to her. Within were yellowed newspaper clippings, which she spread out before her, reading them slowly, carefully. Ten minutes had passed before either of them spoke again.

"This certainly *could* be the right case," she said. "The year is even 1966. Truck rams a bridge abutment, the driver and his three teenage passengers are killed..."

"Cheerleaders on their way to the big game," Talion said. "A perfect fit, and you *know* it...keep reading..."

"Good lord," Vanguard said. "A year later, within miles of the accident - "

"A trucker turns up dead in a ditch with what the coroner calls 'an ungodly amount of alcohol in his system'," Talion said, drenched with self-satisfaction. "*Ungodly!*"

She smiled, gestured dismissively. "This is certainly worth further research, and I owe you a debt of thanks, Mr. Talion. This could be my ticket to a full professorship at a *real* university..."

"The talk-show circuit," Talion said, his gruff voice strangely seductive. "Bestseller list...connect those two incidents to the inception of the 'legend,' and you get another fifteen minutes of fame....Maybe half an hour."

She was nodding, her eyes glazed. "No one in my field has ever isolated the beginnings of *any* urban legend..."

"The core of truth," Talion said.

"At the heart of the beast," she said.

The grizzled trucker sat forward. His good eye narrowed and gleamed. "The 'beasts' are coming out tonight, Doctor. This is it - this is their time."

She looked at the date on the clipping in her hand. "My God, you're right - this *is* the anniversary of their deaths..."

"Once a year," Talion said, sneering, "they come

to claim victims whose only crime is their manhood. Like the Flying Dutchman of yore, they emerge, to wreak their vengeance."

Suddenly he sat forward, and his hand gripped hers, tightly. His face was clenched like a fist.

"Come with me, Doctor. Help me find them. Help *stop* them..."

Jason unlocked the motel room for his fiancée, Jenny Chase, and held the door open for her. Even in jeans and cut-off sweatshirt, Jenny was a stunning young woman, her gold-highlighted brunette hair brushing her shoulders, her features sharply pretty, her big dark brown eyes a lovely contrast to her creamy complexion.

Jenny, train case in hand, stepped in and stopped short, saying, "Oh dear."

She was reacting to the gaudy cupid-themed honeymoon suite before them, dominated by a heart-shaped bed and lots of red satin and mirrors.

"I'm sorry, honey," Jason said, closing the door, carrying a suitcase. "It's the only room they had left."

"I'm so disappointed in you," she said. But there was nothing bitchy in her tone.

"I know," he said. "I'm sorry, I shoulda called ahead. It's just that I wasn't sure how far we wanted to drive tonight."

She pointed accusingly at the heart-shaped bed; even in the suite's low lighting, its red satin winked reflectively. "When I agreed we'd sleep in the same room, on this trip, to save money, you promised you'd book twin beds."

"Baby," he said, "let's turn right around and we'll *un*-check-in and keep driving."

"No," she sighed. "No, I'm in for the night."

"Honey, I didn't plan this - honest..."

Her brow was furrowed over the lovely brown eyes. "I hope not. After we've waited all this time, been so good, and just a few days away from the big day..."

"I'll sleep on that sofa."

She held up a "stop" palm. "No! We're going to sleep in this bed together, and we're going to exercise self-control. We're going to prove our love for each other by doing...nothing. All night long."

Train case in hand, she marched into the bathroom and closed the door. Jason, thinking maybe he should have taken Bobby up on that table dance, stripped to his shorts and was folding his clothes neatly onto a chair when the bathroom door opened and Jenny emerged in a neck-to-floor frumpy robe.

"Is *that* what you're wearing to bed?" Jenny asked, gesturing to his boxers.

"My suit of armor is at the cleaners," he said.

Jenny moved quickly by him, saying, "I don't think sarcasm is necessary," and, still in the frumpy robe, climbed under the satin sheets.

"Oh yes, it is," he said, joining her. "If I wanna preserve my sanity."

"Ready to go to sleep?" she asked, covers up to her neck.

"Soon as I say my prayers."

Her frown was more hurt than angry. "I don't find your attitude amusing."

"I don't find your distrust in your future husband anything to smile about, myself."

"I *do* trust you," she said, doubtfully.

"Right. That's why you're wearing that seat cover to bed."

Now she really seemed hurt. "It's all I have."

"That's what you *always* wear to bed?"

"No. It's just that my nightgown is something... special I'm saving. For, you know - *the* night."

He half-smiled. "And I suppose I just couldn't control myself if I saw you in it."

"Okay," she said, sitting up. "Judge for yourself."

And she got out of bed and opened the frumpy robe, let it slip in a puddle to the floor. She was wearing a sheer baby-blue teddy; her full, round rosy-tipped breasts were visible, her every rounded curve of her was visible in fact, as was the gentle triangle of wispy brown.

"You see," she said. "I do trust you."

And she flounced under the covers.

"Our father," Jason whispered, "who art in Heaven, lead us not..."

Heavyset, hairy Harry Simmons and his friend Earl sat

sipping coffee in a booth at the sprawling I-66 Truck stop, discussing the sexual attractiveness of several waitresses. One of the waitresses in question was a pleasantly plump black woman in her early thirties.

"Nice saddle on 'er," Harry commented.

"I thought you hated coloreds," Earl said. "Didn't you lose your dispatchin' job to a black guy?"

"Yeah," Harry sighed. He lighted up a cigarette. "Now I'm back out here in no-man's land, makin' the long hauls. Musta been one of them quota deals."

Earl smirked. "Didn't have nothin' to do with you screwin' up, and him bein' better qualified?"

Harry leaned forward and shook the cigarette between two fingers at his friend. "Listen, pal - spades ain't better qualified for *nothin'* except maybe peelin' bananas or somethin,' like the black-ass apes they are."

The black waitress swayed by, and Harry turned to watch her fine rear view.

"Love that dark meat," Harry sighed.

Earl chuckled over his coffee. "At least your pecker ain't prejudiced, Harry."

Harry was smiling, shaking his head. "You know what they call them big ol' glorious heinies of theirs? 'Booties.' You know what booty means, don't ya, dickweed? Treasure. Buried treasure..."

Earl was sliding out of the booth. "Catch ya down the line at some other waterin' hole, Harry."

But Harry was still lost in poontang reverie. "I bet they're wild in the sack, man. Savage. They come down outa the trees later than we did, you know. They got natural instincts."

Earl shook his head, grinned, waved. "Later, Tarzan..."

Before long, Harry was heading out to his own rig, in the rear parking lot, when from between two parked trucks, a lovely black girl in her late teens stepped out; she wore a tightly-belted trench coat.

"Hey, big boy," she said. "You up for a romp in the jungle?"

And she opened the coat, flashing him a glimpse of her skimpy jungle-cat pattern bikini.

She was belting back up as Harry, licking his lips, said, "I can make time for you, Brown Sugar. How much?"

"Who said anything about chargin'?"

She slipped her arm in his and walked him toward a parked rig.

"I thought they chased you workin' girls outa the motel," he said.

"We're not in the motel, Harry. We got our own portable playland."

She was guiding him to the ramp of the parked rig.

He frowned at the pretty chocolate face. "How did you know my name was Harry?"

"You told me," she said, her smile beautiful and white. "Remember?"

The door slid up and red light engulfed him. Soon he was within an area that didn't seem to logically fit within the trailer portion of a semi; but he was so caught up, he didn't care - why doubt reality?

And this reality was a jungle-like world of trees, leaves, bamboo, mosquito netting, displayed animal hides. Slipping out of her trench coat, the girl led him into the hut-like canopy of the bed.

"Relax here, Bwana," she said. "Jungle Girl serve you."

Harry stretched himself out on the waterbed. "Hey, you ain't gettin' no argument from me."

The girl plucked a banana from a hanging bunch, waved the phallic fruit under Harry's thick nose. "Bwana like banana?"

"Ain't crazy about 'em...but don't let me stop you."

He could feel his heartbeat increase as he watched her suggestively peel the banana and slowly insert its tip into her mouth. Then she clamped down hard, taking a big bite, which made him jump a little.

Then she tossed the banana peel aside and began unbuttoning his shirt, playing with the thick hair on his chest, nuzzling his neck, sending him into ecstasy.

"Will you be my new bwana?"

"Sure will, Brown Sugar..."

"Old bwana give Jungle Girl fur coat."

Harry frowned. "Hey...what kinda money are we talkin' about here?"

"Coat was gift. Bwana no give Jungle Girl gift 'less bwana wish."

"I mean, I don't mind payin' a fair price...maybe we oughta establish the goin' rate before - "

Her eyebrows raised over big brown eyes. "Bwana

like see Jungle Girl in fur coat? In *nothing* but fur coat?"

"Uh, yeah. Bwana could go for that, just fine." He licked his lips. "Bwana want see Jungle Gal's fur...."

She waggled a finger and gave him a little girl sing song. "Bwana not leave?"

"Bwana ain't goin' no place, Jungle Gal."

She scampered out of the hut-like canopy, and Harry said to himself, "Cute little monkey..."

He was leaning back, elbows winged behind his head, when he heard a terrible bellowing cry, an animal cry, the thundering howl of something huge...

Then it was in the hut's opening, filling it, a huge beast, a *gorilla*...

...only it was an absurdity, a gorilla out of the Three Stooges, an obvious, blatant guy in a gorilla suit.

Except, this was a *girl* in a gorilla suit, wasn't it? What kind of stupid sex play *was* this, he wondered.

"Fur coat my ass," he said, irritably. "Well, *my* fantasy ain't no goddamn girl in a goddamn gorilla suit, so go take that ridiculous thing off - *right now*!"

But then it was on him, and its powerful arms were swatting at him, knocking him around as if he were a ragdoll, and those paws had claws that tore his flesh, and Harry scrambled out of the canopy, screaming for dear life. He didn't see the banana peel.

Harry hit the peel perfectly and sent himself flying, and falling, and landing, with a resounding *whump!*

When Harry looked up, that absurd gorilla face leaned in to fill his field of vision, and Harry began to scream again, a scream that escalated when the phony gorilla yanked Harry's arm from its socket and proceeded to beat him with the bloody thing. In fact, Harry's scream continued, in varying stages of pain and hysteria, until the beast gripped Harry's head in his paws and yanked it off, sending a geyser of blood that painted the ceiling of Harry's fantasy.

Outside the parked rig, a blonde and a brunette, both in cheerleader attire, waited patiently. Ronni filed her nails. Betty sat on the edge of the ramp, swinging her legs like a bored kid. Neither of them seemed to notice the trailer rocking, or the muffled cries of agony, mixed with gorilla snarls, within.

And after a while, the trailer door swung up and open and LaVonne - her jungle bikini traded in for her cheerleader outfit - handed out a large, tied-at-the-top garbage bag, filled with things that poked angularly here and there. Harry's body parts.

Betty took the bag. "Oooo! It's heavy!"

"Put that in the dumpster over there, sweetie," LaVonne said. "White trash."

Dr. Janet Vanguard, at her passenger's request, pulled her little white Geo along the shoulder of I-66. Talion had pointed out a road sign he wanted her to inspect, a sign that clearly read I-666. Which she, of course, assumed was a prank of some kind, adding an extra "6"...

She turned to Talion and said, "I can't believe I let you talk me into coming along on this white-whale hunt of yours..."

"You think I'm crazy?" he asked smugly. "Let's find out."

And Talion got out, even as a semi whizzed by; Vanguard followed, and soon she was examining the sign only to find the third "6" *wasn't* graffitied on!

"Painted on, isn't it?" he asked. "Pretty elaborate 'prank', if you ask me. And every damn sign you see tonight is going to be that way."

"Really?" she said archly. "And this happens every year? Every sign along Interstate 66 transforms itself magically into '666' and nobody notices? Or if they do, nobody believes them?"

"Use that instant camera of yours," he suggested. "See what happens."

She fished her Polaroid out of her big purse and flashed a photo. As she waited for it to develop, she faced Talion and said, "Just what do you hope to accomplish tonight?"

His eyes were crazed as he replied, "These little girls have been taking revenge for nigh onto thirty years...now it's Talion's turn."

She looked down at the developed photo in her hand. The sign clearly read I-66.

"Oh my God," she said, looking over at the sign that still bore its extra "6".

"Never occurred to you that the supernatural elements of these urban legends might hold that 'core of truth' you're looking for, did it, Doctor?"

Soon they were at a booth at a truck stop, and Talion was spreading out a roadmap on the tabletop.

"You aren't expecting us to cover the entire length of I-66 in one night, are you?" she asked.

"Every dot is an incidence," he said, pointing to the occasional red dots on the black line drawn to highlight I-66's path parallel to the Mississippi River. "The first incident was within miles of where they died in that fiery crash. Then they began working their way up to Canada, leaving a trail of bodies. Didn't cross the border - All-American girls, you know."

Vanguard, frowning, shook her head. "Why hasn't the FBI's behavioral unit picked up on this? Technically, at least, these are serial killings..."

Talion shrugged. "The occasional disappearing trucker, or traveler, or hitcher, what's to pick up on? When bodies are found, there's never a similarity of modus operandi. This victim is killed by an arrow, that one's head is cut off, here a dismembered body, there a pureed one..."

Vanguard was aware that eyes of other diners, disturbed by this grisly dinner-table conversation, were on them.

"Keep it down, would you?" she asked him in whisper.

"Over the next fifteen years," he said, ignoring her request, "they worked their way down to the Mexican border - then they turned back again..."

"Where are they now?"

"On their way home," he said.

In the rear parking lot of I-66 Truck stop, between a couple parked rigs, long, tall, cool, laid-back Danny Watkins was confabbing with short, fried, nervous Fred, his friend and occasional customer.

"I don't know, Fred," Danny was saying, feigning reluctance, "I stopped dealin' a long time ago - all I got's my own private stash."

"Don't hand me that b.s., Danny - everybody knows you're still the biggest connection on I-66!"

Slipping his arm chummily around Fred's shoulder, Danny patted the trucker around the chest and waist, gently, with his other hand.

"You wouldn't be *wired* now, would ya, Fred?"

"Hell, no!" Fred said, pulling away. "I wanna *get* wired - so I can make it to Cleveland by five a.m. and not get my ass fired!"

Danny reached in a pocket of his brown, soft leather jacket and withdrew a prescription-type bottle of pills. "Oh-kay...but it'll cost ya a C-note."

"That's highway robbery!"

"Think of it as interstate commerce. Yay or nay?"

"Shit," Fred said, frustratedly, and dug into his pocket for the cash, handing it over, holding out his palm into which Danny placed the pill bottle.

"Be careful now, son," Danny said. "More'n one of those hummers can send ya flyin' into outer space."

Fred popped a pill. "I don't wanna get to the moon - just Cleveland."

Danny slipped his arm around Fred's shoulder again. "Well, if you *do* want a little space odyssey, when your run's over, you and your personal Barbarella pop enough of *these* puppies, you'll be humpin' in orbit."

Fred was already walking away. "That's not my idea of a good time..."

Danny shrugged. "Don't know what you're missin'."

Once Fred was out of sight, Danny withdrew another pill bottle from his pocket and scarfed down a handful of his own product. "One small step for man," he said, smacking his lips, "one giant leap for pharmacology."

Danny was heading toward his own parked rig when a lovely little blonde, no older than her late teens, stepped out from between two other rigs. She wore a tightly cinched trench coat and a coy smile.

"Are you the bad man who gives little girls candy?" she asked.

He ambled toward her. "Stranger things have happened." He withdrew one of the pill bottles from a pocket. "If I bring the snacks, will you provide the party?"

The blonde opened her trench coat and flashed him a look at her cherry-red vinyl bustier and G-string; the only other thing she was wearing, he noticed, were moon boots. Then she smilingly cinched her trench coat back up.

"I'm gonna take that as a 'yes,'" he said.

She led him up the ramp of a parked rig; the door began to slide up of its own accord and a red glow beckoned him.

Inside, however, he found an area larger than you would think might logically fit inside the trailer, a chamber where the walls were painted with starry skies, moon boulders decorated the floor, a moon car served as a bar, and a space capsule with flashing lights sheltered a round bed.

"Whoa!" Danny said, holding onto his forehead, trying to get his bearings. "Those babies are kickin' in quicker than usual..."

The blonde peeked out from behind a boulder. "Ever do it on the moon before?"

"How'd you get in here? I thought you were *behind* me..."

The blonde, stripped to her vinyl outfit, stepped out and approached him. "Anything's possible in science fiction."

"Anything's possible on acid, too."

She looked up at him with big eyes in her baby-doll face. "Is *that* what we're going to do?"

"Naw," he said. "Uppers."

She put her arms around his waist, brushed her breasts against him. "Do you need an upper to get...up?"

"Not with you around, baby."

He was loving this. He'd always been into science

fiction, *Star Trek* and all; wanted to be an astronaut, as a kid. But as a teenager, he'd found other ways to get high.

"I want this to be perfect for you," the blonde said. "Everything you ever dreamed of."

"You know how I'd *really* like it, baby?" he asked, and he whispered to her. She put her hands on her bottom and looked at him like a little girl afraid she'd get in trouble.

"Oooo," she said. "I've never *done* that."

"Great," Danny said. "I can go where no man's gone before..."

"Okay, if that's what makes you happy," she said with a perky smile, and went to the moon cart where a jar of Tang and two glasses of water awaited. She began stirring up two servings.

"That's my wish upon a star," he said. "Short of makin' it in freefall, anyway. You know - doin' it anti-gravity style..."

"Oh, we can do that," the blonde said matter-of-factly. "That's easy. Tang?"

"No thanks - never touch the stuff."

"I'll just hit the anti-grav switch, then. Be right back."

"Yeah. Yeah, you do that."

He watched the little babe wiggle to the capsule and climb onto the bed; as she reached for the control panel, her pretty, heart-shaped, dimpled ass was in the air, displayed just for him.

"The moon is really out tonight," he said to himself. "What a little space cadet..."

She hit the switch and Danny flew suddenly up-ward. She didn't see him hit, but the *splat* turned her head, and when her two cheerleader friends, Ronni and LaVonne, peeked in, all three of them were look-ing up as blood and goo dripped down.

"Ick," Betty said.

"What happened?" Ronni asked, as the gory glop dropped down.

Betty shrugged. "I guess he ran out of space."

Jason, elbows winged out, staring sleeplessly at the motel-room ceiling, suffered in silence as Jenny slumbered peacefully next to him, her brown hair beautifully tousled against the pillow, her creamy bosom spilling generously out of the top of her teddy.

He kept stealing looks at her until finally he couldn't stand it. He leaned in and, ever so delicately, tentatively, kissed her neck.

She smiled, in her sleep, and moaned pleasurably.

So he kissed her neck again. Harder.

And she turned to him and slipped herself into his arms and they kissed; he pulled her close to kiss her again when her eyes popped open.

"Oh my," she said. "This *is* hard for you, isn't it?"

He filled his hand with a full, perfectly rounded breast. "What difference does a few days make..."

He buried his face in her neck, nuzzling her, and she was moaning in delight, really getting into it, when suddenly she had second thoughts and pushed him away.

She gathered the covers around her. "No. Not now. Not tonight. Jason, this is my fault, I shouldn't have tempted you!"

She flew out of bed and slammed herself within the bathroom.

He sighed. Hauled his ass out of bed. Trudged over to the bathroom.

"Look," he said to the door, "I can't sleep, and awake, I'm trouble for both of us. That truck stop next door's open all night. I'll be over there havin' coffee for the next, oh...why don't you join me for breakfast in, say, eight hours?"

And he got his clothes on and left.

The full moon gave the concrete ribbons of I-66 a lovely, lonely glow as Vanguard drove her obsessed passenger from truck stop to truck stop. They'd hit four so far - nothing. No sign of anything unusual.

"Next up is the I-66 Truck stop itself," he said. "It's the one closest to where the girls met their fiery fate back in '66. Where that rapist trucker promised to take them..."

His intensity was amazing.

She said, "You really think we'll find them?"

"Oh, they're out there, tonight. I can smell them."

Her mouth made a wry twist. "Perfume?"

"Brimstone," Talion said.

They drove a while, and Vanguard said, "How do you intend to stop them, anyway? Stake through the heart? Silver bullets?"

"Do I look like the Lone Ranger? Anyway, they don't have hearts."

"What, then? Exorcism? You don't look much like a priest, either."

He was shaking his head, no. "Incantations won't kill them. They're demons. I have to destroy them to send them back to hell."

"Why not Heaven?" she asked. "They were sinned *against*, you know... You remember what the urban legend says."

Talion's grunt was sarcastic, dismissive. "Their search will end when they find a man 'pure of heart'. The man who resists them, frees them."

"That's the way the story goes, in most forms."

He snorted. "Well, I'm here to give the lie to that. *I* resisted them...and they're *still* on their Satantic rampage."

The sound of the wheels on pavement made a steady thrum.

"Are you ready to tell me?" she asked.

"Tell you what?"

"*Your* story... Did they grant you *your* secret fantasy?"

"I'm a common man, Doctor," Talion sighed. "I had a common fantasy. Nothing lurid. Nothing exotic."

"Tell me."

His face was red in the glow of the dashboard lights. "I was hauling produce from Des Moines to points north. She accosted me in a truck stop parking lot, and I'll be damned if she didn't look exactly like Becky Sue Matthews, the girl I loved and lost in high school, and when I followed that little prostitute into the back of that truck trailer, it turned into the backseat of my old Chevy!"

Vanguard tried to keep her eyes on the road, but the hypnotized expression on Talion's face kept drawing her attention to him.

"Buddy Holly was playing on the radio," he said, "and she kissed me, and it was sweet, at first, but then it was shriveling, and she was kissing the life out of me, sucking me dry, and I screamed, and climbed out of there, and I opened the door, and dove into the parking lot...and the bitches almost ran me over!"

As if punctuating Talion's story, a semi streaked by in the passing lane.

"Almost ran me down, in that big truck - the blonde and a brunette and a colored girl, in the cab...and I've dragged my sorry ass up and down I-66 ever since, praying that God would grant me one more night with those Satanic sluts!"

His good hand was raised in a trembling fist. Then he let out some air, relaxed, and Vanguard did the same.

"Thanks for sharing," she said.

In a booth at I-66 Truck stop, Jason sat nursing his

fourth cup of coffee - he was really pushing the "free refill" concept - when Jenny, back in her travelling clothes, slid in across from him.

"Am I too early for breakfast?" she asked, almost timidly.

He wanted to dive into those big brown eyes.

"No!" he said. "Are you hungry?"

"Not really. I...I couldn't sleep."

"I'm sorry."

She was shaking her head. "Don't say that. You don't have anything to be sorry about. This is my fault."

"No," he said, "it's mine."

She was busying her hands with a napkin, fooling with it as she said, "I know you didn't...plan any of that, next door. And I don't know how I could expect you to sleep next to me with me in that...nightie."

She swallowed, embarrassed.

"You ever consider," he said, gently, "that maybe we're just not compatible?"

Her expression was horrified. "No!"

"Jenny, I'm not very religious. You know that. I think I'm a pretty good person, but - I just don't buy any of it, Heaven and hell, life after death..."

Her brow tightened. "I haven't tried to force my beliefs on you."

"I know you haven't. But we gotta live with each other, and how do two people grow old together, if they see the world so differently?"

"I don't understand..."

"We supposedly love each other. We made a commitment. We're on our way to get married! And you treat me like a kid on prom night, tryin' to get laid..."

"I want you to respect me."

He could see the tears welling up in her eyes, but he pressed on anyway; he couldn't help himself - it *had* to be said.

"But *you* don't respect *me*," he said. "That's the *real* problem, isn't it? To you, I'm just some horny asshole -"

A trickle of tear rolled down her cheek as Jenny slid out of the booth. Her chin was trembling, and she was struggling for dignity as she said, "I think you're cruel."

And then she was gone.

The black waitress came over with coffee and said, "More, cowboy?"

"No," Jason. "No thanks. I've had enough."

Soon he was walking across the rear parking lot, shoulders slumped, when a lovely brunette stepped out from between parked rigs. She wore a trench coat and a sexy smile.

"Lookin' for some live entertainment?" she asked.

"No thanks," he said.

He walked on and then there she was, in front of him again.

"First table dance is free."

He swallowed. "Tempting - but no."

He kept walking, and there she was again; how did she move so quickly?

"Business is slow at the club tonight," she said.

"You'd have it all to yourself."

Then she opened her trench coat and showed off her nearly nude, slenderly curvy, devastating sexy body draped in stripper bra and G-string.

"Of course," she said sultrily, "if you've got something better to do..."

He thought about it. Looked toward the motel. Shook his head and said, "Goddamnit, I don't have. Lead the way, beautiful."

And he found himself taken by the hand and led up the ramp into the back of a trailer that opened impossibly into a replica of the strip club where he'd had his bachelor party, an identical foggy, light-flashing, chrome-and-mirror palace, except he was the only patron present.

He touched his forehead, as if checking for a fever. "I've...I've been here before..."

"It's a franchise," the brunette said.

"In the back of a *truck*?"

The brunette leaned in and nibbled his ear. "Don't question it. Float with it."

And she guided him to a ringside seat by the center stage.

"*Welcome to the 666 Club!*" a d.j. announcer's voice bellowed over a throbbing ZZ Top number.

Jason turned and looked back at the d.j.'s booth, but it was empty.

"*We have an out-standing line-up of centerfold lovelies for you tonight, and tonight only, everything's free! You want a table dance, just ask for it! Now, let's get started with bouncing Betty!"*

And down the runway onto the center stage came a blonde so cute it made his teeth ache, decked out in a skimpy cheerleader-style outfit. She began a very sexy version of a cheerleader routine - just for him.

"*You want a lap dance, just whisper in your filly's ear! You want more? Well, let your conscience be your guide...these little gals left their conscience with their clothes! They were put on this earth solely to satisfy your every whim...every desire...every fantasy...*"

"That's all right with me," Jason said to nobody.

In the rear parking lot of I-666 Truck stop, near the parked Geo, Talion was withdrawing two bulky flare guns from a canvas bag.

"What are *those* for?" Vanguard asked him, gesturing with an open palm.

He thrust one of the flare guns into the palm. "They're not silver bullets," he said, "or wooden stakes - but they'll do."

Her head bobbed back as if she were evading a blow. "You expect me to *shoot* somebody? Please."

He got right in her face; his breath mingled coffee and bourbon. "Not somebody - some *thing*," he said. "They're hellspawn. They're born of fire, they'll die of fire..."

"You *are* a lunatic," she muttered. "But what's *my* excuse?"

Then Talion began to prowl the rear parking lot. "If

they're anywhere, they're here...and I *know* they're here. They died within a few miles of this truck stop..."

Vanguard had to work to keep up with him, despite Talion's draggy leg. "Listen," she said, "I don't believe in violence..."

He whirled and faced her. "You believe in the core of truth at the heart of the legend, don't you? You *know* these creatures exist - otherwise, you wouldn't have made this journey..."

And he stalked off, exploring the lot, eyeing each parked rig suspiciously.

She was glancing behind her when she bumped into him; she hadn't seen him stop, frozen to the spot.

"There it is," he said. "That's their home."

And her gaze followed his pointing finger to what, at first, seemed just the rear of another parked semi. But from under the slide-down door came an eerie red glow. "That's just a truck," she said.

"You don't think I can recognize the quarter ton of steel that almost ran me down?" He nodded toward the rig. "But for the sake of argument, check out the personalized plate..."

She did: on it was the number 666. *Nothing* but the number, 666.

Suddenly she realized she was trembling. "So...so, where *are* they?"

His smile was more a sneer. "You know the 'legend', Doctor. Didn't you write a little book or something? They're *inside*..."

"What do you expect me to *do*?"

His eyes were wild. "There are three of them. I'll shoot one, you'll shoot one, and we'll both pray to sweet Jesus I have time to re-load for the third."

Then he strode toward the ramp up to the back of the truck, the gimpy leg not slowing him down a bit.

And she followed.

Stripped to pasties and G-string, the blonde cheerleader was down off the stage giving Jason some up close and personal attention. Then the blonde plucked the pasties off her breasts, baring pert pink nipples, and unsnapped the G-string, revealing a downy tuft as blonde as her bouncing shoulder-length locks. Woozy from her perfume and pulchritude, Jason allowed the blonde to touch him but remained passive.

He closed his eyes, moaning with pleasure as she ground her bottom into his lap, then the pressure eased up, he opened his eyes - and she was gone.

"*Bouncing Betty will be back later,*" the invisible d.j. was saying, "*but right now, feast your horny eyes on Luscious La - Vonne.*"

And now an Afroed black girl, with a generously rounded figure, was strutting down the stage in a purple satin-fringed bikini.

"*Remember, there's no cover at the 666 Club, and no minimum, but there is minimum cover on our foxy ladies! Keep in mind, if you want special attention, just ask and you shall receive....*"

Soon the black stripper was down off the stage and

the bikini was gone and she too removed her pasties and G-string, and dark erect pencil-eraser nipples were stroking his face, mounds of soft firm bosom engulfing him, making him drunk with sweet-smelling female flesh.

Then, in an eyeblink, the black girl was gone and the ZZ Top tune gave way to a romantic Whitney Houston ballad, as the d.j. said, "*And now it's time for your dark dream to step aside, but don't worry - Luscious La-Vonne will be back...right now we want to honor our special guest tonight, here at the Club 666 - this one's especially for you, Jason! Ravishing Ronni!*"

An incredible brunette who looked a little like Jenny was striding down the runway onto the stage, in a lovely sheer teddy. Hell! It was the same teddy as Jenny's!

The brunette had a similar rounded body, and there were no pasties or G-string beneath that sheer teddy, just rosy-tipped breasts and that dark secret between her legs as the dancer gyrated sensuously, gracefully, her eyes gazing down at him with not just the promise of sex, but love.

At times the dancer seemed literally to be Jenny, but then he would blink, and it would be the lovely brunette, again; what a strange, delirious, wonderful, awful dream he was caught up in!

Then, still wearing the teddy, she came down off the stage and straddled his lap and stroked his face sensually, devouring him those bedroom eyes.

When Talion yanked up the sliding door at the rear of the rig, the red glow intensified; but when he closed the door behind them, Vanguard was startled by the glow disappearing, and they were stepping through a doorway into the foggy, music-throbbing chamber of a chrome-and-glass strip club.

"Nice threads," Talion said, with a nasty smile.

And she realized her conservative professorial suit had vanished, replaced by a skimpy gold lame bra that barely concealed her small, well-formed breasts, and sheer red harem pants over a gold lame G-string that left the cheeks of her behind exposed. Her hair was no longer tied back, but full, a dark cascade of curls, her glasses gone, her feet bare.

"What...what's *happened* to me?"

Talion smiled, shrugged. "A marked improvement, I'd say."

"This is insane!"

"No," Talion said, somber again. "It's just that you're inside *his* fantasy..."

And they could see a handsome young man, seated ringside at the center stage, a lovely brunette dancer in a sheer teddy straddling his lap. Two naked dancers, a lovely blonde and a black girl with a '60s Afro, came floating up and began smothering the young man with loving attention, from all sides.

"This world is constructed from each victim's secret desires," Talion whispered. "This guy gets a damn nightclub, and all *I* rated was the backseat of a Chevy!"

They began moving toward the young man, who, strangely, seemed to be having second thoughts; he was gently pushing the brunette in his lap away.

"No," he said. "You're very beautiful, but no..."

"*We have unexpected guests here at the Club 666!*" the D.J. announced.

The three strippers turned with surprise toward the approaching Talion and Vanguard.

Talion planted himself, the flare gun thrust forward. "Remember me, ladies? I'm the little man that got away..."

The romantic song stopped, and a Buddy Holly tune - "That'll Be the Day" - replaced it.

The blonde was suddenly wearing a sweater, pleated skirt, bobby sox and saddle shoes. She was beaming. "Jack! Jack Talion! I've *missed* you so. You *remember* me, don't you? Becky Sue Matthews?"

Talion's eyes half-closed; he seemed almost feverish as he said, "Becky Sue...I've loved you so..."

"The car's right outside," the blonde said. "The backseat's waiting, darling...tonight's the night...I'm ready to go all the way!"

The flare gun in Talion's hand was wavering; but then he had his resolve back. He almost spat, "It won't wash, ladies."

The Buddy Holly tune stopped, with a needle scratch.

"But," Talion continued, his smile an awful thing as he aimed the flare gun, "I *will* let you in on my deepest, darkest fantasy..."

The blonde, the brunette and the black girl were in cheerleader attire now; their latest victim, the young man in the ringside chair, was frozen in time, eyes glazed, hearing, seeing, none of this. The three cheerleaders frowned at Talion, as if he were a mean teacher who scolded them unfairly.

"...I've been dreaming of sending you harlots back to hell!"

"Not just yet, Talion," Vanguard said, lifting the flare gun to her companion's temple. With the young man in the chair frozen, she was back in her professorial attire, again.

He glared at her around the gun at his head. "What's wrong with you? Are you *insane*, woman? This is what we came to do!"

"It's what *you* came to do," Vanguard said. Keeping the gun to Talion's temple, Vanguard turned toward the cheerleaders, focused her attention on the brunette. "Ronni - it's Janet, Ronni. I'm Janet."

"Janet?" Ronni said, stunned. "Baby Jan?"

Vanguard nodded.

"You sure grew up," Ronni said.

"It's time to let go, Ronni," Vanguard said. "You and the other girls. No more revenge."

Ronni frowned, shook her head. "We can't go, Jan...not till we find what we're after..."

Vanguard nodded toward the frozen young man in the ringside chair. "I think you found him."

The cheerleaders took a look at the frozen, slack-jawed Jason Peterson. Was he the man who could resist their hellish charms?

"Naw," LaVonne said. "I can crack this sucker."

"He seems kinda nice to me," Betty said, almost sadly.

"It's our *job*, girl!" LaVonne retorted. "If we can get a rise out of him, he's *soul* food!"

Vanguard asked, "What do you think, Ronni?"

Ronni was thinking about it. The Whitney Houston song began playing, and suddenly Ronni was again in the blue teddy, and the other two cheerleaders were completely, startlingly nude. They converged on their prey, Ronni straddling him, the other girls kissing and caressing him.

Vanguard kept the flare gun pressed to the sweating cheek of the furious Talion; but he too was watching the attempted seduction...

Ronni's teddy was gone, she too was nude, and whispering in Jason's ear.

And then Jason, gently but firmly, lifted Ronni up and off his lap. "No! No thanks..."

He stood, tried to regain his composure. "You girls are really beautiful, but I'm just not into this anymore."

Vanguard smiled at Talion, who was frowning in disbelief.

"I'm *married*," Jason said. "Or anyway, I'm gonna be." And he began to walk away from the beautiful naked girls, saying, "I mean, I don't mean to hurt anybody's feelings or anything, but I got stuff this good waitin' at home...at least I *hope* I still do..."

Ronni's expression, at first one of disappointment, melted into one of bliss. Utter bliss.

"'Bye, Jan," Ronni said.

"'Bye, sis," Vanguard said.

Then the three girls, in the cheerleader outfits, pom poms in hand, were waving, waving goodbye, Betty giggling like a little girl, as they faded away.

And with a whump, Vanguard, Talion and Jason landed on their butts on a bare patch of concrete in the parking lot. The truck had vanished. The two flares were scattered here and there, as were the cheerleaders' pom poms - the only remaining evidence any of this actually happened.

Vanguard, first to her feet, helped Jason to his.

"What the hell happened?" the young man asked.

"Whatever it was," Vanguard said, "want a piece of friendly advice? Don't tell anybody...'less you want it to get around."

Which was, after all, how urban legends got started.

Confused, the young man at first stumbled away, then ran.

Vanguard helped Talion to his feet.

"Guess you had a vested interest in this yourself," he said.

"The core of truth at the heart of the legend," she said. "Why do you think I was so interested in the Stranded Teenagers' Revenge?"

"You blew your second fifteen minutes of fame, kid."

"I don't know," Vanguard said with a shrug.

"There's two of us to claim all this happened...who knows? A book, a movie, talk-show circuit. Partners?"

Talion chuckled, shook his head, taking her extended hand.

"You know, you didn't look half-bad in that wacky outfit," he said.

"Really?" she asked, pleased to hear it. "Aren't there catalogues where you can order stuff like that?"

Then Vanguard looped her arm in Talion's, and they walked toward the truck stop for some coffee.

Jason was careful not to waken Jenny when he returned to the motel room. In his shorts, he climbed under the covers, just hoping to make himself disappear.

But it woke Jenny, nonetheless; she smiled at him sleepily. "You...you came back."

"I love ya, baby. It's not going to kill us to wait a little while. What's a few days?"

She began to kiss him, then turned away. "Ugh! I have sleep breath. I'll be right back."

Still in her frumpy robe, she trundled off to the bathroom and shut herself in.

Leaning back in bed, listening to the sound of running water, Jason felt the glow of relief that his bride-to-be had forgiven him; he wasn't aware, really, how much had been at stake in that "strip club".

Then the running water stopped, the bathroom door opened, and Jenny was in the doorway, wearing only the teddy, and the light behind her was making a radiant silhouette of her womanly curves.

"It's not going to kill us to get a little head start, either," she said.

Jason smiled and looked skyward. "Thank you, God."

Then Jenny was in his arms and they were laughing and kissing and rolling on the bed together, and soon they were making glorious love.

And what the hell is wrong with that?

HOUSE OF BLOOD
a radio play

CHARACTERS (in order of appearance):

BILL HARRISON – real estate agent; middle-aged

ROGER BLOOM – mid-twenties, young husband

LISA BLOOM – mid-twenties, young wife

TODD FERRELL – twenties, cameraman/techie, cocky

FRANCINE WUNDER – early forties, psychic, earth mother type, eccentric, sensual

DR. SIMON QUEST – noted ghost hunter, ex-priest, dignified

NIKKI QUEST – early thirties, attractive, writer, former student of her husband's

SOUND: Chirping birds, wind rustling trees, distant traffic. Plays under first part of narration.

NARRATOR: The house just outside sleepy Middleton, Ohio, was a real bargain for the Blooms. The young couple were thrilled to have a house of their own so early in their marriage, and this was a handsome home indeed, a turn-of-the-century arts & crafts affair, two stories of character and understated grace. They knew that the place had a violent history, but that didn't bother them...after all, it was such a steal...

SOUND: Thunder. Heavy rainfall. Plays under start of next narration.

NARRATOR: Oh, you aren't familiar with the history of the house? Well, it's well-known among afficionados of murder...and the occult. In 1952... or was it '51?...local attorney Regal Bludworth learned that his young wife had been unfaithful.

SOUND: Thunder. Rain.

NARRATOR: In the middle of a night ripped by a terrible storm, Regal arose and went downstairs and found a butcher knife in the kitchen. Up the back stairway he went, to the bedroom of his wife. They say she awoke just before the blade fell.

SOUND: Woman's scream, somewhat distant, as if a memory.

NARRATOR: Of course, many a husband has dispatched a cheating wife, so – horrible though the eighteen bloody wounds had been – that wasn't enough to earn this home the designation of the House of Blood. You see, after Regal Bludworth killed his wife, he crossed the hall and slashed the throats of their two sleeping children, a boy, Adam, four, and a girl, Eve, six. Then Regal Bludworth returned to the rear stairwell where he threw himself down...

SOUND: Regal falling down a wooden stairway. No scream, but terrible.

NARRATOR: ...to his own death. Other mysterious deaths have occurred in the so-called House of Blood, over the years, which is why the place stayed on the market so long...a full five years since the last residents ran from there, putting it on the market, dirt cheap... Which brings us back to the Blooms, who have spent a harrowing week in the house only to return to the office of real estate agent Bill Harrison to express their dissatisfaction.

LISA: (rushed) Mr. Harrison, it's a nightmare, only you can't wake up from it. Every night, it's the same. Ghostly figures move through the house, hazy figures...

ROGER: We've both seen them, but that's just the start of it. There are screams, Mr. Harrison...

HARRISON: Call me 'Bill,' Roger. Please. Lisa. Just calm down. We'll work this out.

LISA: Mr. Harrison...Bill...it never lets up. It's like the victims of that murder are still there, just lingering like...smoke. But smoke that screams...

HARRISON: (reasonable) You're living on the outskirts of town. Really, out in the country...

LISA: Yes, and being isolated doesn't make it any easier!

HARRISON: No, but the kind of sounds you can hear in the country, added to the reputation of the place, might make a person's imagination run wild.

ROGER: Bill. One person can imagine something. Two people can't imagine the same thing. This is real.

HARRISON: (not unkind) This isn't like returning a dress or lawn mower, folks. You've closed on this house. You've lived in it for a week. Your only option is –

ROGER: Put it back on the market. Do it. I don't care if we suffer a loss. I don't know if we can stand another night of that horror show.

LISA: I don't care if we spend the rest of our marriage in a one-room apartment. We have to dump the place.

HARRISON: Look. Let's just...take a breath. Suppose...just suppose you are imagining things...

LISA/ROGER: We're not!

HARRISON: All right, then let's suppose you aren't imagining things. That this is a very real phenomenon you're experiencing. A paranormal event.

ROGER: (insistent) That's what it is.

HARRISON: I've done some research. This is not the first time something like this has come up in the real estate game. Whether what you're perceiving is real or imagined, there are steps that can be taken.

LISA: What kind of steps?

HARRISON: Possibly, we could have an exorcism performed.

ROGER: (arch) Really?

HARRISON: Hold on. Look, it's been a rainy, windy fall, and you live in an isolated area. You know all of the terrible stories told about the place. Whose imagination wouldn't get away from them?

ROGER: What exactly are you suggesting?

HARRISON: Let's bring in a group of psychic investigators to spend a night in the house. Maybe when you're away.

ROGER: Ghost hunters. You have got to be kidding me.

HARRISON: Why, are you kidding me?

LISA: Roger, what can it hurt? Mr. Harrison...Bill... can you put this in motion for us?

HARRISON: Certainly.

MUSIC: Comes up.

SOUND: Windy night. Leaves rustling.

NARRATOR: On a chill Autumn night, just before 10 P.M., a panel truck pulls up in front of the turn-of-the-century home on the outskirts of Middleton.

SOUND: Van engine thrum, then stops.

NARRATOR: At the wheel is Todd Ferrell, several years out of college where he majored in film and video production. Dark-haired, handsome, in sweatshirt and jeans, he is just a little full of himself.

TODD: So, this is the House of Blood. Looks pretty harmless to me.

FRANCINE: You know the old saying – looks can be deceiving.

NARRATOR: Todd's passenger is Francine Wunder, noted physical medium. An attractive redhead in her early forties, Francine is what you might call an earth-mother type, though her caftan cannot conceal her curves.

TODD: I was in an amateur ghost-hunting group all through college, and the closest we ever came to a ghost was some spooky unidentified sounds.

FRANCINE: And yet still you persist in their pursuit?

TODD: Ms. Wunder, I'm on the clock here. I work for Doc Quest, and yeah, I hold out hope that someday we'll make that breakthrough into what's on the other side...but in the meantime? I'll run camera and sound, and cash my checks.

NARRATOR: A car pulls in behind the panel truck, a handsome sedan with a handsome driver, Dr. Simon Quest himself, noted ghost hunter.

SOUND: Car pulls up, engine is shut off.

NARRATOR: In his early fifties, with a nicely trimmed devil's beard, a big man, bulky but not fat in his tweeds, Dr. Quest is accompanied by his lovely young wife, Nikki.

QUEST: Judging by the history of this house, my dear, I think we may have the makings of another book for you. Perhaps another bestseller!

NIKKI: Darling, the book market is so soft right now. I must encourage you to listen to what Todd is saying about a television show....

NARRATOR: Nikki, a lovely brunette with a slender, fetching shape enshrined in dark sweater and slacks, met her husband when he was teaching at a Catholic college. Their love was deep, so deep in fact that Father Quest gave up the priesthood. But the Doctor of sacred theology has never turned his back on the practice of exorcism.

QUEST: I've allowed Mr. Ferrell his gizmos and video gear, but only to facilitate our work. We must never lose sight of our main mission – we're here to help, not to line our pockets. To make this house a home worth living in for the current owners. And to free any lingering spirits from their temporal purgatory and send them onto their next, we would hope, more rewarding plain of existence.

NIKKI: Darling...if it weren't for the books I've written about our investigations, we wouldn't have any money at all. You won't even charge these homeowners for our services.

QUEST: That would be wrong. That would make for what Francine Wunder would call 'terrible karma.'

NIKKI: Perhaps, but doesn't an exterminator charge for ridding a house of bugs or vermin? Isn't your service worth at least that much?

QUEST: It would violate the purity of our mission, my dear.

NIKKI: Simon, our book sales are off. I don't even know if we can get another contract. But with Todd's new approach, we can parley what remains of our fame into reality TV.

SOUND: Van doors slamming. Rear van doors opening. As heard from within a nearby parked car.

QUEST: We'll talk about it later, child. Mr. Ferrell is unloading all of that fancy of equipment of his, and we really should help.

NARRATOR: Everyone pitches in, even psychic medium Francine, as the little band of paranormal investigators enters the house.

SOUND: Front door opening. Some clanking and perhaps a little grunting, indicating heavy gear is being lugged in.

TODD: So the owners are away? Leaving us mice to play?

QUEST: Something like that. Mr. Ferrell, the couple living here have been suffering hell on earth. We're here to help them. Please remember that.

SOUND: Heavy gear being set down.

TODD: Well, they could use some help on their taste in furniture. This great old house ruined by all this bland modern junk.

NIKKI: Maybe it's all they can afford, Todd. I understand they bought this property for a song, because of the...history.

FRANCINE: And the ghosts.

TODD: Hey, Doc – should I set up the laptops on the dining room table?

QUEST: No, use our card table for that. In the living room. The paucity of furniture will be helpful.

NIKKI: Not much to trip over.

QUEST: The dining room table will be perfect for our seance.

TODD: A seance, huh? That is very cool. That will make rockin' TV.

QUEST: (very irritated) Mister Ferrell...

FRANCINE: (interrupting; melodramatic) Something's going to happen tonight.

QUEST: (switching gears) What is it, Ms. Wunder? What is it you sense?

FRANCINE: Can't you feel it? The air hangs heavy with negative energies. Our previous two attempts at 'ghosthunting' were less than fruitful...but here...in this House of Blood...we will be successful.

TODD: If you call encountering a dead maniac a success.

QUEST: In this case, it would be, it most certainly would be. Mr. Ferrell, you are a reasonably intelligent young man, with considerable valuable training. But your attitude troubles me.

TODD: It's just a defense mechanism, Doc. I'm as interested in this spook stuff as you are.

QUEST: Spook stuff. Yes. I'm sure you are...Before you arrange your equipment, let us take a tour of the house. I'll show you where the tragedies took place.

FRANCINE: I would suggest we stay together or in pairs, at all times.

TODD: Come on, guys. Ghosts are harmless. They're souls trapped between dimensions. That's what I believe anyway.

QUEST: I don't disagree with you. But with a house like this one...it's not merely ghosts we could be dealing with.

TODD: What else then?

QUEST: Demons. Evil spirits seeking hosts.

NIKKI: (excited) Simon, do you anticipate performing an exorcism?

QUEST: Much too early to tell, dear.

TODD: That would rock, Doc. That would be something to catch on HD.

QUEST: I won't stop you from recording anything that occurs on this night. But I can't guarantee that I will sanction its use for any commercial purpose.

TODD: Hey, that's a post-production concern. Right now, we're in production mode. Like we were, you know, makin' a movie.

QUEST: (strained patience) Yes...Let us first get our bearings.

NARRATOR: Quickly Dr. Quest walks his team through the downstairs of the house, noting the stairway just off the entryway, the living room to the right, the dining room to the left, the kitchen connecting to the dining room. In the kitchen, Dr. Quest slows his pace.

QUEST: The downstairs is of little concern to us, with two exceptions, both here in this kitchen...that is the drawer from which Regal Bludworth removed a butcher knife. And this...

SOUND: Door opens.

QUEST: ...is the rear stairway that he ascended to do murder, after which he threw himself down to his death... Shall we take these stairs, for our tour of the second floor?

TODD: I've got my mini-HD cam, Doc. I'm gonna be shooting. Okay?

QUEST: Please do. We want a record of our activities...
and those of anyone, anything else in this house.

SOUND: Footsteps, hollow echoey ones, going up
the rear stairway. Four people – two men and
two women.

QUEST: ...Here we are. To the right is a guest bedroom, which does not concern us. To the left,
a sewing room, which is also of no particular
interest.

SOUND: Footsteps of the party of four on carpet.

QUEST: To the left is the master bedroom. This is
where Mrs. Lucille Bludworth met her doom.

TODD: Doc, that sounded pretty corny. Would you
mind taking that again, but maybe say... 'where
Lucy Bludworth was mercilessly butchered by her
own husband'?

QUEST: ...Mr. Ferrell, in life there are no 'second
takes.'

TODD: Okay. You're the one who's gonna come off
cheesy.

QUEST: (dignified, ignoring that) And this bedroom,
here on the right, is where Regal's children were
killed in their beds. Let's step inside.

SOUND: Footsteps on a hardwood floor, again party
of four.

QUEST: The couple living here at the present time have no children, and as you can see, this is a sort of den, a television room.

TODD: Nice flat-screen.

QUEST: Try to imagine the two little beds there...and there....Adam and Eve.

FRANCINE: Biblical names. He was a religious man, Regal Bludworth.

NIKKI: I don't see how a 'religious man' could kill his own children.

QUEST: Abraham was prepared to do so.

TODD: What, Lincoln?

FRANCINE: They are here!

NIKKI: (somewhat alarmed) What?

FRANCINE: I sense two presences. It must be the little ones. Here they were slain. Here they remain.

TODD: Well, at least they have TV.

QUEST: Not amusing, Mr. Ferrell. It is probably too much to expect you to treat the living with respect. But I must insist you respect the dead.

TODD: Like I said, just a defense mechanism, Doc. No offense meant...can I tell you what I have in mind for tech?

QUEST: You may.

TODD: We're gonna have HD minis in both murder rooms. These will capture high-quality sound as well...then another mini in the hall, and on those back stairs, too. All wireless, fed back to the main hard drive system.

NIKKI: That sounds good, Todd. Right, Simon?

QUEST: (grudgingly) It does.

TODD: Can we head downstairs so I can show you how the rest of the gear'll be deployed?

QUEST: Certainly...Ms. Wunder? Are you all right?

FRANCINE: I don't sense them now. They were here. They were here...

QUEST: Come along, Ms. Wunder.

NARRATOR: Soon Todd Ferrell has arranged three linked laptops on the card table set up in the living room.

TODD: Now, I have hand-held meters available for anybody who wants one. I'll be using one when I'm not manning the tech control center.

NIKKI: I'll take one. We used these last time, right? They measure the electro-magnetic field?

TODD: You got it, Mrs. Quest. All entities are energy. Look for fluctuation. You want one, Doc?

QUEST: No, thank you.

TODD: How about you, Ms. Wunder?

FRANCINE: No. I would like to go upstairs and pray in the children's room.

TODD: Sure. I've got another half hour of set-up down here, and then fifteen minutes to half an hour upstairs, setting up the minicams.

QUEST: Will we be ready by midnight?

TODD: The ol' witching hour? Sure, Doc. You can have your seance right on time.

QUEST: I will accompany Ms. Wunder upstairs and join her in prayer.

TODD: Do that, Doc.

NARRATOR: Soon Dr. Quest and Francine have gone, and Todd and Nikki are alone. At last.

NIKKI: (breathy, urgent) Kiss me. Please kiss me. Put your hands on me. Put your hands on me...

TODD: (whispered) Take it easy, baby. Stay cool. There's a time and a place.

NIKKI: We're fine! They're upstairs. It excites me thinking that he's so close and we're...let's do it here. Right here.

TODD: What, on the floor? No way. Behave, sugar tits!

NIKKI: I want him out of my life. Why don't you let me divorce him? Just divorce his ancient ass.

TODD: I told you a hundred times, Nik. You cannot divorce that man. You will lose all your credibility as a ghost hunter.

NIKKI: I can't stand it. I can't stand having his hands on me...

TODD: You think I like the idea? Look, are you willing to really go for it? Like we talked?

NIKKI: (surprised) What, here? Tonight?

TODD: Here. Tonight. If Simon Quest were to die under mysterious circumstances, during a ghost hunt? His grieving widow would inherit not just his money...which you mostly made for him, ghostin' his books...but that big rep of his. You would be the surviving Quest, the beautiful ghost hunter who went bravely on after the tragic death of her beloved.

NIKKI: Is there...do you...have a plan?

TODD: Less you know, the better. But I'll tell you this much. Your boy Todd will place those HD mini-cams right where he can get the best shots...and where he knows just how to stay out of frame...

NIKKI: I'm afraid, Todd. Kiss me. Kiss me.

TODD: Okay, Nik. Just don't get carried away...

NARRATOR: While Nikki and Todd deal with laptops, HD mini-cams, and murder plans, Dr. Simon
Quest and psychic medium Francine Wunder have
gone upstairs to what had been the room of the
two murdered children. In what is now the den, we
find them kneeling in prayer...well, they're kneeling anyway. And kissing...rather passionately.

SOUND: Rustle of clothing as fully clothed couple
make out.

QUEST: (out of breath) No, Francine, dearest...not
here...this is wrong...

FRANCINE: Only in the smallest sense. In the larger
vision, we belong together. Simon, darling, you
must accept that we are soul mates. You know
what my reading said...

QUEST: That we were lovers in many past lives? I
still harbor doubts about reincarnation. There is
still enough priest in me to believe in heaven and
hell and purgatory between.

FRANCINE: (sensual) I would like some ex-priest
in me...

QUEST: Don't blaspheme! Those two children died
here...

FRANCINE: Yes. They did. And they have moved
on, in their innocence.

QUEST: You said you felt something...

FRANCINE: I did. An evil presence when we arrived. Then in this room, two other trapped souls...but I don't think it was the children. Those sweet sad souls have gone on to their next lives.

QUEST: (business-like) And we should move on to our next task. We have a seance to conduct. Darling...now. Get up.

FRANCINE: (reluctant) All right.

SOUND: The two rise.

FRANCINE: (intimate, insistent) Dearest...we do belong together. You must tell that silly girl. That stupid child you married. Tell her and set her free.

QUEST: Divorce her? Impossible.

FRANCINE: Why? You've already been excommunicated by your church.

QUEST: It's not a question of that. I would be a... laughingstock. I gave up the priesthood for her, and now the star-crossed romance has gone bust? No. I have my name, and my mission, to preserve.

FRANCINE: (hurt) Is that more important than us?

QUEST: I don't know. I honestly don't know...

FRANCINE: (hushed) I find myself wishing one of these ghosts, these demons we seek, would strike her down.

QUEST: You mustn't say that!

FRANCINE: She is shallow, she is selfish...she would be better off if she moved on and tried again... perhaps a frog next time, or a beetle.

QUEST: Francine, how can a woman of your sensitivity say such hateful things?

FRANCINE: It's because I love you, dearest...I love you now, as I have loved you through the ages.

NARRATOR: It would seem that not all of the dark forces at large in the House of Blood can be laid at the feet of dead murderer Regal Bludworth. But as the four ghost-hunters work together, to ready the midnight seance, all is calm, professional. Four cameras are set around the dining room table, to capture various angles. An array of candles has been lighted around the otherwise darkened room, providing a flickery, properly ghostly ambiance.

QUEST: Mr. Ferrell, do you have sufficient lighting for your cameras?

TODD: Oh yeah, and I've checked them all. This high-tech gear is amazing. The sound on those minis will even pick up any EVP's.

QUEST: I admit I have my doubts about so called 'Electronic Voice Phenomenon'. But it seems to be accepted by many in our field.

FRANCINE: It's nonsense. If spirits trapped between worlds want to communicate with this dimension, why do so by sounds the human ear can't perceive?

QUEST: Who can say, Ms. Wunder? 'There are more things in heaven and earth, Horatio, than are dreamt of in your philosophy.'

TODD: What, that guy on CSI: MIAMI, you mean?

NIKKI: (Embarrassed) It's a Shakespeare quote...Can we get started? It's a little after midnight already.

SOUND: Outside the house, wind, and rain kick in.

TODD: Cool! Mother Nature providin' some creepy production value. Yeah, let's get started...

NARRATOR: The little group assembles around the table. Even with a table leaf out, this requires some arm-stretching for requisite holding of hands. But they manage. Working together quite well, considering.

MUSIC: Eerie.

FRANCINE: (dreamy trance-like state) I will address you, my spirit guide, Chief Yellow Feather. Are you here, oh honored chief?... The chief is here... Chief, is there any trapped soul in this House of Blood who wishes contact with the physical world?... The Chief says there is such a soul... Tell him, oh honored Chief, that we are here to help him, tell him...

SOUND: Table shifts, lifts up, and sets down with a whump.

TODD: Jeez! Did you see that?

QUEST: (hushed) I saw it. Please maintain decorum.

TODD: Damn table lifted off the ground! Back down again, bam! Is a window open? Did the wind get it?

NIKKI: (hushed, gentle) Todd, please...just go with it...

NOTE: Actress playing Francine will speak in a low, as male-as-possible voice until further notice. Sinister. Strange.

FRANCINE/REGAL: I am here with you. I am the one you seek. You may ask me questions, but first – the failed man of God who assembled you must answer my question.

TODD: (unimpressed) He means you, Doc.

QUEST: I presume I speak to Regal Bludworth. Ask your question.

FRANCINE/REGAL: Good. Can you tell me? Is this hell?

QUEST: We are in a house outside Middleton, Ohio, in the United States of America on the planet Earth. No, I would say we are not in hell, Mr. Bludworth.

FRANCINE/REGAL: Then tell me, priest. Is this purgatory?

QUEST: It may be yours.

FRANCINE/REGAL: Indeed. That thought has a resonance. You see, every night I must do it again.

QUEST: Do what again?

FRANCINE/REGAL: Why kill them, of course.

QUEST: Perhaps...if you could stop yourself...you would be released from this spiritual prison.

FRANCINE/REGAL: Oh, but I don't want to stop myself. As you will see. Because I will kill them again tonight...

SOUND: Table jumps again, whumping down.

TODD: Damn! How is that happening? Is it something you rigged behind my back, Doc? I can shut the cameras down before you answer...

FRANCINE: (normal voice; tired, coming out of trance) What...what happened? Did anything happen? Was I...successful? Did we reach the spirit trapped here?

NARRATOR: Quietly, patiently, Dr. Quest reports to the medium about the conversation they've just had, through her, with Regal Bludworth.

FRANCINE: I remember none of that. But I can tell you this – despite what my previous impressions may have been...there is but one ghost, one soul, one spirit trapped in this place.

TODD: You big ham! Look, I don't mind us dressing things up some, to make a decent TV pilot. But that crapola won't play. (Imitating her) I am Regal Bludworth! (regular voice) Really? Come on!

FRANCINE: (quietly indignant) I don't have to put up with these insults.

QUEST: Indeed, you don't, Ms. Wunder. Mister Ferrell, I would think that by now you would know that we maintain a high level of integrity in our inquiries. There is, and will be, zero fakery.

NIKKI: What the hell is that?!?

NARRATOR: A shadowy figure, without substance yet distinct, like poor television reception, has entered the dining room, having come down the front stairs. The four at the table freeze and watch in stunned attention as a man in pajamas moves past them into the adjacent kitchen...where the light comes on.

SOUND: Kitchen drawer opening. Rustle of silverware.

NARRATOR: Dr. Quest motions for quiet...and for all to follow him...into the brightly-lit kitchen.

TODD: He's gone.

NIKKI: Did we really see that?

FRANCINE: Oh yes.

NIKKI: I thought I heard a drawer opening...but everything seems in place.

QUEST: Not everything...there, on the counter.

TODD: Hell! A butcher knife!

QUEST: And that door to the back stairs...was it open? Did anyone leave it open?... Well, it's open now.

TODD: (excited; not scared) Nobody touch that knife! I'll get a camera. We've got to shoot it.

QUEST: Do so, Mr. Ferrell.

SOUND: Quick footsteps on hard wood floor, leaving.

TODD: (off-mic) I shoulda set up a minicam in that kitchen, too! But I already used every one we got. Gimme a second, gimme a second, I need to check something, gotta rewind here – ghost dude shows up on camera! That's money!

SOUND: Quick footsteps on hard wood floor, coming back.

TODD: (on-mic) Doc, stand near that knife, gesture to it. Man! I think we've really got somethin' here. Caught a frickin' ghost! A real, live ghost.

QUEST: 'Frickin''...perhaps. But not 'live'. We need to go upstairs.

TODD: That thing isn't dangerous, is it?

FRANCINE: I don't believe so. But I have never seen
    so vivid a manifestation. Have you, Simon?

QUEST: No. Never. Shall we?

SOUND: Footsteps on stairs as they go up.

QUEST: (quietly) Bludworth said he must repeat his
    vile act every night. I suggest we start with the
    master bedroom.

SOUND: Footsteps of the foursome on carpet.

NARRATOR: But as the four ghost hunters enter
    the bedroom, there is no sign of their ghost in
    pajamas. To Dr. Quest and his wife Nikki and
    cameraman Todd, there's no sign of anyone. But
    to Francine Wunder...

FRANCINE: Do you see them?

QUEST: No. Anyone?

NIKKI: No.

TODD: I see a made bed. So what?

FRANCINE: I see a couple. They are sleeping. Rest-
    fully. They are hazy, but...I can see them. I do not
    think the man is Regal Bludworth.

TODD: So ol' Regal caught his wife and her boyfriend
    in bed together? But I never heard about any boy-

friend being here or getting himself killed...

FRANCINE: No. These are...I'm not sure who they are. They are friendly.

QUEST: You said only one spirit inhabited this house.

FRANCINE: I must have been wrong. I'm...I'm confused. Mine is an imperfect science.

TODD: No kidding.

FRANCINE: Let us leave them in peace.

TODD: What, so the ghost in p.j.'s can hack 'em to death?

FRANCINE: If so, we can't stop it.

TODD: (upbeat) But we can record it.

QUEST: Let's check the children's room.

SOUND: Footsteps of the four on carpet.

FRANCINE: I sense no spirits here. I see no manifestations. Not the children, not Regal Bludworth.

TODD: So, what now?

QUEST: I suggest we position ourselves at key spots – I'll take the top of the back stairs. Mr. Ferrell, return to the murder bedroom with your handheld camera. Nikki, you take the children's room. And Francine, you roam, picking up whatever... transmissions...you can.

TODD: Okay, Doc.

NIKKI: All right.

FRANCINE: As you say, Simon.

SOUND: Footsteps on carpet, heading away.

NARRATOR: Nikki shuts herself in the den, the former children's bedroom, to wait. But for what? The ghost of a killer with a butcher knife?

SOUND: Door opens.

NIKKI: Oh!...Damnit, Todd, you scared me.

TODD: What, you were expecting Regal Bludworth?

NIKKI: You're supposed to be in the murder bedroom.

TODD: Never mind that. This is our chance. I'll shove that pompous-ass husband of yours down those back stairs and blame it on these spooks or the excitement of the ghost hunt or whatever.

NIKKI: (frightened) Todd, not here, not now...not after we saw that, that...whatever it was, in the kitchen.

TODD: (upbeat, fast-talking) It's the perfect cover for us. My God, we got a dead guy who'll take the rap for us! And we'll wind up with footage worth God knows how much – we caught a ghost on HD, Nik! And your old man is about to hit the cutting room floor.

NIKKI: But it's so risky...so dangerous...

TODD: Look, I know just where the mini-HDs are positioned on those stairs – and just how to trip the old boy and not get caught on camera.

NIKKI: But...what if the fall doesn't kill him?

TODD: Easy peazy. I'll just break his neck after the 'ghost' knocks the camera out of the way... Hey, how come the old boy is calling that New Age witch 'Francine' all of a sudden? And she's all 'Simon' with him...(nasty laugh)...Maybe you got some competition, Nik.

NIKKI: My husband has about as much interest in sex as a castrato choir boy. But do look out for her... she's the wild card in this. If she sees you...

TODD: If she sees me shove the doc? Then Regal Bludworth will just have to claim another victim.

SOUND: Thunder and rain, up and then, as narration begins, down and playing under the next sequence.

NARRATOR: For perhaps half an hour all is quiet. Dr. Quest takes a position near the open back stairwell. His wife Nikki waits in what had been the murdered children's bedroom. And in the master bedroom, where over half a century ago Regal Bludworth had killed his slumbering bride, is cameraman Todd Ferrell, waiting for the right moment to deal with Dr. Quest. But where is the psychic, Francine Wunder? Ah...there she is. Downstairs. In the kitchen.

Taking that butcher knife off the counter. Walking through the dining room in a zombie-like trance, butcher knife poised to stab. Slowly...so slowly... moving up the front stairway. So quietly does she move that Dr. Quest, at his rear stairway post, does not notice her reach the top and glide into the master bedroom.

TODD: Francine! What the hell are you doing?!?

(NOTE: Until further notice, Francine will again speak in the male register, sinister seance voice of Regal Bludworth.)

FRANCINE/REGAL: I will not be your cuckold!

TODD: (Quietly) Put the knife down. Wake up!

NARRATOR: For a moment, like a signal flickering in and out, a couple in the bed appears before Rod's astonished eyes. But the man and woman do not wake or react as Francine drives her butcher's blade again and again into the bed, as if the couple were only an apparition.

SOUND: Knife plunging into mattress, again and again.

NARRATOR: Todd rushes into the hall...

TODD: Doc! Doc!

SOUND: Heavy footsteps on carpet as Todd runs to Quest.

QUEST: (urgent) What is it, Ferrell?

TODD: (rushed) Doc, your psychic's come unglued, she's got that butcher knife and she's walin' away, killing the damn mattress in the murder bedroom!

QUEST: (hushed) Wait...she's coming out of the bedroom...

TODD: My God, Doc, she's going across the hall – into the kids' room! Nikki! Nikki, look out!

SOUND: Running footsteps of two men on carpet. Door opens. Then a scream that cuts off in a gurgle, followed by the thud of a body hitting the floor.

QUEST: (aghast) Francine – what have you done?

TODD: (flipping out) She cut Nik's throat is what she's done! You bitch! I'll –

FRANCINE/REGAL: You'll die.

TODD: Put that down! (almost orgasmic) unghh... unghh...uhghh...unghh...

SOUND: Stabbing interposed with above "unghh's," as Francine stabs Todd to death, then his body hits the floor.

QUEST: (Trying to be strong) Francine...dearest....

hear me...I know you are still in there...the demon has you...I will cast him out! Out satanic spirit! By the power of all that is holy...

FRANCINE/REGAL: Do you truly think that a defrocked sinner of a priest like you has any such authority?

SOUND: Quest screams, but it becomes a death gurgle. Then he falls to the floor.

MUSIC: Big, dramatic, then down, down.

FRANCINE: (muted, coming out of a trance)...Simon? Simon? Oh dear God! What have I done? What...have...I...done?

NARRATOR: The medium flings the bloody blade to the floor...

SOUND: Knife clatters.

NARRATOR: ...and runs from the room, where the slashed and stabbed remains of her co-workers are strewn. Fleeing the horror, she means to go down the front stairs, but something freezes her at the top...a voice that emanates from...herself.

FRANCINE/REGAL: Join me.

FRANCINE: ...What?

FRANCINE/REGAL: Join me in this house. How lonely I have grown. Join me. Go to the rear stairs. Go. Now.

SOUND: Francine's footsteps on carpet.

NARRATOR: Francine stands at the top of the stairs. A man at the foot of those stairs, in blood-spattered pajamas, smiles serenely and crooks his finger...

FRANCINE/REGAL: Join me.

SOUND: Francine throws herself down the stairs. Again, no scream, but terrible.

MUSIC: Big, dramatic, then fades.

SOUND: Chirping birds, wind rustling trees, distant traffic.

NARRATOR: The following morning is a sunny one, a few puddles and fallen branches the only proof of the storm the night before. In Bill Harrison's real estate office, seated across from him again, are the young couple, Roger and Lisa Bloom.

HARRISON: Another rough night, I take it?

ROGER: (frazzled) God yes. Same freaking drill – ghostly figures, screams, just unbearable.

LISA: We talked over your suggestion to bring in a team of ghost hunters and decided against it. I mean, it didn't do any good five years ago, did it?

ROGER: Just added to the horror...and to the body count. No, put the ungodly pile on the market.

Sell it to Hollywood, why don't you? The damn place makes that house in Amityville look like a bed and breakfast.

SOUND: Chairs scrape the floor as Roger and Lisa rise.

HARRISON: There's nothing I can say...?

ROGER: No, we're out of here. We're packed up and on our way. (off-mic) We'll arrange for a moving van. Get contact info to you....

SOUND: Wind rustles trees. Perhaps a distant wind chime.

NARRATOR: That night, just before 10 P.M., as it does every night, a panel truck pulls up in front of the turn-of-the-century home on the outskirts of Middleton, Ohio. A car pulls in behind the panel truck, driven by Dr. Simon Quest himself, noted ghost hunter. Like Regal Bludworth, he and his team are residents of the House of Blood, who – unlike the Blooms – do not have the luxury of moving out.

MUSIC: Sting.

MERCY
a radio play

CHARACTERS (in order of appearance):

MERCY – eighteen. Vixen who gets religion, not in a good way.

ROD – captain of the football team who makes a bad decision.

NURSE – walk on.

PASTOR STRICKLAND – sixtyish, apparently well-meaning, but extreme Fundamentalist views

CINDI – initially unpleasant classmate of Mercy's; girlfriend of late Rod, blames Mercy for his death

RANDY JOHNSON – self-styled retro j.d.

DAN DICKEY – philandering guidance counselor,

late twenties.

PETER BISHOP – spoiled rich kid, eighteen. Brief.

OSCAR PIKE – nerd computer guru, eighteen.

SOUND: The happy sounds of high school kids at a kegger-type party. Drunken laughter, girls and boys. Beer pouring. Generic rock or hip-hop music.

MERCY: (a little drunk) Listen, Rod – you round up as many of the guys on the team as you can... first-string only...I'm no slut! And pile into my van. We'll go out to the Hollow and I'll...take one for the team...

ROD: Mercy, you can't mean this. I mean, I heard you were kinda wild, but –

MERCY: Sounds like a good time, doesn't it? You don't think I can handle it? Try me!

ROD: Okay, okay, I'll call your bluff.

MERCY: I don't bluff. Remember that when we play strip poker.

ROD: ...I'll round up the guys...(off mic)...Meet you out front in five...

MERCY: (to herself) Touchdown.

NARRATOR: Mercy Mathers had, once upon a

time, been a good little girl. As a child, she had platinum blonde hair, sky-blue eyes, a perfect pale complexion, and a smile that would melt the heart of a misanthrope. But after her mother and father died in a plane crash, when she was just thirteen, Mercy had gone to live with her wealthy, elderly grandmother. Grandma provided Mercy with two things: everything she wanted, and no supervision. And when puberty came calling, the good little girl grew up and out and every which fetching way, the most beautiful perfect blonde any red-blooded boy or man might dream of. The kind of young woman who seemed utterly unattainable. But the thing was...Mercy was attainable. Very attainable. She loved attention, she loved to party, and the worst kept secret at Clarion High was that everybody's favorite cheerleader, the prom queen, the girl most likely to succeed, was in particular the favorite of any number of boys. She'd never gone steady, Mercy, because she liked variety. She liked fun. The good little girl quite liked being bad.

SOUND: Party sounds muffled. Outdoor ambience. Guys talking, laughing, excited, drawing closer to the mic.

ROD: Okay, Mercy. We're game if you are.

SOUND: Guys hooting, hollering in agreement. "Oh yeah," "Game on!"

MERCY: (drunker) I was born game. You boys may be conference champs, but I am gonna rule your asses. You are mine!

SOUND: More whistling, hooting, "Bring it!," "It's on."

MERCY: Save your energy. You're gonna need it. Get in.

SOUND: Van door opens. Sound of guys piling into van. More male boasting, adlibs.

MERCY: This is gonna be the best homecoming ever.

ROD: Hey, Merce. You better let me drive. You're a couple sheets to the wind, sweetcheeks.

MERCY: Rod, I am doin' all the driving tonight. Otherwise, you and your jock pals can find some other way to end a perfect evening.

ROD: Okay but take it easy. Lot of cops out tonight, looking for party animals. A DUI wouldn't look cool on your permanent record.

MERCY: Yeah, yeah, yeah. Get in and buckle up.

ROD: (off-mic) Oh-kay...

NARRATOR: The Hollow was everybody's favorite make-out spot, but it took any number of back roads to get there.

SOUND: Vehicle traveling fast, making a fast turn

on gravel.

ROD: Merce! Take it easy.

MERCY: Don't be a pussy...

NARRATOR: Mercy would have been fine if she hadn't passed a slow-moving vehicle...

MERCY: Get outa my way, farmer!

SOUND: Gunning vehicle.

NARRATOR: ...on that hill.

ROD: Mercy!

SOUND: The worst car crash ever heard. Tearing metal, screaming (young) passengers.

SOUNDS: Hospital hallway.

NURSE: Pastor, she's just woken up. She's heavily medicated, and dazed, so please...be gentle when you talk to her.

PASTOR: I'm here as much as a family friend as in my official capacity. Her late father was on the church board. What does she know?

NURSE: Nothing. Not about her friends, or her grandmother, either. If she gets upset, ring me. And don't talk with her long...

SOUND: Door opens, closes. Hospital sounds muffled now, then fade away. Footsteps.

MERCY: (weak, even groggy) Pastor Strickland...is that you? Pastor, the last I remember...

PASTOR: Take it easy, young lady.

SOUND: Chair pulled up. Sits.

PASTOR: We're just going to sit here like old friends and take our time with this. Give me your hand, child.

MERCY: My friends...Rod...the others?

PASTOR: They're with the Lord. At least I hope they are.

MERCY: Hope they are?

PASTOR: If they were right with God.

MERCY: And if not?

PASTOR: (soothing) Then I'm afraid they're burning in Hell, dear.

MERCY: (alert, alarmed) They're dead? They're all dead? And I'm alive...

PASTOR: (mildly amused) Well, this isn't heaven, child. It's just Iowa. You're going to be fine. That air bag saved you. But all the passengers...and the driver of that combine you hit...well, we'll pray they were right with God.

MERCY: My Grandmother. Where is she? Has she

been here?

PASTOR: Now, you don't have to worry about your grandmother.

MERCY: Good. Good. She won't judge me. Everybody else will, but she won't...

PASTOR: I won't lie to you, child. She was concerned when she heard. You know, you've been unconscious for a week.

MERCY: Call her, would you, Pastor? Tell her I'm okay. That I'm not in a coma or anything.

PASTOR: I'm sure she knows, dear, where she is.

MERCY: Why? Where is she?

PASTOR: She's left this vale of tears, God be praised.

MERCY: What?

PASTOR: (gentle) She had a fatal stroke the night she heard.

MERCY: Oh my God...

PASTOR: Yes. Let us pray.

MERCY: Pastor, she's dead, too?

PASTOR: She walks the green pastures with the Lord. I know she does because she prayed with me before she died. The Lord forgave her. She was born again. Washed in the blood of the lamb.

MERCY: Oh, my God...what have I done? I've sinned...I've been such a bad girl...

PASTOR: It's too late for those boys, Mercy. But not for you. You can get right with God.

MERCY: I'm going to jail, aren't I?

PASTOR: No.

MERCY: Pastor, I was drinking. I was drunk on my ass.

PASTOR: That kind of language, young lady, is hardly the first step on your path to redemption.

MERCY: My what?

PASTOR: Those boys in that van, who died with you, who died in sin? For the sake of our community, for the sake of their parents, the sheriff has declined to press any charges against you.

MERCY: That's crazy...

PASTOR: No. To the community, those eight members of the Clarion High football team were fine young men. Let them set an example in death that they did not in life. That they were drinking and on their way to defile a sweet young thing like you, Mercy, well...what lesson would that teach?

MERCY: Maybe that God struck them down for sinning.

PASTOR: That's an interesting thought. A topic worthy of discussion. Why don't you come live with Agnes and me? Our daughters are grown up, and I could be a father to you, you could have the guidance you need.

MERCY: Thank you, Pastor, but...I'll go back home. I'm eighteen. I can finish the school year and then decide what's next for me.

PASTOR: That's a very grown up decision, dear. May I suggest that you start attending services again? Your grandmother never missed a one.

MERCY: All right.

PASTOR: And you can study with me, privately, if you like. The Scripture. Why, before you know it, you'll be a theological whiz.

MERCY: Why do you want me? I'm a bad girl, Pastor. I was drinking. I invited those boys. I was going to...I was going to do bad things with them.

PASTOR: You're confessing your sins. What better start is that? You can be born again, child. All those sins washed away.

MERCY: But I'm weak. What if I sinned again?

PASTOR: There is no limit to the Lord's forgiveness.

MERCY: But what if I slip? What if I'm not right with the Lord when I die?

SOUND: (chair scrape) I think you know the answer to that, child.

NARRATOR: And so, Mercy turned over the proverbial new leaf. She went home to the gothic near-mansion where she and her late grandmother had lived, so big and empty and foreboding now. Yet somehow it seemed just right her new life, living alone, her spare time given to reading the Bible. Several evenings a week, she and Pastor Strickland studied and discussed scripture. She dressed more conservatively now, often in angelic white, but her natural beauty came screaming through. But when she returned to school, the welcome of some classmates was less than warm. Like Cindi Wesson, who had been Rod's steady girl...

SOUND: A bell rings quickly followed by bustling high school hallway sounds between classes. Talk, movement, a little laughter.

CINDI: Hey! Skank!

MERCY: Cindi, I understand how you feel...

CINDI: No, you don't. I think you're evil. Oh, I know all about this new goody-two-shoes act of yours. You're all churchy now. But that doesn't mean you aren't going straight to Hell.

MERCY: I'm not going to Hell. I've been saved. You can be, too.

CINDI: Oh, my God!

MERCY: Yes, your God. He loves you. He'll forgive your sins.

CINDI: My sins? You were gonna gang-bang the first string of the football team and got 'em killed instead, because you were drunk as a skunk! If you weren't designed for Hell, who was?

MERCY: I'll pray for you.

CINDI: (off-mic) Don't do me any favors, scuzz queen.

RANDY: (off-mic) Hey! Merce.

SOUND: Locker shutting.

MERCY: Oh...Randy. Hi. You look nice today.

RANDY: Yeah, it's a retro thing. Black leather like James Dean.

MERCY: Who?

RANDY: Just another stud who died in a car crash.

MERCY: ...I have to get to class.

RANDY: Bad joke. Look, some of these clowns around here are treating you pretty rotten. When's the last time you had a little fun?

MERCY: I've sort of given up fun.

RANDY: Aw come on, baby. Let's hook up. What do you say?

MERCY: I'm not that way anymore, Randy. But if you want to come over to my place, tonight, and study, that would be cool.

RANDY: Yeah, study what? We're seniors. We already know we're graduating.

MERCY: How about something a little more spiritual?

RANDY: What, Bible school?

MERCY: Yes. It's never too late to get right with God.

RANDY: Uh...your grandma croaked, didn't she?

MERCY: Yes. She passed away.

RANDY: That's a shame. So, then, you're, uh...living alone?

MERCY: I am.

RANDY: Okay. I'm cool with a little Bible study. I could stand to get straight with the Man Upstairs, I guess.

MERCY: That's wonderful! Stop over at seven. We'll sit by the fire, have snacks...

RANDY: Yeah, I'm salivating already.

NARRATOR: So that evening, a cool autumn night, Mercy puts on a white dress and makes crackers and cheese and starts a fire.

SOUND: Several hard knocks at the door. Door opens.

RANDY: Hi, babe.

MERCY: You surprised me! I was listening for your Harley.

RANDY: Hey, I only live three blocks over. Nice night like this? Thought I'd just have a nice walk out under God's majestic sky.

MERCY: You look great – no biker leathers?

RANDY: So ya like me in a jacket and tie? Hey, it's Sunday school, right?

MERCY: You're teasing. Come on in.

SOUND: Door shuts.

NARRATOR: Soon Mercy and her guest are nibbling snacks and having soft drinks as he listens to her talk about the need for him to get right with the "Man Upstairs".

RANDY: Yeah, baby, I could see gettin' cool with the Almighty...I done bad shit in my time, and what the hell, I could go for this Born Again trip.

MERCY: You're not just saying that?

RANDY: No. You gettin' a little warm? I am. Why don't you slip out of that dress?

MERCY: No, Randy, I...

RANDY: Hey, you were talking about sacrifice before! Like that dude you read me about that was
up for killin' his kid 'cause God told him to! God
likes sacrifice, right?

MERCY: He does.

RANDY: Well, then, give it up, baby. Sacrifice a little
bit to Randy.

MERCY: I don't think you're sincere.

RANDY: Hey, my frickin' sincerity is sticking out
all over the place!

MERCY: Pray with me, Randy.

NARRATOR: So they prayed. And Randy asked for
forgiveness and he got right with God, and soon
their kneeling position became prone and Mercy
made the sacrifice. She enjoyed it. It was like
old sinful times, but for a good cause. Randy fell
asleep there in front of the fireplace, and Mercy
– still naked as God had made her – slipped into
the kitchen and found the biggest butcher knife
she'd ever seen. She was raising it in two hands,
clutched in her prayer-like grasp, when Randy
awoke and looked up at the blade pointing at his
bare chest.

RANDY: Mercy! What the hell!

MERCY: Randy, you're right with God now. But what if you slipped? What if you slipped?

RANDY: No!

SOUND: The knife stabs deep.

RANDY: No...(gurgling)...muh-mer-see...

SOUND: Stabbing. Again, and again and again.

NARRATOR: Living alone as she did, Mercy performed the clean-up herself, at her leisure. That she and Randy had both been nude had been helpful. But disposing of him was problematic.

MERCY: (to herself) Can't go dragging Randy off and just dropping him somewhere. Might be seen... God would understand, but would the police?

NARRATOR: So she went to the body of the boy she'd saved from hell, took him by the ankles, and dragged him to the old-fashioned claw-foot bathtub. Somehow, she got him up and over and in. Her father had been in the grocery business and she'd seen sides of beef cut up often enough as a child; and she was just about the least squeamish person in Biology class. So cutting Randy into pieces was difficult work but less disturbing than you might think. She sang "Amazing Grace" as she worked, and had two epiphanies: one, she had nice enough a voice to join Pastor Strickland's choir; and two, saving Randy from Hell by offering herself to him...by using the perfect body God had given her as a sort of offering...suggested that path to redemption the Pastor had spoken of. Mercy had found her calling...

MERCY: (to herself) Okay...now what?... Of course, tonight is garbage night...

NARRATOR: And so Mercy tidied up – the parts that had been Randy fit nicely in three triple-bagged garbage bags, taking up two of her grandmother's garbage cans...with room for another bag from the kitchen on top. Hauling the trash cans out to the curb took only minimal effort. And cleaning the tub and the hard wood flooring was a breeze...

SOUND: Morning sounds – birds chirping, cars starting. A garbage truck rumbles toward mic, stops down the street. Throughout next dialogue sequence, garbage truck keeps moving and stopping, as cans at the curb are emptied in back of the truck. Phone rings.

MERCY: (sleepy) Hello?

PASTOR: (telephone) Sorry to call so early, child. But I wanted to remind you about Bible studies this evening.

MERCY: Thank you, Pastor. I hadn't forgotten.

PASTOR: (telephone) You're still in bed, aren't you child?

MERCY: Afraid so.

PASTOR: (telephone) Well, go to the window and look at the beautiful Fall day the Lord has provided, and get your pretty little bottom off to school.

MERCY: Yes, Pastor. Thanks for calling...

SOUND: Bed springs. Feet pad on floor, then window opens, letting morning sounds in, including garbage truck, about a door away now.

MERCY: (to herself) What a lovely day. Thank you, God. Thank you.

SOUND: Garbage truck louder, stopping nearby. Garbage can being emptied into back of truck. Out front of Mercy's house. Another can, its contents thudding noisily into back of truck.

MERCY: (sincere – no irony) You're welcome, Randy.

NARRATOR: The absence of Randy Johnson at school the next day went unnoticed – neither his failing to return home the night before, nor his failure to be in class today, were at all out of the ordinary. Today was like any other day at Clarion High, except for an appointment Mercy had been putting off, with Mr. Dickey, the guidance counselor. After school, in his third-floor office.

DICKEY: Come in, Mercy! Come in. Sit right there on the couch.

MERCY: All right, Mr. Dickey.

DICKEY: Please, Mercy. We don't stand on cere-
mony, remember? Not old friends like us. Call
me Dan.

NARRATOR: Mr. Dickey – Dan – wasn't just a counselor. He also taught a few classes of algebra. For
a teacher, Mercy supposed, he was pretty young
– late twenties? He had a wife and a little baby at
home. And last year, in this office, she had earned
an A from Mr. Dickey in a subject that up till then
she'd been failing...until her oral exam...

DICKEY: You don't mind if I sit next to you, here
on the couch?

MERCY: No, Mr. Dickey.

DICKEY: Dan. Make it Dan. We're overdue for a talk
about this terrible tragedy.

NARRATOR: And for half an hour, with hardly a
word from Mercy, the counselor counseled her –
assuring her that she need feel no guilt for making
this one small mistake..."One small mistake,"
Mercy thought, that had cost Clarion High most
of its first-string footballers!

DICKEY: Oh, I'm afraid I've gone on and on...do you
have anywhere you need to be?

MERCY: No, I'm living alone now.

DICKEY: That's right! That's right, I heard that...do you mind if I shut the door?

MERCY: I don't mind, but I think all the office staff is gone already.

SOUND: Dickey getting up off couch. A few footsteps.

DICKEY: Everyone does seem to have skedaddled. But still, better we preserve your privacy. Delicate subject.

SOUND: Door closes. Lock click. Quick footsteps. Dickey sits down again.

DICKEY: I understand you've had something of a... religious conversion.

MERCY: Well, Grandma went to Pastor Strickland's church regularly. Sometimes I went, too. But I never took it seriously till now.

DICKEY: You're, uh...born again?

MERCY: I'm right with God.

DICKEY: So you, uh...your sins are forgiven?

MERCY: Oh yes.

DICKEY: Well, that's wonderful. Mercy, uh...about last year...our little relationship...

MERCY: It wasn't a relationship exactly.

DICKEY: No, but you were very warm to me, and

I hope I was, uh, understanding in return, and, well...now that you have this newfound faith, I'm wondering if you must, uh...are you compelled to...?

MERCY: I'm not going to tell on you, Mr. Dickey. Dan.

DICKEY: (very relieved) Good, I...well, that was inappropriate, last year, and I'm really sorry.

MERCY: It was sinful. You're a married man. You have a small child.

DICKEY: I am. I only wish I could make amends to you, somehow.

MERCY: You need to make amends with God.

DICKEY: Yes! Yes. I'm a pretty religious person myself, actually. That would be a fine solution. Shall we...pray together?

NARRATOR: And once again, Mercy got on her knees in Mr. Dickey's office. But this time so did he. They knelt together. Prayed. And, with Mercy's prompting, Mr. Dickey indeed, got right with God. Just after he got right with God, however, Mr. Dickey put his hands on Mercy...in an inappropriate manner...

MERCY: You see, Mr. Dickey! You've slipped already.

DICKEY: You're so lovely...such an angel...(out of breath) Air...I need some air...

NARRATOR: Mr. Dickey got to his feet and went to the window.

SOUND: Window raises. Night sounds.

DICKEY: I'm not a nice person, Mercy. I'm really not.

MERCY: We'll pray again. You will be right with God, Mr. Dickey. You will be.

NARRATOR: So they prayed there at the window, in the crisp fresh air, until dusk turned into a starry evening. When their prayers had ceased, Mr. Dickey took her in his arms.

MR. DICKEY: You're a special young woman, Mercy. Very special.

NARRATOR: There wasn't much time. Mr. Dickey was faltering. Before he could slip from grace, Mercy gave him a firm but loving shove...and he slipped from the window...

SOUND: Dickey screaming, then SPLATTING.

NARRATOR: ...to the hard cement three stories below.

MUSIC: Up.

NARRATOR: The tragic "suicide" of guidance counselor Dan Dickey attracted no more attention than the disappearance of Randy Johnson, who had after all been threatening to "blow this pop stand" for years. So Mercy became convinced of the righteousness of her calling. As fall turned into winter, Mercy saved a number of troubled souls from perdition. Take that spoiled rich kid, Peter Bishop, who took advantage of his parents being away to invite Mercy over to try out his new hot tub.

SOUND: Jacuzzi bubbling.

PETER: Ah, it feels good to be right with God, you sweet thing...so gooood...

NARRATOR: The hot tub provided Mercy with the chance to perform her first Baptism. Peter was a dissipated youth, but holding him under would have been a problem. When the opportunity to wrap her legs around his neck presented itself, that problem disappeared along with Peter's sins...

SOUND: Jacuzzi bubbling. Splashing, growing more and more frantic.

PETER: No, Mercy! No, Mercy! (gurgling)

SOUND: Bubbling and splashing, then bubbling, then easy waves. Click of Jacuzzi motor shutting off.

NARRATOR: With the buds of May displaying themselves in colorful profusion, Mercy went on a picnic with gifted nerd Oscar Pike, whose computer skills were for sale to his fellow students.

SOUND: Outdoors, birds, breeze, maybe a distant dog bark; running water of a nearby stream.

OSCAR: Yeah, Mercy, you wouldn't believe how much dough I got stashed away, L.O.L. Selling porn site codes to tweens, fixing grades in the school's data base. Man, there's nothing I can't do online.

MERCY: But Oscar, you can't get right with God with a few keystrokes.

OSCAR: (disappointed) I thought you'd be impressed...D.F.I.!

MERCY: Oh, I am by your skills. Your mind. But intellectual values pale next to spiritual growth. I could never be with a boy who wasn't one with the Lord.

OSCAR: Well, uh...B.T.W., I'm willing to learn!

NARRATOR: And there, in the cool shade of a magnificent oak, with a babbling brook nearby, sharing a picnic lunch on a checkered tablecloth with not even an ant to disturb them, she schooled Oscar in the ways of righteousness, and he confessed his many (though to Mercy somewhat boring) sins.

OSCAR: So, uh...I'm free of sin now, right? Now maybe we could, W.T.F...I dunno...

MERCY: How about a skinny dip?

OSCAR: O.M.G., yeah!

NARRATOR: And soon, swimming under the sun as God had made them, they splashed and kissed, and she rewarded him.

SOUND: Splashing, frolicking.

OSCAR: I can't believe this! Woot! This is frickin' great! R.M.S.! The most beautiful girl in school... the most beautiful girl anywhere...and she's mine, all mine! Nailed it!

MERCY: (having fun) How long can you stay under? I'll time you...

OSCAR: Okay! W.T.F.N.?

SOUND: Oscar goes underwater with a big splash. Then sounds of struggle, splashing, gurgling, gurgling, gurgling.

OSCAR: (underwater) W.T.F.! W.T.F.!

NARRATOR: And performing this second Baptism was much easier. Mercy barely needed both hands holding Oscar under...and, after, when he floated on his belly like a fish without a loaf, he seemed so peaceful. He had left these earthly woes behind, on his laptop hard drive. He was in a better place.

SOUND: School hallway, bell rings, kids bustling, as before.

CINDI: Mercy! Hey, wait up.

MERCY: (sincere) Hi, Cindi. You look nice today.

CINDI: Yeah, well...look, I wanna make amends.

MERCY: (hopeful) Oh?

CINDI: I was wrong about you. I thought this I-found-hay-zeus thing was just an act. Something you put on to try to make people think you were sorry for what happened last fall.

MERCY: I am sorry.

CINDI: (no irony) Yeah, I think you are. I know we'll never be friends, but I just wanted you to know... no hard feelings.

MERCY: Bless you for that.

CINDI: I mean, with all these deaths lately, it makes you think. Sorta...re-evaluate. It's almost like God has it in for poor little Clarion.

MERCY: No! God loves everyone here and everywhere.

CINDI: Sometimes He has a funny way of showing it. I mean, first Peter Bishop...I mean he was an awful person, but...to get boozed up and fall asleep and drown in your own hot tub. Ewww. Then Oscar Pike goes swimming by himself, like he could swim, and the poor nerd drowns, too?

It's an epidemic!

And our guidance counselor kills himself? What kind of way to guide impressionable young minds is that?

MERCY: The Lord moves in mysterious ways.

CINDI: No shit!

MERCY: Cin – if you ever want to talk, you can come over to my house. Sometimes it helps to just... unburden yourself.

CINDI: Okay, maybe I will. (laughs) I been thinkin' maybe it's time to take the "sin" out of "Cindi".

MERCY: Never too late.

CINDI: Anyway, I was gonna mention...I signed up for that church retreat this weekend.

MERCY: Awesome!

SOUND: Bell rings.

CINDI: (off-mic) I'll see you there!

SOUND: Narrator's speech below, drop in some car engine noise and a car door slamming at appropriate points.

NARRATOR: Mercy had already been looking forward to the Bible study retreat out at the church camp grounds.

In jeans and tee-shirt, she drove out there late Friday afternoon, pulling up the gravel drive into the open space set within a cathedral of sun-shimmering trees. She was surprised that only one other car was there – Pastor Strickland's. Was she early?

SOUND: Outdoor sounds.

PASTOR: (off-mic) Mercy! Mercy, come inside the lodge house!

SOUND: Footsteps on gravel. Door opening, closing.

MERCY: Where is everybody?

PASTOR: The rest of the kids won't be coming till tomorrow around noon. This is just my little surprise.

MERCY: Oh?

PASTOR: After meeting so often at my house for our Bible Study sessions? Figured this would make a nice change of setting. We can get a jump on this retreat.

MERCY: (game) All right.

PASTOR: You can bunk in the girl's wing, and I have my own quarters. It'll be strictly, uh...

MERCY: Kosher?

PASTOR: Yes, perhaps not the exact word I might have chosen. Do you have your Bible with you?

MERCY: I do.

PASTOR: Let's sit by the fire. I have sandwiches made and soft drinks. We'll dig in...to the food and to our studies!

NARRATOR: For several hours, Mercy and Pastor Strickland talked scripture and theology, and she was very pleased when he praised her for how much she'd grown. Several times he put his arm around her, and she had a momentarily queasy feeling...but she guessed this was just fatherly affection on the Pastor's part.

PASTOR: I'm so proud of you, Mercy. Of what you've accomplished over these months, on your path to redemption.

MERCY: I have worked hard.

NARRATOR: Then, when he sent her off to her bunk, he gave her a kiss on the cheek that maybe lingered a little too long. Or was that her imagination? She was just starting to undress when she sensed something and turned.

MERCY: Pastor! You scared me.

PASTOR: Not my intention, child. Not my intention.

NARRATOR: But he had scared her, as he stood there in the doorway, in an old-fashioned dressing gown. Purple and satin, sashed with a yellow droopy belt. Like the old prize fighters used to wear before starting the match.

PASTOR: You are such a beautiful child. Do you know this verse? 'Thou art fair...though hast doves' eyes within thy locks...thy lips are like a thread of scarlet...thy two breasts are like two young roes that are twins, which feed the lilies.'

MERCY: I...I don't know that one.

PASTOR: The Song of Solomon. Continue.

MERCY: What?

PASTOR: Please...continue...disrobing. Let me feast my eyes on God's great handiwork.

NARRATOR: Oh dear. It seemed now the Pastor was slipping. How ironic that Mercy would have to save him... She slowly removed her things, and he watched her with half-lidded eyes, trembling, unsteady, as if he might fall over. Then she was before him as God had made her. But, of course, after puberty had finished the job.

PASTOR: Now, dear...behold your maker.

NARRATOR: The Bible said that man was made in God's image, but Mercy hoped that wasn't true in the Pastor's case. This man was a skinny, awful creature with splotchy pale flesh mottled with splotchy white hair. His pitiful erect manhood shook like a scolding finger. Mercy had never seen a naked man so old, so wrinkled, so...disgusting.

It was difficult for her to reconcile this shriveled beast with the kind reverend who had schooled her in the ways of goodness.

PASTOR: Take my hand, child. You will make your offering to me under God's great sky.

NARRATOR: Mercy took his hand, and the perfect naked young woman and the ghastly older man walked into a pleasantly cool evening under a million stars and one glowing ivory moon. The sky was God's handiwork at its greatest – the Pastor was more like an off day. At Strickland's command, she lay on the grass before him.

PASTOR: Perfection. Perfection. There is a God... there is a...(pain) God!

MERCY: Pastor! What's wrong?

PASTOR: My pills...they're in my room...get them child...

MERCY: First you must ask for forgiveness for the sin you were about to commit.

PASTOR: Luh...lord...forgive me!

MERCY: Good. Now ask my forgiveness.

PASTOR: I'm sorry. I am only human. A frail imperfect man...ow! I need my pills! Don't just lay there...get up! Get my pills!

NARRATOR: Watching Pastor Strickland die wasn't any worse than cutting up Randy Johnson's body in that bathtub. Mercy felt a kind of serene goodness, sitting there naked, watching him gasp and groan and froth. He'd done something terrible, and was paying for it; but he was right with God, so it would be worth the suffering.

PASTOR: (weak) Damn you...damn you...

MERCY: Bless you, Pastor.

SOUND: A groaning death rattle from the pastor. Night sounds. A distant howl of some animal... fade to morning sounds again. (No garbage truck.)

SOUND: Phone ring.

MERCY: (sleepy)...Hello?

CINDI: (telephone) Mercy, it's me – Cindi. You want a ride out to the campgrounds?

MERCY: Campgrounds?

CINDI: (telephone) The church retreat? I can pick you up.

MERCY: (still a little sleepy sounding) Uh, no thanks, Cindi. I'm a little under the weather.

CINDI: Too bad. Well, I'll say hello to your pal, the preacher man.

MERCY: (flat) Do that, please.

CINDI: Hey, you sound funny. You haven't lost your faith all of a sudden?

MERCY: Not at all. Not my faith. Or my calling.

MUSIC: Ominous sting.

NARRATOR: So before we say an amen to our dark little sermon, let me remind the randy boys among you...and the dirty girls, as well...that Mercy is still out there, right now, among you...saving souls. And to those boys especially, I must offer this friendly counsel – think twice when some beautiful angel offers herself to you in sacrifice. It might be our little Mercy...ready to send you screaming to your maker.

A Look At: Murder— His & Hers: Stories

Nine enthralling short crime and mystery fiction stories from talented husband-and-wife duo Max Allan Collins and Barbara Collins.

This entertaining collection ranges from a late-night craving which drives a pregnant private eye out to a convenience store and into a hostage situation to a womanizing senator who tries to replace his dead mistress with a lookalike and a cat with an accusing gaze.

Each tale features the twist ending that fans will relish, while also being a little old-fashioned.

"Boasts a plot twist that Hitchcock or even Rod Serling fans will savor. Recommend this highly to all fans of mystery short fiction." – Booklist

AVAILABLE NOW

About the Author

Max Allan Collins was named a Grand Master in 2017 by the Mystery Writers of America. He is a three-time winner of the Private Eye Writers of America "Shamus" award, receiving the PWA "Eye" for Life Achievement (2006) and their "Hammer" award for making a major contribution to the private eye genre with the Nathan Heller saga (2012).

His innovative Quarry novels were adapted as a 2016 TV series by Cinemax. His other suspense series include Eliot Ness, Krista Larson, Reeder and Rogers, John Sand, and the "Disaster" novels. He has completed twelve "Mike Hammer" novels begun by the late Mickey Spillane; his audio novel, *Mike Hammer: The Little Death* with Stacy Keach, won a 2011 Audie.

For five years, he was sole licensing writer for

TV's CSI: Crime Scene Investigation (and its spin-offs), writing best-selling novels, graphic novels, and video games. His tie-in books have appeared on the USA TODAY and New York Times bestseller lists, including Saving Private Ryan, Air Force One, and American Gangster.

Collins has written and directed four features and two documentaries, including the Lifetime movie "Mommy" (1996) and "Mike Hammer's Mickey Spillane" (1998); he scripted "The Expert," a 1995 HBO World Premiere and "The Last Lullaby" (2009) from his novel The Last Quarry. His Edgar-nominated play "Eliot Ness: An Untouchable Life" (2004) became a PBS special, and he has co-authored two non-fiction books on Ness, Scarface and the Untouchable (2018) and Eliot Ness and the Mad Butcher (2020).

Made in the USA
Middletown, DE
27 January 2021